Armed and Outrageous

Note from the author:

When I created the Agnes Barton Senior Sleuth mystery series, I had a dream—and the dream became a reality. I portray zany characters that are over the top. Not only was that intentional, but it was deliberate. I have worked with senior citizens for a long time, and if I have learned anything, it was that you just never know what they will do, or what they will say at any given time. So before you say, "Senior citizens don't act like that," I challenge you to visit a nursing home. Furthermore, not all senior citizens are feeble or confused; many are, but many more don't fit this description. Keep your mind open, and enjoy the series for what it was meant to be, a fun read. Belief is in the eye of the reader.

Thanks to my many readers who have followed the series—you are my constant cheerleaders. Feel free to contact me on Facebook, Twitter, or join my email newsletter located on my website: http:// madisonjohns.com.

Also by Madison Johns

Book cover
http://www.coverkicks.com/
Completely re-edited and revised February 2014.
Editor: Melissa Gray
Proofreader: Cindy Tahse
Internal Design: www.cohesionediting.com

Armed and Outrageous

by
Madison Johns

Dedication

I dedicate this novel to every senior citizen whom I have cared for in either a nursing home or hospital. If not for their quick wit and spunky personalities, this novel would never have been possible.
In memory of Rosa Lee Hill and Rose Hamilton.

Acknowledgements

I'd like to thank the following people in no particular order: William Johns, Andrea and Luke Kalkman, Barbara Pappan, Robert Walker, Mel Piff, Terry Crawford Palardy.

I'd also like to acknowledge everyone on Facebook. I could never have done any of this without you! Friends have come and gone through the years, but you have stuck by me no matter how crazy it's been, most of you, anyway. Smiles.

Chapter One

My internal alarm clock went off at five, as it does every morning. Reluctantly, I pulled my feet out from under my comforter. I had forgotten about the air conditioner and left it set on sixty-five the night before, but heck, older gals have been known to get pretty heated at night. Not that it mattered much, but I wake up every morning wringing wet. Most mornings, I feel like a wet dishrag.

First thing in the morning, standing isn't an easy task, and today was no exception. I grabbed my bedside table with one hand, pushed the other against my mattress, and stood. I heard a thump and looked down; my denture cup had hit the floor, and not only had it opened, but my dentures had bounced beneath the bed like an angry crab. I hoped the damned things hadn't managed to break into pieces. If I had to take them to be repaired—again—it would make the third time this month.

It's a crying shame to feel so achy and sore every morning. I'm only seventy-two, and that's not old. It was strange how my perception about age changed over time.

I flipped on the light switch and knelt on the floor in search of my false teeth. I finally spotted them hiding amongst the dust bunnies that I hadn't even known were there. I used my grabber to reach the dentures; of course, I'd leave the dust bunnies for another day. The grabbers were the only practical thing I had gotten out of physical therapy; those grabbers that could also be useful for pinching my best friend, Eleanor, when she gets out of line.

I examined my errant, runaway dentures. I sighed in relief when I saw they were still intact, although loaded with ancient cat hair. My cat, Duchess, sheds enough in one week that I could use it to knit a blanket for the homeless.

I plopped my dentures back into my denture cup, and as I waddled across the cold, wood floor and into the bathroom, Duchess wound herself around my ankles as if trying to trip me for laughs. This cat will be the death of me one day, literally. I think she is secretly an assassin, a ninja cat.

First things first; I had to pee. Once done, I walked to the shower, adjusted the temperature, and pulled my rose flannel nightgown off. I stepped in carefully and let the hot water pound my achy body. As is her habit, Duchess wasn't far away. I wondered why cats are so fascinated with water when they hate it so much. Then I pondered human nature, and I understood, sort of.

I could hear what sounded like my answering machine, but decided that if that's what it was, they better just leave a message because I wasn't hurrying a bit. I don't think the word hurry is in a senior citizen's vocabulary. I stayed in the shower and scrubbed myself until the water became lukewarm.

One thing I can't stand is a smelly old woman. Not that I considered myself old, by any means. I'm Agnes Barton, and I can still turn a head or two around this sleepy town of Tadium, Michigan.

I grabbed the grab bar attached to my bathtub, a staple in any senior's house, and clambered out. I toweled off and surveyed my reflection in the mirror while Duchess jumped into the empty tub. Sure, I'm no prize, but considering all I had been through in my life, the mirror told me outright: "Agnes, you're none the worse for wear." My blue eyes still twinkled whenever I batted my eyelashes—which were still there to bat! I may have bags under the eyes, but who at my age doesn't? I have a crease that starts at the corner of my nose and runs all the way to my chin, but my lips are still full and inviting when I smile. Age spots are plentiful because of all the time I've spent in my garden during the summer months all these years, but I think that's understandable.

I picked up a brush and ran it through my wet, silver hair. I decided last year to let nature take its course, and stopped coloring it altogether. I snapped on a pair of pearl earrings, the clip kind. Never was one for the other kind. I have a jewelry box full of costume jewelry left to me by my mom, God rest her soul. I wear her jewelry every day. It makes me feel like she's still with me.

I put my underclothing on; no granny panties for me. Today, I was wearing bright pink bikini panties with a matching push-up bra. I laughed out loud. I still remember the shocked look from the young lady at Victoria's Secret in Saginaw when I bought them. She giggled when I told her, "They're for me, dearie, and not my granddaughter." As if all women my age have grandchildren. With that thought, I wrinkled my forehead.

No, I can't think about that today; it would ruin my whole day.

I pulled a purple and pink paisley silk blouse and purple pants on and slid my swollen feet into a pair of white ballerina-style flats. Next, I gave my hair a quick smoothing out before I put a tube of pink lipstick in my pocket.

I walked into the living room and inhaled deeply. I admired the knotty pine walls in the living room, one of the reasons I had bought this house. A cabin by the lake is what I had always wanted, but I ended up buying a house across the road from Lake Huron.

It's nestled in the woods, with just enough sunlight streaming through to help my garden grow. I have one of the best gardens in the area, and that isn't an exaggeration. The proof is in the soil. I had it tested once; it's loaded with nutrients and minerals, creating a perfect balance for growing ideal plants.

The previous owner grew marijuana, or wacky-weed as it's commonly known. Around these parts, they call it funky flower. I heard he had the best crops around until the law shut him down. It's too bad because these days, it's used for medicinal purposes.

I could see the answering machine light flashing.

I walked past the confounded blinking light with ease. The shower had done its magic, and my limbs felt much better. I moved into the kitchen and pushed the white lace curtains aside before opening the window. Listening to the call of the mourning doves made me smile.

Duchess jumped up on the counter and glared out the window, making soft mewing sounds. I knew if able, she'd snag a mourning dove for breakfast. She sure knew how to carry mice into the house and release them. They were always still alive. I call it the catch and release program. It takes me weeks to locate and capture them. I use the traps called Tin Cat. They work better than Duchess.

I filled the cat dish while Duchess meowed loudly; it sounded like a cannon blast to my ears. In all my days, I have never heard a cat meow so loud or often as Duchess.

I made coffee and waited, listening while it dripped into the glass coffee pot. Anticipation getting the better of me, I poured myself a cup before it was finished, adding a liberal amount of french vanilla creamer. Stirring it, I finally walked over to the answering machine, pushed the button, and sank into my black leather sofa.

"Agnes … another missing person's report … just hit the airwaves," the voice started softly, pausing briefly. "Not far from here, another young woman. Need you to be prompt. Twelve."

Eleanor Mason, quite a gossip, couldn't at all contain herself when she found out any bit of news.

Another missing young woman. I played the words over in

my mind, frowned, and asked Duchess, "Has the whole damn world gone mad?"

I finished my coffee, shut off the coffee pot, and headed out the door, settling myself in my red Mustang. No sedan for this old woman. I'm what folks like to call eccentric. I have a rose tattoo on my right shoulder, too; got it for my sixtieth birthday.

I drove up the road to Roy's Bait & Tackle shop, the only place in this sleepy town where you can get an early edition of the Tadium Press. Tadium is just another small town on the eastern side of Michigan, on Lake Huron, ten miles from East Tawas.

The only place you can stay in Tadium is Robinson's Manor, a bed and breakfast. Some would say the old place was one of the most haunted houses in Michigan. The mansion was left empty for years after the entire family was murdered in 1968, a murder that remains unsolved, even today.

It seemed a bit odd that the Robinsons didn't build a house of that size on the lake instead of in a dark forest across US 23, a half-mile drive through the woods. However, it did make for an enjoyable drive in the springtime when white trilliums blanket the ground; not a fragrant flower, but a protected one. Once you reach the end of the drive, it opens up to a clearing surrounded by a well-tended garden framed by maple trees. The current owners, Frank and Frances Bowdine, encourage their guests to help pick fresh produce in the summer. The original owner, the unfortunate John Robinson, had relocated from his native Charleston, South Carolina. He put his fortune into the construction of the white-pillared house. It had two stories, with a rooftop deck for chairs and such, and from that height, one can see over the tree line to Lake Huron.

Robinson's Manor is always booked throughout the year. Maybe it's the mystery; maybe it's the hope of seeing something out of the ordinary. It was rumored that the ghosts of the Robinson family still walk the grounds at night.

I pulled into Roy's Bait & Tackle shop, climbed from the car, and stepped inside. Fishing poles, lures, and nets covered the warped walls entirely, while air filters bubbled in the minnows' tanks. I wrinkled my nose at the overwhelming, stagnant smell of the place.

Roy Garrison, the owner, was here, like always. He's a married man, but that doesn't stop him from flirting. His wife is a sweetheart of a woman and does rosary at one of the local nursing homes.

Roy, a long-time resident of Tadium, inherited the property from his granddaddy, him being the only one in the family who had any interest in the old bait shop. In truth, his Granddaddy Mac had raised him. Roy's father, Axel, was far more interested in spending money on women and whiskey than bringing his paycheck home to feed the family—one of many reasons Roy's mother ran off, leaving little Roy with his granddad.

Roy's bald head seemed to be shinier than the sun today. *He must be rubbing something on it to make it so,* I told myself, *because that big knob is normally not near so shiny.* I inwardly laughed, knowing I could check my makeup in the mirror of his forehead.

Roy wore blue jeans held up with red suspenders over a white T-shirt stained brown under the armpits. It was enough to make me want to vomit. I have always hated an unkempt man. I smiled, despite how I felt.

"Morning, Roy."

Rubbing one of his hands over his hairless head, he smiled. "Well, saints preserve me. I do believe an angel has descended from heaven to astonish me with her rare beauty."

I tried hard not to roll my eyes. Surely, they would somehow be stuck in my head never to return if I did. What an ass. Does he really think women want to hear that kind of crap? If he's looking for a fool, it's not me, but I smiled just the same. I wanted to get the paper so I could leave before he came up with yet another, equally unimpressive comment.

"I'm here to buy the morning paper, is all. So, if you please, be a good boy and fetch it for me." *Just like the dog you are.* I could not help such thoughts racing in whenever I was around Roy.

He played along with the suggestion, and right on cue, he stuck his tongue out, nearly touching his chin, and panted like a dog. He wobbled over toward the stack of papers while I rightly feared he'd come back with it between his teeth and gums!

"Please, don't put that paper in your mouth," I said, my voice indicating how horribly un-amused I was by his doggy antics. Thankfully, he used his 'paws' rather than his mouth.

He turned abruptly. His demeanor had changed. "I wasn't going to fetch it doggy style," he snapped. Returning to the counter, he shouted, "That'll be fifty cents, Milady."

I dropped two quarters onto the counter and watched as they bounced off to Roy's obvious irritation, noted by the narrowing of his eyes.

I picked up my paper and left, as Roy called out, "Hon, why don't you come back here; you can bend over, and I'll show you doggy style."

I shook my head and continued toward my car.

Chapter Two

As I sat in the car and stared down at the front page of the Tadium Press, the headlines jumped out at me. Not that hard considering the newspaper only measures twelve-by-twelve. Small town news usually consists of garage sales and arrest reports, not missing tourists.

Missing Person Reported

I read it out loud as stated: "Tourist Jennifer Martin reported missing by birth father, William Martin, President of Automated Industries, Detroit, MI. She came into Tadium area vacationing with friends. Late Tuesday night, she walked alone, presumably, to Quick Stop and never returned. Sheriff Peterson indicates there is no reason to believe foul play is involved at this time.

"Meanwhile, William Martin adamantly stated, ⊚I know my daughter, and there is no way she'd just up and leave. Jennifer has a medical condition requiring regular medication. Without it, her life may be in jeopardy"

"The Sheriff's Department will continue to look into the matter. When questioned further about the other missing persons cases in the area, they wouldn't comment.

"In this reporter's view, we need to start locking our doors at night. Living in a small town is hardly a reason to take chances. Sure, most of the missing women are from out of town, but for how long?"

My hands shook, and I remembered all too well how many missing young women there were, including my granddaughter, Sophia. She had come to visit me last summer, and when she had gone jogging on US 23, poor dear, she had simply disappeared, never to return. Sophia was an honor student and had just graduated from Saginaw Valley State University with a BA in nursing.

Sophia had curly brown hair, and I remember how she would cry as a child when I brushed it. She had the kind of baby blue eyes that almost jumped out at you, and her tan skin and freckled face simply glowed. Two huge dimples appeared when she smiled, displaying a dazzling set of teeth. Men showed her attention, but she shrugged it off, as if unaware of her unique beauty.

"Gram, I don't have time for men. I plan to go back to school," she'd so often tell me.

Sophia had a well-toned body and jogged regularly. I remembered the last time I saw her. She'd been wearing a pink and white striped jogging suit, and she had her hair tied back into a ponytail. I was in the garden that day. I remember glancing up and waving as Sophia ran north on US 23. That was the last time I saw her.

One year now. Is that all it's been?

I started my car and drove to Eleanor's house. I knew it wasn't noon, not precisely, but I also knew Eleanor wouldn't mind if I showed up a little early.

Sunlight split through the gathering clouds over the lake. Not many waves today either, just a slight slapping of water against the beach. It reminded me of a postcard. Although the sun had begun to blind me a bit, reminding me what a night owl I used to be. Years ago, I would stay up well past the witching hour, waiting for my husband to return from his night shift as a state trooper.

Dark memories tried to surface, but I couldn't allow myself to think about them.

I shook my head to clear the bad thoughts as I turned into Eleanor's driveway. Her house wasn't much to look at from the front. It was more of the backyard. When I found the door not locked, I rolled my eyes, and I walked in. *I shouldn't be upset,* I chastised myself; after all, most of us small town residents didn't lock our doors. *Call it small-town comfort,* I thought next, *but these days, comfort may kill you.*

I walked through the house and noticed the lingering smell of bacon and eggs, both cooked too long, although the kitchen looked to be scrubbed clean.

I eyed the beast of an old ironwood stove Eleanor used to heat her house. I would have replaced if it were up to me. Eleanor's too old to be going out in the dead of winter to get wood from the woodshed. She'd just turned eighty-two, after all, but you couldn't tell it from the way she acted.

Eleanor had two church benches with green and yellow plaid cushions that she used in the dining room; this cheap man's version of a dining area fronted the glass patio door. Outside was a deck overlooking the lake.

I slid the door open and found Eleanor leaning against the white fence that completely wrapped around the deck and extended all the way down to the lake.

If you looked up at the house from the lake, you'd notice how the triangle windows upstairs looked like a pair of gigantic eyes, or maybe it was just me who saw these things. I was always one to see more into inanimate things than the average person.

She didn't turn at my approach.

"Why in the world, Eleanor, would you leave your door unlocked?"

Eleanor turned around with an indignant expression on her face. Her large frame was squeezed into a matching mustard-colored shirt and capri pants. On her feet, she wore white flip-flops. I couldn't understand how she could walk in the blasted things.

Eleanor had blue eyes that simply danced, and her well-wrinkled skin was covered with large moles, as if she collected them. Her thin gray hair was curled today—her hair appointment had been only yesterday. When she laughed, which she did often, her whole belly shook.

"Why would I lock the door? I knew you'd be coming straight here after getting the paper. How is Roy this morning?" She giggled and tried unsuccessfully to stop.

"You're the one who has eyes for him, not me, Eleanor."

"Really? Do you think he would be interested?" Her eyes danced suggestively.

Ignoring her chatter, I held up the newspaper and handed it to her to read. She carried it to one of her white wicker chairs and sat, reading the article before handing it back to me.

"It said the same thing on the news this morning. The girl's father is on his way here, too," Eleanor said, putting her hand against her mouth as if someone else could hear her. "Word is that he is staying at Robinson's Manor while he's here."

"Put your hand down, and start acting serious for once. How in the world does he think he can get in there? They are always booked this time of year."

"There is one suite that is always empty. I heard they remodeled it real quick like just to accommodate him."

"Certainly not ... *the* suite?"

"One and the same."

"The suite where Mrs. Robinson was raped and murdered?" I couldn't believe it. "Nobody in their right mind would want to stay in ... that room. Maybe he doesn't know."

"Beats me, but word is he wants to be close to the place where his daughter went missing." Eleanor's face reddened like she was about ready to burst, as she added. "Not far from Quick Stop. It was the party store she was going to on Tuesday."

I frowned. Like I needed Eleanor to tell me, but I didn't want to make her feel bad, so I let her think she was the one with the juicy tidbit of information.

I stood and walked back through the house with Eleanor hot on my heels. "You won't find anything there. If the police haven't found anything, what makes you think you will?"

"Eleanor, I'm a concerned citizen, and it's my God-given right to get to the bottom of this. It could be related to Sophia's disappearance. What if all of these cases are related?"

Eleanor put her hand on my shoulder and gave it a squeeze. "Honey, I know you want to believe that, and I'm not saying you're wrong, but it's a long shot. I hope Sophia is still alive, too; But, Agnes, it's been a year."

I wiped away a tear before it could make its way down my cheek. "I know you're right, but I have to do this."

"Would you like company, at least?"

I gave Eleanor a strange look. "I'm not sure you will fit in my Mustang."

We both laughed while Eleanor retrieved her keys. "I'm driving," she said

"I don't think th-that's a good idea," I stammered.

"Don't be silly, Agnes. You might want to move out of my way. I would hate to lose a good friend at my age."

Eleanor went into her garage and backed out her gray, 1980 Cadillac Seville. It only had 50,000 miles, but that was hard to believe with the damage on the body—part of the reason I wanted to drive. They say a Cadillac is built like a tank, one of the main reasons I had raised money and bought her the car.

Eleanor hadn't had much luck in her life until she inherited her house from a nephew who'd died unexpectedly a few years back. Her only son, Edward, wouldn't have anything to do with her. We had met at the Mikado bingo, quite a distance from where we lived. We were surprised to learn we lived only a mile from one another. I was immediately taken in by her quick wit, and I thought of her as a sister I never had—the perfect partner in crime.

Eleanor opened the car door for me. "Don't be afraid; I promise I can see much better with these new glasses."

I had my doubts about her driving skills, but I climbed in nonetheless. Right on cue, Eleanor hopped in, cranked the engine, and slammed her foot on the pedal. Rocks flew up and tinged the roof; hot tin roof came to mind. She tore off down the road toward Quick Stop. She swerved and didn't stay in her lane, but we made it there without incident, thanks to the grace of God.

"Pull over here. It looks like a good spot to start searching," I said.

Eleanor pulled over and parked on the shoulder. Lake Huron wasn't visible from where we started searching, and trees lined the road.

"What exactly are we looking for?"

"I'm not sure yet," I said, getting out. "I just feel this is as good a place as any to start."

I walked north on US 23, toward Quick Stop, and noticed skid marks. They were wide and might have come from a truck or van. They extended from the start of the pavement and stopped just on the other side of the double yellow line.

When I glanced toward the other side of the road, I made my way over there, hoping to find a clue. I had made it a few feet when I spotted what looked to be blood on a blade of grass. Going past that, I walked toward the trees, but before I reached them, I tripped on something. I thought it was a rock or hole in the ground at first, but it was a shoe!

It was an athletic shoe with a silver chain with the initials J.M. attached to it. I knelt, and noticed the shoe had a black mark extending from the side all the way to the toe.

Pulling out my cell, I dialed 911 to report what I had found and agreed to wait for the sheriff to show up. He showed up ten minutes later.

Sheriff Peterson stopped his car and crossed the road. His black hair was plastered to his head, and he was wearing dark sunglasses on his face. He reminded me of a big city cop you'd see in one of those movies I'm so fond of, minus the trim body, but cops never seem to look like that in small tourist towns.

He shook his head in irritation when he saw me. "What are you doing here?"

Not feeling one bit intimidated, I started speaking. "I think I have found something related to the recent missing woman."

"What in tarnation are you talking about? If you've been watching the news, you'd know she hasn't even been officially listed as missing." He scratched his head, as gnats were flying about and his nose began to drip. Taking a tissue out of his pocket, he rubbed it under his nose, temporarily stopping the clear liquid from dripping further. "Are you suggesting we may have missed something?"

"You said it, not me, Sheriff." Leading him to the blade of grass I'd found earlier, I knelt to rub his nose in what I had found. "For one thing, this blade of grass appears to have blood on it." I carefully stepped around it and walked to where the shoe lay. "I also found an athletic shoe here." I pointed down.

Sheriff Peterson walked to the spot I indicated. "So this is your vital evidence? A shoe and a drop of blood?"

"You missed it, of course, but it could be the shoe the girl was wearing when she was kidnapped. That blood looks fresh."

"Agnes, now listen here. There's no evidence anyone was kidnapped. It's just a shoe, for Pete's sake, and there's no way of knowing if that's blood."

"So you're shirking your responsibilities and not looking into it? In my days, it would be your responsibility as a member of law enforcement to … investigate further."

He looked back across the road, waiting for the traffic to clear. The five or six cars coming through slowed down as they passed us.

"Of course, I'm gonna look into it." He crossed the road and returned with plastic bags and gloves. Kneeling, he snipped the blade of grass with a pair of scissors and placed it into a small plastic bag. Picking up the shoe, he placed it into a larger bag. Snatching his gloves off, he walked back to his car as I followed.

"Sheriff, where was the woman staying?"

"Why do you want to know that?"

"I would like to find out if she's here with friends. I want to ask them some questions. Perhaps, dealing with an old broad like me, they'd impart more information than they would to you … maybe?"

Putting his face close to mine, he barked, "You know I can't tell you anything like that. This is official police business. Go home, and let us do our job."

I pursed my lips, which suddenly felt dry. "What you want and what you get are two entirely separate things. I fully intend to look into the matter myself," I assured Sheriff Peterson. As I walked back across the road to Eleanor's car, I shouted over oncoming traffic, "Oh no, sir, Sheriff. I'm not about to let it go this time."

The bungling sheriff tossed the bags he'd collected onto his passenger seat, gingerly worked his bulging stomach beneath the steering wheel, and quickly pulled away. Peterson put his cruiser into a tight U-turn, wheeled about, and sped toward East Tawas.

Chapter Three

Where are we going now?" Eleanor asked, making herself comfy on the passenger seat of the car.

I glanced up the road a spell and noticed a dirt path that appeared large enough for a car to fit down. Getting in on the driver's side, I started Eleanor's Cadillac, driving toward the path.

"What in the hell are you doing? This isn't a road, Agnes!"

I didn't say a word, just continued down the path. Tree branches scraped across the car and slapped against the windows. I didn't care. I needed to get to the bottom of this before another young woman was snatched. Besides, it couldn't possibly hurt Eleanor's car. It couldn't look any worse than it already did.

"You're crazy," Eleanor said as she laughed. "You talk about my driving."

"I know this path leads somewhere." My hands gripped the steering wheel so hard that my knuckles turned white.

"If you get us stuck in here, we'll be trapped forever. They won't find our corpses until winter. I don't want to be a corpse." Eleanor pouted.

I would have looked at her and made a smart comeback, but I was having trouble keeping control of the car. Every branch seemed to pull the car off the path.

I reached a clearing in the woods and tore up the grass when I hit the brakes. I saw a log cabin. It was small but well-kept, with a brick chimney that ran down the right side. I hadn't heard about this place, which surprised me. Thanks to Eleanor, who always keeps me up-to-date on the local gossip, I had heard about most everything in the area at one time or another.

I stopped the car, stepped out, and approached two young men sitting at a campfire with a blue enamel coffee pot on the fire in front of them, most likely boiling water for their morning coffee.

The two young men looked at me with wide eyes, and I knew why. Between one of the young man's fingers was a joint, and the smell of marijuana hung in the air as if a cloud surrounded their heads.

"Enjoying your morning buzz, boys?" I asked, smiling. "I don't give a hoot about that. Why, you know, in my day … well, forget about that. I never touched the stuff."

"Sure, Agnes! Whatever you say," Eleanor said, standing behind me.

I popped a glance over my shoulder and gave Eleanor the evil eye to make sure she understood that I disapproved of her interruption. I then glanced back at the young men. "I was wondering if either of you knew the missing woman, Jennifer Martin?"

"Who's askin'?" a young woman standing in the doorway of the cabin pointedly asked. Her blonde hair appeared tousled, and she had black eyeliner smeared beneath her eyes. She wore only a large white Sick Puppies T-shirt. Exactly what that meant was lost on me. Puppies were supposed to be cute, and I couldn't think of anyone who'd want a sick puppy.

"My name is Agnes, and Jennifer is like a granddaughter to me. I'm not the type to be waiting for the police to tell me something." I spoke in my most sincere voice. I knew how to lay it on thick when need be.

"You don't want us. You need to drive down the road a spell. There's a log cabin right behind Lodge's Sporting Goods," the young woman said, to the annoyance of the two fellows at the campfire.

I glanced at the men and noticed one of them was now busy studying the ground, avoiding my eyes. I, of course, walked straight over to him. "Can I speak to you for a moment?"

He glanced up at me, tears swimming in his green eyes, and he nodded. Standing, he stretched his nearly six-foot frame up. His blond hair was spiked, and he wore cutoff denim shorts. His muscular frame made me think he might, at one time, have been an athlete.

"Leave us," he barked at his friends. The woman glared at him, but his friends left, walking down a wider lane on the opposite side of the cabin—clearly, a better way out than the way we'd driven in.

He walked away and stepped onto the cabin porch, obviously in order to have a post and a handrail to lean against.

"My name is Agnes," I repeated, now having to look way up at him. "Can I get your name?"

"Kevin Marks," he replied. "I've been waiting for someone to come around asking questions."

"So, you're saying the sheriff hasn't been out here to talk to you?" I couldn't believe it. Obviously, nobody at the Sheriff's Department took Jennifer's disappearance seriously.

"If they did, it wasn't to talk to me."

"Can you tell me what happened? I'd appreciate any help you could give me."

He took a deep breath, expanding his broad chest even further. "Jen wanted to walk up to the store to clear her head. I wanted to go with her, but she wanted no part of it. When she didn't come back, I didn't think anything of it at first until … well, until I saw she had left her medication behind."

I started to get the feeling there was something he wasn't telling me, so I pressed on. "So, you had a lover's spat then?"

With tears standing in his eyes, he continued. "We were just friends. He made sure of it."

"Who are you talking about? Who was stopping you?"

"Her father!" He spat out the final word. "I wasn't good enough for her, and he made sure he pressed the point home. He even pulled me aside and offered me money to leave her alone."

"How did you react to that?"

"I told him to shove it up his ass. I may only be a farmer's son, but I plan on going to college. I have a scholarship to Michigan State University. I've played football my whole life, and my coach seems to think I could go pro."

"Doesn't sound to me like you're a loser. Is there something more you can tell me?"

"Her father has control issues. I doubt anyone would be good enough for his little girl."

"Were you the one who called the police?"

"No, he did. If she missed one phone call, he would call the police to hunt her down."

"Did she leave anything behind?"

Rather than answer, he turned and walked into the cabin. I turned to exchange a look with Eleanor and found her impatiently frowning back at me. I ignored her and turned back around as the young man returned. He held up a mauve backpack.

"Everything is in there, including her medication. She seemed to do okay, but if she doesn't get it regularly—who knows what might happen."

"Thank you, Kevin. I hope we can find her before that becomes an issue."

Eleanor stood by the car, fanning herself with a magazine, waiting. She raised an eyebrow, glancing at the backpack I was carrying. I didn't say a word. I just got inside the car as Eleanor scrambled to get in the passenger door, which took a few minutes longer. While I drove down the wider lane on the opposite side of the cabin, Eleanor couldn't contain her questions any longer.

"What do you have there, Agnes?" she asked, with a sheepish grin on her face.

"It's the missing girl's backpack."

"What? He just gave it to you?" Her mouth gaped open, and I hoped a fly would find its way inside.

"Of course. Why not? I'm family, after all."

Eleanor laughed so hard her belly jumped as if making popcorn inside.

"Where are we going next, Agnes?"

"Taking you home." My face felt tight. I hoped that, for once, she'd just let this go. I loved Eleanor, but I didn't want her attached to my hip.

"Oh, no, you're not," Eleanor said. She puffed out her chest in indignation, resembling a hen. "This is the most exciting thing I have ever done, and I won't let you spoil it for me."

"I hate to remind you that you're not as swift on your feet as you used to be."

"I know that, but nobody would suspect two old ladies digging up clues." Eleanor rubbed her hands together.

I nodded in agreement. "I suppose you're right, Eleanor, but it could get dangerous. Are you still game?"

"Throw me in the frying pan and consider me cooked, Aggie."

"Hopefully, our goose won't get cooked." It was the understatement of the year because nothing we ever did turned out the way I hoped it would.

Pulling into Eleanor's driveway, we exited the Cadillac. I was holding the backpack tightly in my hand, and the sun beat down on us from directly overhead.

"It's much too hot, already," I muttered out loud, a habit of mine. I talk to myself all the time. They always say just make sure you don't answer yourself, but I do that, too.

Sometimes you're the only one who'll give you the answers you want to hear.

When we entered the air-conditioned house, we both exhaled loudly. I was relieved that we were out of the blasted heat.

I set the backpack down and took the items out, carefully setting them on the counter. Spotting the medication, I was shocked that such a young woman would have a serious heart condition. Most likely, she'd had it since birth. It was no wonder her father was so frantic to find her. If they didn't, her life would indeed be in serious jeopardy.

I examined the items laid out on the table. Two tall bottles filled with shampoo and conditioner, toothbrush and toothpaste—the normal toiletries you would find in anyone's vacation bag.

I raised an eyebrow when I spotted a small, red velvet box. Upon opening it, I realized Kevin hadn't told me everything. This made her disappearance all the more puzzling.

Chapter Four

By the time Eleanor and I had tea before us, we sat listening to some God-awful Hank Williams music. Eleanor loved him, whereas my taste in music is quite the opposite. I preferred a good pop tune the kids listen to these days, like Britney Spears. I'm not too old to shake a tail feather, yet.

I had a brilliant idea, and as a result, a wicked grin formed on my lips. I thought it over a moment, and then I shared the idea with Eleanor.

"I'm going to Robinson's Manor to question the missing woman's father, which would likely be a complete bore for you, Eleanor." If only I could persuade Eleanor to stay behind; not that she'd get in the way. In fact, she might even be an asset. Eleanor, despite her age, attracted men with her loud personality and winning smile. Perhaps, the missing girl's father might just open up to Eleanor sooner than he would for snoopy me.

Eleanor rolled her eyes about. "You mean Robinson's Manor, the bed and breakfast?"

"Is there another Robinson's I don't know about?" I said, as I nodded and tried not to visibly shake. *Think about the father who is missing his daughter, not about the place where an entire family was murdered in '68.* "Eleanor, is there any way you would stay behind while I speak with the missing woman's father?"

"Not a flippin' chance." Eleanor laughed. Her belly shook as she struggled to get out of her chair. "Besides, Agnes, someone needs to keep you out of trouble." She winked.

I helped my friend out of her chair just like I helped her with everything she needed.

Eleanor had only held one job in her lifetime, and that was for a mere six weeks. It'd been a job at a paper factory, all before she was married. Once she became Mrs. Mason, she had been forced to quit because they didn't want any married women employed there. In those days, with no unions and no laws to protect a worker, she had no choice in the matter. That's how it was back then.

Years later, when Eleanor found out that her husband, Wilbert, had cheated on her, she wigged out and chased him with a butcher knife. When the police showed up, they merely insisted he leave temporarily, for his own safety. In those days, domestic abuse was hardly a crime. It was best kept between the married couple since, frankly, law enforcement simply didn't want to get between a man and his wife.

Eleanor had moved into her mother's house shortly after, but in those days, there weren't any decent jobs, especially for women.

A few years back, Eleanor's son, Max, tried to put her in a nursing home, but I wouldn't have it. I helped her fill out the court papers so she could keep her independence.

Max never visited his mother, a shameful thing. Maybe she hadn't been the best mother, but what was she to do?

When I married my high school sweetheart, Tom Barton, I thought we'd be together forever. I never contemplated he'd die from a heart attack at age forty-two.

Tom was a state trooper, and it would be more likely that he would die in the line of duty. I still remembered when the police came to the door and informed me of his death. I was shell-shocked. He didn't die violently. They just found him in his police cruiser, dead. It took the cold autopsy results to determine the cause of death.

We had married at nineteen and had two children, Martha and Stuart. Both were over eighteen when their father died. Not one to hold anyone back, I insisted the children go to college, as planned.

After my husband had died, I had a terrible time coping. At least my children were grown and away at college, although that fact did add to my loneliness. There were days when I barely made it out of bed. I had no desire to. After all, my husband had passed away, and nothing would ever bring him back.

I had gazed around my recently-remodeled kitchen with ire and wondered if that had contributed to his death. He had, after all, done most of the remodeling work himself with the help of Kevin Bower, our neighbor. The house where I had once raised my children now seemed like a tomb that kept me confined. It still hurts, even now.

Six months later, I was forced to make hard choices. I needed a job, a good one. I thought back to all the crummy jobs, and wondered why I hadn't gone to college. I was only forty-two at the time.

I started my own business, cleaning houses. In short order, it became more interesting than I could have ever dreamed.

All over town, my clients' business was quickly my business, and I learned more about my clients than I could ever have imagined a cleaning lady could! I did so simply by listening to their gossip. They vented and raged on the telephone or with someone visiting while I moved around them like an invisible person.

I learned to keep my mouth shut and ears open, all the while keeping an expressionless face. No way would they ever know I was compiling data about them.

Two months after cleaning the offices of Attorney Andrew Hart, I struck gold. I gave him a few tips, and we made a deal. I continued my cleaning duties while working undercover for him.

Being an investigator for a lawyer was no easy task. First and foremost, I couldn't tell a soul, and second, my boss was Andrew Hart. I felt attracted to him, but he was married. He had sealed the deal before he became a hotshot lawyer, and I knew he wouldn't risk losing half of what he had worked for just for a fling. Nor would I begin to settle for such a horrid and messy arrangement; and besides, he never once gave me more than a passing look.

Of course, Hart didn't know what he was missing, but I was careful to keep my desire for him concealed. Regardless of my hidden feelings for my boss, those became the best days of my life. After Tom, of course—since Tom's passing, you understand. Oh, yes, I loved the job. Loved to be the first person to greet Andrew with fresh, brewed coffee poured and waiting for him.

He smiled at me every morning, and a glimmer shone from his brown, bedroom eyes. The edges of his dark hair had just begun to turn a light gray, and I longed to run my fingers through it. He was fit and trim. Although only five foot eight, it completed the already impeccable package. I never knew the name of the aftershave he wore, but it reminded me of fresh rain and cinnamon. Maybe it was the coffee. He smelled so good, it made me weak in the knees, which was something I hadn't felt since Tom.

Remembering those days sent a tremor through me. I'd heard his wife had died of cancer five years ago, but I stopped myself from looking him up. He had barely noticed me, after all. But I still had my fantasies, and the last thing I wanted was to repeat our history of me wanting him so much and him never even noticing me, especially not now that he wasn't even married anymore.

I forced myself back to the present. "If you want to come with me to Robinson's Manor, you better be ready now, Eleanor," I said, walking out the door.

"Don't you dare leave without me, Agnes Barton."

Eleanor hobbled out the door after me, and I sat in the car waiting for her to make herself comfortable next to me, while contemplating the long list of helpful facts and information I might squeeze out of the father. After all, I'd done pretty well with the boyfriend.

Chapter Five

The journey to Robinson's Manor took only five minutes, as it was just a few miles away. Turning onto the paved road, I shuddered when two squirrels darted across the drive.

"I don't know what bothers me more, meeting Jennifer's dad or going to the manor," I mused. Eleanor knew the reason why. I quietly added, "Why in the world would anyone in their right mind turn a house with such a dark history into a bed and breakfast?"

"Why would anyone sleep all night there?" Eleanor asked.

"People's fascination with the supernatural is why. You can find a ghost hunter type show any night of the week on the tube." I gripped the steering wheel tighter. All the tiny hairs rose on the back of my neck. "For all we know, there is a murderer amongst us. A real, cold-blooded killer who raped and murdered Mrs. Robinson before finishing off the rest of the family with a claw hammer."

"Just because they never found the killer … that fact doesn't mean he or she is still around here, Agnes."

"Woman?" My eyebrows rose.

"It could be a woman."

"How'd you figure that?"

"Could be a couple. I've heard of cases like that." She gripped her black purse. It looked more like luggage to me, and I wondered what in the heck she kept inside.

The car surged ahead as we cleared the woods, and an array of multicolored roses welcomed us as I drove past. Majestic maple trees loomed in the distance and it occurred to me how easily someone could hide among them.

I parked in the rear, where the parking lot was hidden behind the white-columned mansion. Curious glances shot from the deck, striking my heart.

This could be a small town anywhere in Michigan, but it wasn't. This tightly-knit community was so shrouded in mystery that it reeked. I am sure that most who passed by our town on their way to East Tawas never gave it much thought, but they didn't know the truth. The real truth was that this miniscule town had all the makings of the infamous Peyton Place, USA.

Most of the community was of a certain age—folks fighting their advancing years with unusual vigor. Many businesses had come and gone through the years, but most of the seniors stayed.

Walking toward the back deck, I saw more familiar faces than unfamiliar ones. Robinson's Manor catered to more people than just their guests. It sure looked like they were able to draw the local folks for lunch. They offered a full menu, including the most sinful desserts I have ever tasted. My favorite is the hot fudge sundae.

I scolded myself. I wasn't here for dessert. I was here on business.

I pulled the back door open, trying to keep a low profile. I didn't want to draw any more attention than necessary, but the door creaked and made such a racket that everyone looked up and stared straight at me.

I sucked in my breath when I saw Dorothy and Frank Alton seated closest to the door.

"Look, Frank," Dorothy said. She cackled like she always did, which reminded me of a witch— not that much of a stretch, if you ask me.

Frank either had his hearing aid turned down or was ignoring his wife. He continued to eat, not even looking up from his bowl of soup.

Dorothy swatted his arm with her napkin. "Frank, did you hear me?"

Right on cue, he fidgeted with his hearing aid. He was turning it up. I knew it. He probably turned it down to drown her out. That's what I'd do.

I guided Eleanor through the crowd before she could say anything. The two women had gone more than a few rounds before.

"Why did you do that, Aggie?" Eleanor asked. "I'd like to give that woman a piece of my mind."

"Yes, I know, but we're here on a mission. Remember?"

Eleanor sighed, rubbing her knuckles. I'd hate to see Eleanor and Dorothy scrap again. Usually, it was a once a month occurrence.

I spotted William Martin seated along the opposite wall. He looked just like his picture in the newspaper.

I walked across the room and noticed another man was seated with him. Undaunted, I continued toward the table and waited until the men noticed me.

William Martin was every bit the hotshot businessman I expected, but his clothing screamed, "On vacation," complete with khaki shorts and loose, white tropical shirt. I even noticed his deck shoes when I walked up.

"I hate to bother you, but are you William Martin?" I asked.

He seemed to be surveying me before he spoke. "Yes, I am. Who are you?"

"My name is Ag—"

"Her name is Agnes Barton, investigator extraordinaire."

I snapped my head around and looked into the warm, brown eyes of Andrew Hart. I held my breath for a full two minutes, feeling faint.

He jumped up, pulled out a chair, and guided me onto it. Thank God he did, because I almost fainted—that would have been a scene.

I saw Eleanor dart across the room, returning with a glass of ice water and a cloth. She placed it against my head, always the consummate nursemaid.

"I'm so sorry. I don't know what happened." I fanned myself with my hand.

"Maybe you should go to the doctor," Andrew suggested, concern filling his eyes like honey.

"I'll be fine. I was just a ... uh..."

"Bit shocked to see me after all these years, perhaps?"

I smiled. "I suppose it could be that." I turned to look into William's eyes, worried that he would be irritated with the intrusion, but he smiled kindly.

"What do you want with me?" William asked.

"I heard about your daughter's disappearance, and I was hoping I could help."

He frowned. "Help how?" He looked me in the eyes, his hope evident.

"May I ask you some questions?" I took a sip of the water, the condensation dripping onto my shirt.

"William, let me assure you," began Andrew, "Agnes has a knack for finding out things. She was an investigator for my law office in Saginaw years ago, and she is good at what she does."

I anticipated his response. "I know what you may think. I'm some old woman, so what can I possibly do, right?"

He let out a breath I felt clear over on my side of the table. "The sheriff isn't taking my daughter's disappearance seriously."

"He didn't when my granddaughter went missing last summer, either. I think their disappearances could be related, and there have been others."

"How many others?"

"At least three that I know of, all of them under the same circumstances. They go for a walk or jog north on US 23, and they vanish into thin air."

"Jennifer is special. She's on medication, and if she doesn't get it … well, it may endanger her life."

"I understand." I shifted in the chair. "Have you received any ransom notes?

"No. I wish I had because I'd pay whatever they asked."

"Has anyone threatened you?"

"I own a large company. It comes with the territory."

"Lately?"

"Nobody has ever threatened my family before."

"So you're married, then?" asked Eleanor, who had joined us, batting her eyelashes.

She's such a buttinski, I wanted to say, but kept it to myself.

I rolled my eyes. "This is my dear friend, Eleanor Mason."

Eleanor shook William's hand, lingering longer than William was comfortable with, judging by the look displayed on his face.

"Yes, I'm married, but I don't see what that—"

"Are you cheating?"

He stood. "Cheating? Who in the hell do you think you are, asking me that?"

I stood, too. "I'm trying to help you. If you can't give it to me straight, maybe you really don't want to find your daughter."

He sat back down and glowered at me. I knew I had struck a nerve.

I, too, plopped back down. "Do you know anything about your daughter's social life?"

"Not really, no. You see, I work long hours and travel frequently."

"I see. Do you know Kevin Marks?"

"No."

I leaned forward. "That's strange. He told me that you offered him money to leave your daughter alone."

"When did he tell you that?"

"Earlier. He seemed pretty upset about it, too. He mentioned how overprotective you are."

"Did he, now? Did he mention why I might feel that way? That he took advantage of my daughter and got her pregnant last year."

"Jennifer has a baby?

I knew my face had flushed with shock. This was a situation where I couldn't mask my facial expressions. I was also a terrible liar, but managed to spin a tale or two if it would help me attain information.

"No, she had an abortion. She is very sick, too sick to go through a pregnancy."

"Is that what she wanted?" I couldn't believe he'd be that cold.

"I did what any caring father would do, and in the end, she realized it was the right decision."

Young Kevin had the father pegged.

"I really need the names of any of her friends that you can come up with."

"It might take a while. How can I reach you?"

I gave him my card and stood. "I will await your call." I nodded at Andrew and, with Eleanor following, made for the door.

I held my breath as emotions threatened to come to the surface. Damn, but Andrew still looked good after all these years. His Bermuda shorts and white linen shirt clung to his body like a glove. No beer belly in sight. He obviously kept himself in shape.

I'm too damn old to be thinking what I'm thinking. It's possible he had remarried, or maybe he was the type to date younger women. He certainly had the body for it.

Chapter Six

I kicked back on the deck, sitting on Eleanor's lime green lawn chair, and groaned when fibers that worked loose stabbed me in an unmentionable place. The sun had set in the west, leaving a spectacular view with rays of orange, gray, and pink that spread across the horizon. My mind traveled a bit, and I thought of Andrew. I needed to stop it. I'd probably never see him again. Damn, but he looked good.

"Are you listening?" Eleanor stood with her hands on her hips, tapping her foot in irritation.

I was grateful for the distraction. I needed to think about something else.

"Have you heard they have a back door store in town?"

I snapped my head up. "Back door store?"

"It's a bikini shop that has certain adult products in a secret back room."

"Who told you that?"

She chuckled. "I overheard it, is all." She coughed. "It's not like I've ever been there before," she added quickly, maybe a little too fast for it to be true. She'd been there, all right, but why was she mentioning it?

"Is that supposed to mean something to me, or are you suggesting we make a trip over there?"

Eleanor nodded. "Oh, come on, Aggie, don't be so old-fashioned," She said, yawning. "We'll have to wait until tomorrow, though. I'm bushed."

"Okay, we'll go there tomorrow."

"You promise?"

"I promise."

I walked inside, grabbed my purse, and headed out the door and back home.

It felt good to be home, and all I could think about was taking a long, hot bath.

Making my way into the bathroom, I turned on the water and tossed in some bath beads. I'd risk the UTI. I then retrieved the phone. I mean, what in the hell would happen if I fell in the bathtub and couldn't get out? It would be mighty embarrassing—for the paramedics.

I know I should get one of those lifeline devices seniors wear, but I'm not that old yet. I knew a woman who had one, returned it, and fell a week later. She had to crawl to the phone. I shuddered. That wouldn't happen to me, though, I hoped.

I slipped my clothes off and folded them neatly in a chair. I could still wear them another day. It's not as if they were dirty. Not that I don't have a washer and dryer; I do. It's just another thing I don't have time for. I'd much rather spend my days in the garden.

I eased myself into the lavender-scented water, and just as I started to relax, the phone rang.

Grimacing, I reached for the phone, fumbling with it and nearly dropping it into the bath water. That's what had ruined my last phone.

I leaned my head over the tub and put the phone to my ear.

Before I could even say hello, someone started talking. "Aggie, are you okay?"

I froze. "Who is this? I'm fine. Why?"

"This is Andrew. When it took so long for you to answer ... well, I just wondered, is all."

Damn, how in the hell did he get my number? I suddenly felt more naked, if that made a lick of sense.

"I hope you don't mind that I'm calling. I know you were hoping William could supply you with a list of Jennifer's friends.

Unfortunately, William can't help you with that. He didn't want to admit how little he knows his daughter. Plus, William didn't appreciate your insinuation that he's cheating on his wife."

"Is he?" The sarcasm dripped from my words. Had I thought better of it, I would have made an effort to mask it, but that wouldn't be me.

"You haven't changed a bit."

"It comes with the territory. No man who's faithful to his wife gets so damn sensitive when you ask him if he's cheating. Being defensive about it tells me that he has something to hide." I tried to think straight. "Is she Jennifer's mother?"

"No, she's someone he hooked up with ten years ago, after his first wife disappeared. William's new wife is quite a bit younger than he is."

"What else is new?"

"Now, that's not fair, Aggie. We're not all like that."

He had a way of making me feel bad. "I was sorry to hear about your wife's death, Andrew."

"Thanks. I'm sorry I can't help you further. Jot down my number in case you need to contact me."

I laughed, looking down at my bath water. Poking my toes up, I could see the wrinkles already forming. "I can't right now."

"Why not?"

"Because I'm in the bathtub, that's why not. I just got in here, and it's where I plan to stay."

I heard static. I must have shocked him. *Did he hang up?* I thought. I hung up the phone. *Of all the nerve.*

The phone rang again, and I answered it. "Hello." I grimaced when I heard Andrew's voice. I certainly didn't want to talk to him now.

"Sorry about that, Aggie. I heard you say you're naked in the tub, and I dropped the phone."

"Oh, the horror. A seventy-two-year old woman naked in a tub." I wished I could reach through the phone and strangle him.

"I didn't mean it like that."

Annoyed, I changed the subject. "So, how exactly did Jennifer's mother disappear?"

"He said she ran off. But she left a note behind, so the police never got involved."

"Starting to sound like a coincidence? How did he get a divorce if she's missing?"

"It's possible to divorce someone without them signing or being present."

"Did he get a divorce?"

"Damn, Aggie. He's married. I went to the wedding."

"You two are that chummy?"

"I've handled some things for him through the years."

"Like what?"

"I can't tell you that, Aggie. You know that."

I frowned. "You'll have to call me back tomorrow. If you have any useful information, leave a message on my answering machine because I plan on being out the entire day."

"Doing what?"

"Don't you worry about what I'll be doing. I'm on the case now, and I plan to see it through. I just wonder what else William is hiding."

"Be careful, Aggie. I'll talk to you soon." He hung up without giving me time to say another word.

What in the hell does he mean, talk to me soon? I had no intention of talking to him again.

I soaked in the tub, but I felt too hot now. I stood, being extra careful not to fall, and toweled off. I pulled my teeth out and plopped them into a denture cup. Dropping an Efferdent inside, I filled it with warm water.

I padded into the bedroom, pulled my nightgown over my head, and crawled into my bed. Pulling my blanket over me, I glanced at the clock and noticed it was only eight o'clock. No wonder I wake up so damn early.

* * *

I awoke at four thirty to the sound of birds chirping. Jeez, it wasn't even light out yet. I hadn't slept well. Every time I looked at the clock, only an hour had passed by. That's the way it was all night.

I couldn't stop thinking about Andrew. I berated myself because I knew there was no way he felt the way I felt, and even if he did, we were both too old to do much about it. Not that I felt old. I just hadn't had thoughts like this in years.

I swung myself out of bed, trotted into the kitchen, and made coffee. My head hurt like hell, and I popped two Tylenol, breathing deeply of the brewing coffee.

Opening the curtains, I saw dense fog surrounding the house. Duchess chose that moment to join me, and she rubbed her head against me, purring. I poured my coffee, and while stirring in my creamer, the phone rang. I picked up the phone and listened to a recording about the appointment I had scheduled for my physical the next day. I called and canceled it so I wouldn't be charged for not showing up again. I had no idea why Dr. Thomas insisted on me going, since I've felt fine of late.

I had forgotten about the appointment. It seems like I have been forgetting about a lot of things, lately.

I smiled and walked to the couch and sat down. I turned on the TV, flipping through the channels. I laughed when I saw only infomercials were on, mostly for male enhancements. If you aren't getting any by four thirty in the morning, chances are you're not going to be getting it, and no male enhancement product is going to change that.

I popped in a DVD and watched a horror movie. It was one of those movies based on a book by a popular author somewhere out east. I never liked his books much, but the movies always turned out to be pretty good.

Hollywood-created monsters never scared me much. It's the real-life ones that do. There are plenty of monsters hidden behind smiles of seemingly-normal folks. I still can't shake the feeling that whoever killed the Robinson family may still live nearby. I wonder why they had never caught the person responsible, although I had heard they reopened the investigation.

Yawning, I drank my coffee, and before long, I was going back for more. As I watched the movie, I realized how unrealistic it seemed. Something coming out of the mist seemed unlikely at best, but with the fog being so thick this morning, I decided it might be best to keep myself indoors until it lifted. You can never be too careful.

Chapter Seven

I was jarred awake by the sound of someone pounding on my door. I struggled to rise and noticed the TV was off. I must have flipped it off, but I don't remember when.

Eleanor's smiling face greeted me when I opened the door. I noticed her car parked precariously close to my Mustang—within inches. I silently prayed she hadn't swiped it. I would have heard that, though, I suppose.

It felt hot outside, and I noticed dark clouds hanging low. I hoped it wouldn't rain, which would make it even muggier, although I couldn't imagine how it could get any muggier. I moved away and Eleanor stomped inside. Closing the door, I saw she wore a blue floral dress with white tights. At least, that is what I thought they were, at first.

"Eleanor, are you wearing compression stockings?"

"Yes, the doctor had a nurse put them on me yesterday, and to tell you the truth, I can't get the damn things off. But I need to wear them because my legs have been swollen lately." She pouted. "You don't want me to get a blood clot, do you?"

"Of course not. It's just ... why didn't you wear pants?"

"It's going to be ninety today." She stood with her hands on her hips and a look of annoyance creasing her face.

I wrinkled my brow. "What time is it?"

"Noon."

"I need to throw some clothes on," I said while walking away.

I changed into beige crop pants and a short-sleeved jungle print shirt. I pushed my feet into my white flats, brushed my hair, and tried to rearrange it so that I could fill in all the spots where it was thinning. My hair had always been fine, but the last few years it had become thinner. The medications helped about as well as dousing it with seltzer water.

I returned to the living room, where I was greeted by the sight of Eleanor bent over, her behind in the air, searching through my refrigerator. She popped her head up. "Do you have anything to eat in here?"

I walked over and pulled out leftover roast chicken and mashed potatoes and made a plate for her, then popped it into the microwave.

She moved to retrieve it when the microwave beeped. She then carried it to the table, where I had set a place for her.

I sat across from her, gnawing on an energy bar while she ate the remainder of my food. I needed to get some groceries. "I'll have to drive to East Tawas to Walmart before long, but it's summer, and tourism's in full swing. I dread it."

"Traffic will be horrible. One of the reasons I haven't gone yet," Eleanor said between bites.

"I suppose you want to go to that back door store today, eh?"

"You promised," Eleanor said, and nodded.

I waited for Eleanor to use the bathroom and wash her hands, which took another fifteen minutes. She walked back wearing lipstick, a God-awful color, too—bright red. She hardly had the complexion for it. She had it smeared well past the line of her lips. I handed her a tissue so she could dab it, but it didn't look much better when she was finished. I shrugged, thinking God help anyone who dared make a comment.

We walked out the door, and I locked up. I held my hand out, waiting for Eleanor to put the keys into my hand, which she did with some reluctance.

I walked past my car, hoping it had no scratches or dents. When I saw it didn't, I got in and backed out the driveway.

"Humph," Eleanor muttered. She sounded like a spoiled child sometimes.

"What?" I asked.

"You don't trust me. You thought I hit your car."

"I trust you, Eleanor. It's your lack of driving skills that bother me. I hope you didn't mow anyone down on the way over here."

"Meaning?"

"You shouldn't be driving."

"And why the hell not, may I ask?"

"Your eyesight isn't the best, for one, and you have the reflexes of a sloth."

"Oh, of all the nerve, Aggie. Really! Like you're so perfect. What woman your age drives around in a hot red Mustang?"

She was really burning me. "Do you want to go or not? If you keep arguing with me, I'll just turn this car around and go back home."

"Okay, Mom!" Eleanor chuckled.

"Where is this place? Because I've certainly never heard about it before."

"Keep driving, and I'll tell you where to turn."

I drove a few miles, and across from the bend on US 23 stood the bikini shop, aptly named, "Bikini Shop." How original. We parked up front, and just when we stepped out of the car, I saw Dorothy Alton drive by. I mentioned it to Eleanor, and she gasped while I added, "Oh, great. I hope she doesn't know what this place is. Why in the hell are these sorts of stores on the main drag? I bet nobody knows about the backdoor because it would be closed up quick, like that bed and breakfast that turned out to be a swinger's club."

Bikinis hung from racks outside with the blow-up rafts and other assorted toys. This seemed more wrong all the time. I shuddered to think what other kinds of blow-up toys they'd have inside ... perhaps in a closed-door room.

We walked inside and began to move the bikinis around the racks as if we planned to buy one. I think the cutoff for wearing a bikini is forty, younger for anyone who'd had a C-section.

A young woman with flowing blonde hair approached us. Her golden skin had quite a glow to it. I wondered if she had oil on it, and the unmistakable odor of cocoa butter settled the argument—tanning lotion.

Eleanor held up a pink and white polka dot string bikini with a thong bottom. "Miss, do you have this in my size?" she asked with a straight face.

The girl's eyes became large. "I-I don't know, but I don't think ... so."

"Oh, I see. This is some kind of discrimination then, is that it? There's plenty of plus-sized people who need swimwear too."

I decided to step between the two women before things got ugly. I leaned forward. "We're here because we would like to purchase from the back room."

The girl's eyes darted back and forth, and I just knew she wished she were anywhere but here.

"I'm sorry. I don't know what you're talking about."

I firmly said, "You don't sound convincing, dear, and you look ready to swallow your tongue, which, while my friend and I would find amusing, would bring a shitload of paramedics down on your store. You know, if Sheriff Peterson found out about your back room, he'd lock this place up. You know how small-minded people can be in small towns."

"I'm not sure why you two would want to go back there. You're both so..."

"Old? Were you gonna say old?" Eleanor snapped. "You think older gals don't like to have a little fun?"

"Are you two together? I mean, like, a couple? I'm not one to judge, but you two look like an odd pair, is all I meant."

"You have no idea how right you are, child," I said, stifling a laugh.

"Remember the first time we made love, Agnes?" Eleanor asked me.

"You were drunk. How could you remember anything?"

"Oh, my God, I can't believe you said that, and after all these years."

Eleanor threw her hands upward as if calling on the rapture.

I declared, "Eleanor, I know what you're thinking, and you'd best hope the rapture isn't upon us 'cause you'd be going to Hades!"

"Follow me, then." The young woman walked towards the back, pulling the beads aside that covered the door. It reminded me of the sixties.

Five girls looked up and hastily put whatever they were holding away, and they all retreated out the door.

"We sure know how to clear a room, don't we, Aggie?"

I pulled a picture from my purse and handed it to the sales clerk. "Have you ever seen this girl here?"

The girl took the picture and started laughing. "Of course. Her name is Jennifer. She came in with some friends last week. Why?"

"She's missing."

"Oh, God," the girl said. "She's the one I read about in the paper." She frowned. "That's just awful. Are you, like, family?" She handed the picture back to me.

"I'm looking into her disappearance, is all. If you have any information that you can remember, it may be helpful."

"None that I can think of offhand, but the owner will be in soon, and she could help you. She spent a lot of time with them while they were here."

"Thanks. We'll just browse until the owner gets here."

I joined Eleanor. She had busied herself staring into a glass case like a kid in a candy store. Most of the toys were in glass cases with boxes of items along the back wall.

I read the name of the company off one box: Fun Factory. *What an odd name for a company that makes sex toys,* I thought.

"Look, Eleanor, these are all made by Fun Factory."

Eleanor giggled. "I see that, Agnes." She tucked her chin with a sheepish grin on her face. I think that's the closest I'd ever seen Eleanor come to blushing.

"Fun Factory is all about fun because if it's not fun, it would be named something else, like the Non-fun Factory," I said.

"I think it's a fitting name," Eleanor agreed.

As I moved on, I saw massagers. I think that sounds like a better name. Maybe I am old-fashioned, but the word vibrator sounds too dirty.

They had a wide variety of items. Many looked like animals in vibrant colors: hot pink, green, and purple. I'm quite sure if you used most of them too much, that's what your skin would look like: purple. That could make an interesting conversation with the doctor tomorrow.

Eleanor was giggling over in the corner, and I saw why. She was holding what they called a pink banana. It looked so pretty too.

"Look, Agnes, it says on the package that you can boil it for sanitation purposes." Her belly shook, and tears rolled from her eyes. "Imagine someone coming over and looking into the pot and wondering what you're cooking."

"Serve 'em right for being so damn snoopy."

Eleanor agreed, adding, "I can think of a few friends who I'd love to pull that kind of prank on!"

I found more items of interest, like a green wormy, and held it up for Eleanor's inspection. "What exactly you'd do with this I have no idea."

"And I'm pretty sure I don't care to know either, dear!" Eleanor grimaced.

I burst out laughing when I saw the rubber ducky massager. They even had one dressed in S&M clothing. That would take a bath to another whole other level. I saw rubber whips in vibrant colors. I wondered if smacking Eleanor with one would keep her in line. I doubted it. Knowing her, she'd love it. She was so incorrigible.

Then I spotted an item I knew I had to have, a lipstick vibrator. It'd be easy to conceal, and who would ever know the difference?

I picked my items and pulled Eleanor with me as we went to the counter and made our purchases. I saw a woman walking in and guessed it was the owner, judging by the way she bolted behind the counter.

She smiled at us as if women of our age were in here all the time.

"Excuse me, but are you the owner?" I asked.

She rubbed a hand through her cropped hair and nodded. Her expression was somber. *She thinks we're here to cause problems, I can see it in her eyes,* I told myself.

I flashed her Jennifer's picture.

"I heard she disappeared. What do you want to know?"

"Your employee said you spent a lot of time with her while she was here."

"I did. I thought she was here to shop, but she started asking questions about her mother."

"Her mother?"

"Yes, she figured she might be in the area. She showed me her picture, too."

"Did you recognize the woman in the photo?"

"It was an old picture, so it's kind of hard to say. So many people straggle through the area. She told me her mother left when she was ten, but she believed her father had something to do with her disappearance."

"You couldn't help her?"

"No, but I told her to check out Hidden Cove. It's a restaurant on Lake Huron. You can't miss it. The view is amazing."

"Who did she come in with?"

"She came in with a young man. I overheard her mention the name Kevin."

"Anyone else?"

"There were four of them all together, another couple, but they could be brother and sister because they shared some of the same features."

"Good observation, and thanks."

We started walking to the door, and I stopped when she spoke.

"I hope you don't plan on telling anyone about the back room."

I turned. "Nope, finding Jennifer is all I'm concerned with." I patted my bag. "As you can see, I made a purchase." I added, with a smirk, "Like I'd tell that lame-brained sheriff anything."

We walked outside, and I helped Eleanor back into the car. This heat was too much for her. She was already having problems breathing. The humidity today was even making it hard for me to breathe.

I jumped into the car, cranked up the engine and air, and stopped by Fuzzy's, the local ice cream shop.

We made our way inside, sitting at a table because the booths just didn't allow enough room for Eleanor to sit comfortably. Ironic, if you think about it. Anyone who came here often wouldn't fit in a booth. Kinda makes you wonder why they had them. It would seem like it'd be bad for business.

Most folks ordered at the counter, where you could choose from thirty different flavors of ice cream from within a glass case. Red and black licorice ropes dangled alongside the cash register, and nostalgic metal signs hung on the walls. Lake Huron was visible from the large glass window etched with the name Fuzzy's. Today, the water proved quite choppy, with gray clouds gathering in the distance. Picnic tables lined the deck, but most days it was too hot to eat outside.

Sally, the girl who works at the counter, came to our table. She smiled, and I noticed how perfect her teeth looked.

"Sally, did you get your braces off?" I asked.

She blushed. "Yes, isn't it great?"

I admired her glowing face, which was so pretty I couldn't help think it belonged on a magazine. She had only recently gotten a tan, and a few freckles were visible.

"We'd like the usual," Eleanor said.

Sally nodded and sprinted across the room. Eleanor had her eyes glued to her shapely butt.

"Honestly, Eleanor, I think you're a closet lesbian."

"What'd I do now?" She laughed. "You gotta admit, she has a rockin' shape."

"Rockin'? Since when did you start using words like that?"

"If you took the time to listen to the kids these days, you'd hear that and more, like HPOA."

"And that means what?"

"Hot piece of ass."

My mouth hung open, and I gulped. I was shocked. I knew Eleanor well enough to know that I constantly needed to prepare myself, because one never knew what might fly out of her mouth at any given moment, but sometimes she still managed to shock me. I couldn't believe she had repeated those God-awful words. Maybe I am old-fashioned. Then again, maybe I'm not, because ever since leaving the backdoor store, I had been thinking about trying out the lipstick vibrator, while thinking about Andrew.

I smiled when Sally returned with our desserts: a banana split for Eleanor, and a pineapple sundae with all the works for me. Problem is, it would probably set me back twenty bucks. Tourist towns were known to be mighty pricey.

I gazed across Lake Huron and watched the boats far in the distance. I had never been on a boat, aside from a charter fishing boat with Eleanor once. Fishing was never my thing, but watching Eleanor's face light up when she caught a perch warmed my heart. Watching her trying to catch the little bugger when it fell on the deck was priceless.

Her antics never ceased to amaze me, one of the reasons we were friends.

We had just started spooning in our delicious concoctions when Dorothy and Frank Alton walked in and hugged Sally, who's their granddaughter.

Eleanor froze with her spoon midway to her mouth, and chocolate syrup dripped down and rested on her cleavage. Frank's gaze was drawn to that spot as if on radar, openly staring at Eleanor's now chocolate-covered chest. Dorothy's eyes grew large when she saw Frank ogling Eleanor. Her nostrils flared, and she resembled a bull about to charge when, all of a sudden, she started to bark; or so it seemed.

I immediately thought, *Oh, my God, where is that yapping coming from?* Then I recalled Dorothy's dog. Surely, Dorothy hadn't brought her Shih Tzu in with her? Sure enough, she held the yapping dog, oddly named Zeus, in her arms.

I'm pretty damn sure that allowing a dog into an eating establishment remained illegal in Michigan, unless it was a seeing-eye dog. And I felt confident that this pint-sized annoyance to the eardrums wouldn't qualify.

"Get that damn dog outta here," Eleanor said to Dorothy. "It's not my problem your husband knows a good-lookin' woman when he sees one."

Dorothy cleared her throat. "Good-looking? Miss Melanoma?"

What I saw next baffled my mind.

It seemed to happen in slow motion. Eleanor tackled Dorothy, dog and all. They scuffled on the floor and rolled around, resembling a pair of flailing fish while the dog yipped and yapped up a storm, an annoying accompaniment to Frank's laughter.

Eleanor got in a few punches, but Dorothy yanked her head back and spat in Eleanor's face. At this point, even Zeus had sense enough to retreat from the pair.

Dorothy managed to make it to her feet, but as she tried to stagger away, Eleanor snatched her wig from her head. Gasps were heard about the room, and Eleanor lifted her head up and walked away.

"I so showed that bitch," she said gleefully.

Dorothy wasn't through, yet. I could see it when her eyes glazed over.

She planted a tub of ice cream over Eleanor's head, and cackled when Eleanor couldn't immediately get it off.

I jumped up and removed it before Eleanor could suffocate. I was in no mood to do CPR.

Seeing Dorothy minus her wig, I hid a snicker. She had hair. She just hadn't had it done this week. It looked dirty, flat, and in sad need of coloring.

Dorothy Alton had always prided herself on looking put together. You could tell by the clothes she wore. Her shirts and pants always matched. Her shoes matched her pants, and her hats matched her shirts. She was every bit the princess her family thought her to be, or a legend in her own mind. I believed she thought she was both.

When she spoke now, though, she sounded more like an owl screeching than a princess, and I saw her nails were razor-sharp, evident by the deep scratches on Eleanor's arms.

As for Eleanor, ice cream covered her head and had run into her cleavage—making for a complete hot fudge sundae. Eleanor stuck her tongue out toward Frank in a suggestive manner. Dorothy tried to dash toward her again, but Frank held her back.

"Calm down, Dorothy," he said.

Dorothy began bawling like a baby, always the drama queen. "Did you see what she did?" Dorothy mumbled, between sobs.

"I'll take you to the hairdresser so you can get your hair done."

"Okay, but look at what she did to my clothes."

"I'll buy you new clothes in Saginaw."

"Oh, Frank, but that's a long way." She glanced at Sally. "Can you drive us after work?"

"Sure, Grams, whatever you want."

I watched while Dorothy swooped Zeus up and left with Frank. He didn't look happy. This would no doubt set him back a pretty penny.

Sally ran into the back and returned with a mop bucket and two wet towels. She handed the towels to Eleanor, who then tried to clean the ice cream off.

I picked up the mop and mopped the floor while darts shot from Sally's eyes. She took the mop from my hands and finished the task herself.

"Oh, this isn't doing any good. All it's doing is making me more sticky," Eleanor whined.

"Serves you right, Eleanor," I said.

She pouted while I laughed. She really was quite the mess.

Sally walked over to me and spoke between clenched teeth. "You two so owe me." She dropped her head in her hands. "Like I want to spend my day driving clear to Saginaw and traipsing around with those two all day." She wiped her hands with a towel. "You think they're bad here, try being trapped in a car with those two on a road trip."

God forbid Dorothy buy clothing at Walmart like the rest of us, but I didn't say a word. There were no words that could excuse Eleanor's behavior, but she couldn't help herself, being uncontrollably impulsive by nature.

"Come on, Eleanor, I'll drive you home." I put money down on the counter, far exceeding the twenty I thought it would cost.

Eleanor hung her head and turned to Sally. "I'm awful sorry, Sally. I guess I'm banned again."

"See you next week," Sally replied.

Chapter Eight

I dropped Eleanor off so she could take a shower, and I drove back to the campsite where I had last seen Kevin. I knew it might be a long shot, but I hoped he'd still be there. He'd left certain details out when last we spoke, and I wanted him to clarify a few things for me.

Driving up the trail, I noticed an ambulance and the sheriff's car parked by the cabin. I parked my car, ran towards them, and saw Kevin being strapped onto a stretcher.

"What happened?" I asked Sheriff Peterson.

His face turned red when he saw me, but it didn't dissuade me a bit. "I was just here yesterday and..."

"What in hell for?" Sheriff Peterson asked.

I tried to see Kevin's face, but the sheriff blocked my view. "I'm waiting," he said.

I tried to see around him, but it was impossible. How did a sheriff this out of shape ever get elected, anyway? If this is who we had to count on to protect us, we were in big trouble.

"I was asking him questions about Jennifer. He was sorta seeing her." I contemplated telling him about the backpack Kevin had given me. Oh, what the hell. "He gave me Jennifer's backpack."

"Really? And where would that be now, Agnes?"

"At Eleanor's house."

"What? I told you to butt out. This is police business. I told you not to interfere, and now you are withholding vital evidence."

My heart began to pound. "Evidence? I thought you said she wasn't missing."

"I received a complaint about your interference in this case!"

"Now you're making stuff up? No one would... "

"William Martin, Agnes."

I needed to think, but I wanted to know what had happened to Kevin. "I planned to give you the backpack." I stalled while rational thought eluded me. "I just wasn't sure what to do with it. You were so insistent that I bug off..."

"I know, but that was before William filed the missing person's report with the Michigan State Police this morning." He scratched his head. "I just hate it when they take over."

"So, the state police are in charge of the investigation now?"

"Yes, but it will be a joint venture."

"What happened to Kevin?"

Sheriff Peterson's eyes darkened slightly. He didn't want to answer. I knew it. However, I also knew how much he hated being ousted by the state police, maybe enough to share information.

"Someone used him for a punching bag."

"He was beaten up?"

"Yes. Pretty bad, too. He's going to the hospital." He scratched his head. "Give me the backpack, and I'll take it to the State Police Post."

I'm not sure if it was how he said it or what, but I hesitated. What if he failed to give it to them? What then?

"Okay. Follow me to Eleanor's house and I'll give it to you. I'll be making a call to the trooper in charge of the case tomorrow."

"Why?"

"Maybe they'll be more appreciative of my efforts. Plus, I have additional information that may help them in the investigation."

"That's not necessary, Agnes. I told you I'd take it there, and I will."

"In my opinion, William Martin may be responsible for Kevin's current condition."

His eyes searched mine. "What makes you think that?"

"He told me Kevin knocked up Jennifer last year and she had an abortion. I came here today to ask Kevin if it's true."

"I think the timing could be a bit off. Like I said, Mr. Martin was at the Police Post."

"Okay, if you insist, but he runs a large corporation. Someone like that could have someone take care of Kevin while he is elsewhere."

"You can't just go around making assumptions like that unless you have proof." He glared at me. "If Kevin is one of the last people to have seen Jennifer, it would seem plausible her father would want to question him."

"Question him, or torture the poor kid? Jeez, Sheriff."

"We don't know that he did this, Agnes."

"You would think that, but men like William Martin are different."

"I'll follow you to Eleanor's and retrieve the backpack." He added, "I'd like to be home on time tonight."

I stepped outside and felt a chill as if being watched. I got into the Cadillac and drove back to Eleanor's house, followed by the sheriff. Once there, we walked into her house, and we both froze in our tracks.

Eleanor stood buck naked in front of a fan. We were shocked, but from the look on Eleanor's face, she couldn't have cared less. I'm not sure who was more shocked, the sheriff or me. Sheriff Peterson turned his back, and I'm sure he planned to gouge his eyes out later.

Her rolls and sagging skin covered most of her private parts, but it was a sight I could have gone without myself.

I handed the sheriff the backpack, and he ran out the door without saying a word. I heard him stumble in his hasty retreat. There was something about the sheriff's demeanor that I just didn't trust. He was hiding something. I wish I knew what.

"Eleanor!"

"What?" She smiled. "I was hot, and I needed to dry off." She giggled. "If I knew you were bringing a man, I'd have made my bed."

"You're not very choosy, are you?"

She paused as if lost in thought. "Not at my age."

"I left to question Kevin again."

"Without me? No fair." Sticking her lower lip out, she looked even funnier.

"Someone—they don't know who—beat the boy senseless, and he's on his way to the hospital."

"You think Jennifer's dad tried to off him?"

"Yes, that'd be my first guess, but he has an alibi. He was at the State Police Post filing a missing person's report."

"Likely story."

Eleanor disappeared into the other room, then returned, dressed in a low-cut black shirt with matching capri's, still wearing her white compression stockings and tan canvas shoes.

"What's up with the sudden show of skin?"

"It worked earlier. I like men to leer at me. It reminds me of working the streets in Saginaw."

"Did that actually happen or is it another one of your stories?"

"Wouldn't you like to know?" She pursed her lips in indignation.

I rolled my eyes and watched while she trounced outside and climbed in the car. She must have thought we were going somewhere. "We both think too much alike, Eleanor, but I'm running out of leads," I said to the empty room. Kevin was en route to the hospital. Jennifer had been looking for her mother before she disappeared, and her dad had made a complaint about me. Was he responsible for his ex-wife's disappearance? The girl's father sure seemed to be touchy about my prying questions. I looked out at Eleanor, who was sitting in the car, waiting for me, awaiting the chase. Let the games begin, she must be thinking.

I got in the car and roared up US 23 toward what looked to be my last lead, Hidden Cove.

It was a strange name because there were no coves anywhere near here. It sounded like a catchy name, though, and when I pulled into the paved parking lot, I saw it had an amazing view. There were only a few cars in the driveway. When I saw a Mercedes parked in the lot, I hoped William Martin wasn't here.

I walked inside, and sure enough, he was sitting at the bar with Andrew. With Eleanor in tow, I strutted over to them.

"Hello, William," I purred. "Fancy meeting you here. I heard you filed a missing person's report for Jennifer today."

William didn't even look up, the bastard.

"Is there any truth to the fact that Jennifer was in town searching for her mother?" I baited him.

"You just don't quit, do you?" William said between clenched teeth.

Our eyes met in the mirror behind the bar. "I'd hoped to question Kevin, but someone beat me to it, and beat the hell out of him while they were at it." I touched his shoulder. "You know anything about that?"

He jumped from the bar stool and pushed me to the ground. "You meddling old bitch! If you know what's good for you—"

Swoosh. Eleanor swung her big black purse and caught him alongside his head. He thumped to the floor, and Andrew helped me to my feet.

"Are you okay?" Andrew asked. "Damn, but you have good reflexes," he said to Eleanor.

William was laid out on the floor, unconscious. We all looked down at him. "Eleanor, what in the hell do you have in that bag?" I asked.

"Wouldn't you like to know?" She smirked. "Looks as though I saved your ass, so we're even, again."

"Even?" Andrew asked.

"We sort of had an episode at the ice cream shop today," I said.

"Somehow, I think you two have an episode everywhere you go." He inhaled loudly. "I think you two better scat before he wakes up."

"I'm not about to go anywhere," I insisted. "I came here to get information, and I'm not leaving until I get what I came for."

He raised an eyebrow. "She knocked the man clean out. How are you going to get any information from him?"

"It was self-defense," Eleanor insisted. "Plus, he knocked poor Aggie to the floor."

William was coming to, and Andrew helped him to a chair. The manager brought a plastic bag filled with ice and pressed it against the large bump on William's forehead.

"I think we should get you medical attention," Andrew said. He helped William to his feet and out to the car.

I watched William closely the whole time, and the look in his eyes was chilling. He was a man capable of anything. I hadn't expected him to push me to the ground like that, but I shouldn't have touched him. I imagined myself next on his list should he have his way.

Chapter Nine

I smiled at the manager, shrugged, and sat on a barstool. I ran my hand along the bar and felt the smoothness of the wood. It was made of mahogany, and I caught my reflection within its shiny surface. The high-backed black leather bar stool was cool against my back. It felt refreshing.

I saw pictures scattered along the walls, local pictures. I knew some of the faces. They were holding their catches, not all noteworthy. No swordfish here in Michigan. They held up perch, trout, and salmon.

I said in a stentorian voice, "I remember when you could catch perch by the bucketfuls from the dock in Tawas." This got the attention of the bartender, a spritely young woman I knew as Carly.

"It's not like that anymore," she replied.

"And I wonder why? Are they all fished out, or is there an environmental reason?" It was a dialogue we shared each time I came in for a drink.

"Hi, Agnes," the manager said.

I was taken aback, thinking, *Do I know him? Keep talking, Aggie, maybe he'll say something that will remind you.* At my age, I could get away with just about anything. I call it convenient confusion.

"I'm sorry, but I'm at a loss. I think I bumped my head on the floor when I fell."

"Oh, my God, Aggie," Eleanor said. She began to pant, sounding like a dog that had run for miles. "I think you may have a concussion! Somebody call a doctor, quick." Her eyes searched the room as if there were more than the four of us here.

"I'm fine," I insisted.

I saw Eleanor wink, and suddenly, I felt faint.

"Oh, I'm sorry, Mr. Manager, I think I may faint." I threw my hand to my forehead and let myself slump to the floor. Lucky for me, the manager caught me before I fell. Thank God. I worried he would let me fall on the damn floor. That just wouldn't do—these were new pants.

If Eleanor deserved an Academy Award, I deserved painkillers.

I saw his name badge said Jim. Oh, God! Jim, little Jimmy from little league, twenty-five years ago. It came back in a flash. Jimmy Paxton had been the smallest boy on the team, but that boy could run. I believed his speed came mostly from his daddy's belt. Fathers didn't spare the rod in those days.

His warm blue eyes looked at me with concern when he helped me to a chair just as Trooper Sales strutted in. The trooper's face, although striking, meant business.

His dark hair was rammed under a cap that cast a shadow on his face. His slender body and under-average height didn't detract from his appearance, which was obvious from the way Eleanor was gawking at him. I knew him to be a fair trooper.

I began to massage my hip, which had suddenly begun to throb, for real this time. "Damn karma," I whispered to Eleanor. "It's what I get for feigning feeling faint."

"What happened in here?" Trooper Sales asked Jimmy.

"Agnes came in and spoke with a man seated at the bar, and he pushed her to the floor."

Trooper Sales pulled his notebook out and began to jot down the information. "Did you happen to overhear their conversation?" He raised an eyebrow.

I stood. "Now listen here, what are you trying to say?"

He gave me the eye. "We have a man with a lump on his head at urgent care who said one of you knocked him out." His gaze seemed to penetrate Eleanor and me with an intensity I hadn't expected.

Eleanor stepped forward. "I hit him with my purse, is all." She began to fan herself with her hand. "He shoved an old lady to the ground. He was out of line and out of control, and I had no idea what he might do next. It was self-defense!" Her face turned red, and she tipped her head down, then raised it again, displaying tears in her eyes.

The trooper narrowed his eyes. He turned to Jimmy. "Is that how it went?"

"Yes, and I think she needs to see a doctor because before you came in, she nearly fainted."

"She seems fine now."

This damn man isn't so easily fooled, I thought. It's like he sees right through me.

"Is that what they taught you in Saginaw—that it's acceptable to knock old ladies around?" Jimmy asked.

"Jesus, Jimmy, the man's daughter is missing. He's kind of on edge."

"I have reason to believe he is impeding the investigation into his daughter's disappearance," I countered.

"In what way?"

"His daughter was seeing Kevin Marks, and when I went there to question him further, an ambulance was there. Someone had beaten that poor boy terribly, someone with a temper." I smoothed my hair back. "I think William may have had something to do with it."

"So you have been snooping around again?" He raised his hand, halting me from saying anything further. "The Michigan State Police are handling the investigation, and we don't need your help. If you continue to involve yourself in this case, you're going to find yourself in trouble."

"Seems to me you'd appreciate the help. When my granddaughter went missing last year, the police just sat on their laurels. If you won't do anything to keep girls around here safe, I guess it's up to the citizens to take action."

"I'm sorry to hear you feel that way, Agnes. I'd hate to lock an old lady up, but I will if you give me no other choice." He strolled back out into the parking lot and took off.

"This is a bunch of crap. He threatens to arrest me but doesn't do a damn thing about William. I could have broken something when I fell," I said indignantly.

"Those troopers don't care about us. I bet when we drive through town later, he'll be at Tim Horton's for a double dipped doughnut," Eleanor said, nodding.

I handed Jennifer's photo to Jimmy. "Jimmy, do you recognize the girl in this picture?"

"I can't help you, Agnes." He never even glanced at the picture.

"Why not?"

"I gave the information to the man that pushed you down, already. She was in here asking questions about her mother before her disappearance."

"Well, what did you tell him?"

"I told him to check Roy's Bait Shop."

Ice ran up my spine. "Come on, Eleanor."

I ran out the door with Eleanor in tow, got into the car, and raced toward the bait shop. "I sure hope we get there before William does."

"He's at urgent care, didn't you hear?"

"Man like that probably has goons working for him. That's probably how Kevin got beat up while William was filing the missing person's report."

"You think he'd hurt Roy?"

"They hurt Kevin, and William's proven to me he has a violent streak. You saw what he did to me."

"I wouldn't worry about Roy, though. He's not the type to let somebody get the best of him. He was in the Marines." Eleanor nodded emphatically to prove her point.

I pulled into the bait shop and saw two black Impalas in the lot. I dialed 911 and jumped out of the car while Eleanor shuffled inside her purse. I didn't wait. I had to save Roy.

When I opened the door, I saw Roy on the far side of the room with a hunting knife in his right hand, jabbing at one of the men.

"You bastards picked the wrong person to harass," he said angrily.

I could see he had a cut across the top of his forehead that was seeping blood. I sized up the four men surrounding Roy. They were tall with dark complexions, Italians I think. They pushed him against the counter, while another man struck Roy in the stomach. Roy grunted and almost fell, but they held him up. It was clear to me they weren't through with him yet, as he took another blow to his face.

I stood there, as if watching a movie. I felt rooted to the spot. I would be an even easier target than Roy, but I hit the floor when I heard a gun explode, and the bullet struck a net above the men's heads, showering them with seashells. One of the men fell, and the other two tripped as they tried to scramble away. I heard another explosion. The bullet struck a metal pan on the wall this time and ricocheted in the small shop until it struck the only man left standing right in the ass.

"Freeze, suckers!" Eleanor shouted. She walked forward with a menacing look on her face. Her eyes darting between the men, she curled her lips back into a snarl. She was holding a pink gun in her shaking hand.

"You better listen to her," I shouted.

I'm not sure if they felt intimidated, but they lit out into the back room. We heard clattering, followed by screams and a growl. I could hear them kick the back door open, and we watched through the windows as the trio ran for their cars, leapt into them, and screeched onto US 23.

Roy's face mirrored mine.

"Eleanor, where in the hell did you get that gun?" I asked.

"I bought it."

"When? Where?"

"In Saginaw. Aw, don't worry. It's legal. I have papers to prove it."

"Well, put it away before the police get here."

Eleanor shoved the gun back into her purse, and I looked expectantly at Roy.

"You have a dog in the back room?" I asked as I shook, looking through the open doorway. I could see two glowing eyes peeking from the darkened room. I gulped hard.

"No, a coon."

"You have a flippin' raccoon back there?" Eleanor asked.

We dodged behind the counter for safety.

"It's much better than a dog, and twice as mean," he informed us. He looked up at the dangling net. "I'm sure glad you didn't kill me, Eleanor. You don't seem to be a very good shot."

She put her hands on her hips and tapped her foot. "I was nervous."

We heard sirens blazing up the road, and gravel scattered as the cars parked.

"I don't think we should mention the gun or the raccoon," I whispered to Roy and Eleanor.

They nodded in agreement. Roy crossed the room, closed the back door and finished up by sitting down on a chair. I found a paper towel and applied pressure to his head. I couldn't find anything else clean, and I feared he would get an infection.

Sheriff Peterson ran into the shop, gun drawn, followed by the stone-faced Trooper Sales.

Paramedics were the next to enter. I moved so they could attend to Roy.

"What happened?" Trooper Sales asked. His face tightened, and his voice took on a serious tone. "Anyone else hurt here?

I imagined him after his shift, stopping at Hidden Cove for a stiff drink.

"We were planning to go fishing later, and um, when we walked in, four goons were putting a pounding to poor Roy here." Even as I lied, I wondered why lying to this trooper was so hard.

"Hmm, is that how it was, Roy?" Trooper Sales asked.

"They saved my life! I mean, if these two ladies hadn't come in when they did, I woulda been toast."

"Did the men say what they wanted?"

"No, they just attacked me."

"I guess they were surprised when we walked in, and they scooted off like a buncha little girls," Eleanor told them.

I was about to choke on my tongue when I added, "I called 911 when I didn't recognize the cars."

"I see. It'd probably be best to stay outside next time you think a crime is happening," the trooper suggested. "I would sure hate to explain how two old ladies got offed playing Super-sleuths."

Roy was helped onto the gurney. "Agnes, please do me a favor and work my shop until I get back. The keys are hanging on the nail over there." He pointed at the wall.

"I can't do that," I said. "I don't know anything about selling bait and tackle."

"Oh, please! This is my busy season," he implored.

"Sure thing, Roy," Eleanor said with a shrug. "Hell, it's the least we can do." And, seeing my disapproving grimace, she said to me, "What? It sounds like fun."

"What about the, ahhh ... dog in the back? Does he ... need to be fed?" I asked.

"There is some fish in the cooler over there. Just throw it back there and close the door quick. He doesn't cotton to strangers."

The sheriff and the trooper gave me an amused look.

"At least this will keep you two out of trouble," the trooper said. The sheriff patted him on the back, laughed, and together, they left.

Chapter Ten

The neon sign of Roy's Bait & Tackle flashed to open. It flashed like the light would go out at any moment, which I'd be happy about. It was enough to cause a person to go into a panic attack. It could have just been me, though, because I wasn't happy that I was stuck minding the shop while Roy was at the hospital. Eleanor busied herself by polishing her gun. It made me more than a bit nervous, but what the heck. At least we'd be prepared if the goons showed up again.

I sprinkled food in the minnow tank. It seemed pointless, really, because they'd be dead soon enough. I glanced toward the worm box with a less than enthusiastic expression. We flipped a coin, and I won the honor of being the first person to dig worms out. Just my luck.

I swept the floor and picked up the seashells that had fallen victim to Eleanor's gunplay. I piled them into the sink so I could wash them because they were covered with dirt, and some had not been completely shattered.

I had placed a bell over the door earlier. If someone wanted to come back to finish the job, I wanted a forewarning.

The bell rang, and Jack Winston walked in with a woman half his age.

He's my age.

He left his wife when his children were quite young and stayed gone for a number of years. He then returned, and they seemed happy enough until her death five years ago. Ever since then, he'd been bringing a different young woman around with him everywhere he goes.

In general, he was a male chauvinist.

His hair was slicked back today, and he stroked his mustache. It had enough wax on it to stay in place if there were a hurricane.

Why in the hell was he here?

He reminded me of a cartoon. He was dressed too nice to be going fishing, wearing black dress pants and a tropical dress shirt— silk I think.

The redhead accompanying him wore shorts so short they were practically jammed up the crack of her ass, and she had a rack that would make most men visibly drool. You could see her silver dollar nipples through the clingy white T-shirt she wore.

I knew that simply nudging Eleanor wouldn't stop her gawking.

"Hello there, Agnes," Jack said. He opened his eyes wide and smiled.

I wanted to smack the smile off his face.

"Why does it smell so fishy here?" He sniffed the air. "Is that you, Eleanor?"

She tried to grab him from behind the counter.

"Ignore him, Eleanor." I smiled at Jack. "Have you found a cure for your erectile dysfunction yet?"

"I don't need anything. The Johnson is working just fine. Isn't that right, honey?" He pulled the woman close.

The girl blushed. "It sure is, baby." She giggled.

"Did you hear that, Eleanor? He has a name for it—Johnson!"

"How disgusting," she replied.

"Compliments of a little blue pill, no doubt," I added.

"Summer school must be taking a break," Eleanor said to the woman.

The girl's bottom lip trembled, and she seemed to be at a loss for words. "Baby, do we have to stay here?" she asked in a whiny voice.

"No, sweetie pie, I just heard the old crones were minding the shop, and I had to see it to believe it." He smiled, guiding the barely-legal girl out the door. He rubbed his fingers along the exposed skin of her ass, and I had to choke back vomit.

"I'd take my gun and shoot myself in the head before I'd let that man touch me," Eleanor said.

I nodded, as an amused Andrew entered the bait shop, followed by a man and two young boys.

Andrew stood back and watched as the two boys, who looked to be age five and six, jumped around the shop excitedly. I panicked when I saw them looking at the worm case.

"Settle down, boys," the man with the two boys said.

"We have a nice tank of minnows over here," I suggested.

"Worms are better," Eleanor offered.

"Minnows have always been the way to go," I countered as I smiled playfully. I hated this sales crap.

"Worms are more fun." Eleanor grinned down at the children. "We have some fat, juicy ones in there. It's so cool when you grab one of those slippery buggers." She danced her fingers along the counter for emphasis.

"Daddy, can we get worms?" one boy asked.

He nodded. "I always liked worms when I was your age. I'd like twelve of your juiciest worms."

Eleanor beamed, and I wanted to give her a pinch.

"Agnes would be more than happy to help you."

I made my way to the case, opened it, and saw I'd have to dig into the moist soil to retrieve them. I picked up a Styrofoam container and scooped some dirt into the bottom. Holding my breath, I worked my fingers into the dirt and pulled worms out, placing them into the box. What I really wanted to do was gag.

"These suckers are kind of hard to pull out," I said. I yanked one of the fat suckers a little too hard and flung it into the air. It landed in Eleanor's cleavage.

Laughter echoed as we heard her scream. She pushed her hand down her shirt, searching frantically for the worm. Panting loudly, she finally pulled it out. "What in the hell are you trying to do? Give me a heart attack?"

I handed the container of worms to the man, and he dropped money on the counter. Tears of laughter continued running down his face as he led the boys out the door.

Andrew chuckled. "You two should go on the road. You're a couple of comedians."

Eleanor sat down and pouted.

"Oh, stop it, Eleanor. You deserved it, and you know it."

"Deserved it?" She puffed her chest up.

"You egged them on."

"I'm not speaking to you right now. I'd never do something like that to you." She smiled at Andrew. "Isn't this the hot-shot lawyer you used to cream your pants over when you lived in Saginaw?"

I held my breath. *She didn't just say that,* I said to myself as I cringed. But she did, and I wanted to throttle her. "Ignore her," I softly pleaded with Andrew. "You know, she's just trying to get back at me."

I walked to the sink and washed my hands for at least ten minutes. I was hoping that if I stayed there long enough that Andrew would just leave, because I sure as hell didn't want to face him.

Finally, I turned, and he looked more amused than ever.

I strutted past him and walked to the door, flipping the open sign to closed. After all, it was after five. My lips suddenly felt dry for some reason. I turned, reaching into my pocket, and pulled my lipstick out to apply some, but I dropped the tube. It fell to the floor, and I heard a familiar vibration. Freezing in horror, I realized that it was the lipstick vibrator! The one I'd bought at the backdoor store earlier in the day. I must have put it into my pocket by mistake.

I froze and wanted to die. I wanted God to take me that very instant.

I have never been so mortified! Andrew had immediately bent over, picked it up, and turned it off before handing it back to me. I stood there like a deer in headlights.

"I think you dropped this," he said.

I snatched it from his hand. "We're closed. Maybe you should leave."

"Well, that's a hell of a business motto. What if I wanted to buy some worms?"

"It's Eleanor's turn."

"How about going somewhere for a drink?"

"I smell like fish."

"Really? Is that what that smell is?" His smile widened.

I almost wanted to send Andrew into the back room. I wondered how much and how loud he'd scream.

I bet the raccoon was hungry. I pulled a fish from the cooler and tossed it into the back room, slamming the door quick.

"What in the hell is back there?" he asked.

"You want to find out?"

His smile faded.

"It's a 'coon, a mean one," Eleanor chimed in.

"You mean a live raccoon?"

"He has a real nasty disposition," I added. "What are you doing here?"

"I thought I'd check out the tip the manager at the bar gave us. William is recuperating in his room."

"It's dirty business," I said.

"What is?"

"This whole thing stinks to high heaven."

"You've lost me."

"We followed up on the same tip he was given, and there were goons here pounding Roy, but they ran off when we came inside."

"I shot one of 'em in the ass," Eleanor proudly added.

"Eleanor, would you quit supplying him with information. For all we know, he's somehow ... some way involved."

"Is that what you think, Aggie? You think I'd be party to something like this?"

"You're his friend," I reminded him.

"And a former lawyer," Eleanor added with a grimace.

"Ahh, I see... Everybody knows lawyers are slime. Is that what you think?" Andrew asked.

"You said it, not me, mister," Eleanor crowed as she rejoined the fray.

Andrew stomped to the door, where he did an about-face before he left. "I thought you knew me better than that, Aggie," he said angrily. He flung the door open, and it slapped the wall.

When he tore out of the lot, it felt like a piece of my heart went with him.

Chapter Eleven

When we locked up Roy's Bait & Tackle shop, I was in a sour mood. Running a bait shop sure had its drawbacks. I still can't believe I had touched a slimy worm. I hoped the other girls wouldn't hear about our adventure. The last thing I needed was to be the talk of Tadium.

"Oh, stop it, Aggie."

I glared at her. "It's all your fault, and you know it."

"Who, me? What did I do?"

"You didn't need to blabber on like that in front of Andrew." I limped toward Eleanor's big heap of junk Cadillac. "I'd never do anything—"

"Oh, you better stop right now. You were the one who threw a worm down my shirt, remember?"

She yanked the car door open and sat inside. When I joined her a few minutes later, she glowered at me. "Who cares what Mr. Fancy Britches thinks, anyway? It's not like he's interested in you."

"What makes you think he's not?"

"Come on, Aggie, you don't still have the hots for him, do you?"

I glanced at my reddening face in the mirror and fanned myself. I felt like I'd been stricken with a hot flash, which I still had on occasion.

I cranked up the air conditioning. "Okay, you win. I still have the hots for him, but I didn't want him to know. Certainly, you can understand that, El."

"At least the cat's out of the bag now, and, dear, he won't forget you now for sure," she said as she patted my hand and chuckled. "You should have seen the look on your face when the lipstick vibrator went to buzzing. I swear, your face contorted like some kind of zombie."

"I'd rather not remember, if you don't mind." I turned up the radio loud enough to discourage Eleanor from further commenting on my embarrassing scenario. More blasted honky-tonk. It grated on my already frayed nerves, and my hip was beginning to nag at me.

I drove Eleanor home for the second time that day, and then made my own way home. When I got there, I limped in the door and made my way toward my bathroom, where I ran a hot bath. I noticed a large bruise along my right hip. "So that's why it hurts so damn much," I said aloud. But the bruises to my ego hurt even more.

I brought my phone with me and sank into the tub.

I heard my phone ring, and I saw Andrew's name displayed on the caller ID, but I didn't answer it. Let the answering machine get it. I had no intention of answering any calls from him just yet.

I soaked for as long as I could, but when the water became tepid, I rose from the tub and slipped into my dressing gown. From the bath, I walked into my bedroom. I eased myself into bed and fell fast asleep within minutes.

I'm not sure how long I slept, but I awoke to the sound of my car alarm going off. I got up, retrieved my remote starter, and pressed it several times in an effort to stop the alarm, but it was no use. I then opened the front door and hit a button again to silence it. I hadn't given it a second thought how dangerous that might have been. Someone could have been lurking in the darkness.

I was, after all, investigating a disappearance, possibly a murder or two.

I stumbled my way though the living room, and as a sharp pain shot up my hip, I fell to the floor. I couldn't move, and crawling back to the phone wasn't an option because I had left it in the damn bathroom. I closed my eyes while wondering if I would die on this floor. I had Eleanor's Cadillac. There was nobody to check on me. I had no one. A cold sweat crept over my skin and my breathing became labored I fought to keep myself from fainting, but I could not be sure if I'd be successful or not.

* * *

I woke up confused, and I tried to get my bearings, although I hadn't opened my eyes yet. Where was I?

My scrambled mind recalled the details. *I'm not on the floor in my house, though*, I thought. I felt the mattress beneath me, and knew I was lying on a bed, but it wasn't my bed. The mattress was much thinner and harder, and the blankets rough against my palms. When I opened my eyes, I saw Eleanor's concerned face hovering over mine.

"You're not going to kiss me, are you?" I asked.

"Of course not," Eleanor snapped. "You gave us quite a scare."

"Us?"

"Yes, Andrew just left to get more coffee."

I gulped. Why is he here? "What happened?"

"Andrew got concerned about you and tried to call you, but when you didn't answer, he was afraid the goons were going after you next." She took a breath. "So he stopped by to make sure you were, you know, okay."

"I don't remember much, but yeah, he called when I was in the bath. I forgot to call him back. Went to sleep instead..."

"When he came over with some lame excuse," she said with a wink, "he saw your Mustang's windows were broken out, and he kicked your door in just like a hero in a film."

Andrew walked into the room and smiled, handing a coffee to Eleanor.

"Why did you kick my door in?" My voice rose an octave.

"You didn't answer, so I thought something was wrong." He took a sip of his coffee.

Eleanor chuckled. "Good thing, too, because he found you passed out on the floor."

"My poor car."

"Your poor car? What about poor you? I'm just glad you are in one piece," Eleanor said.

"I remember hearing my car alarm, and I shut it off. I had an awful pain in my hip, and I fell. I had left my phone in the bathroom, and I knew there was no way I could reach it." I shuddered at the idea that whoever broke my car's windows could have been outside when I opened the door.

Andrew's face looked solemn. "I think it was a warning shot across your bow, so to speak."

"It will damn sure take more than a broken window to scare me." I'd be damned if they'd scare me off.

"They broke all your windows, not just one," Eleanor added.

My head began to pound with every word they said, as if they were driving nails into my head.

"You both need to be careful," Andrew added.

I folded my arms across my chest. "It all leads to William, but you know that, don't you?"

Andrew gave me a stern look and a shake of the head. "Let's wait and see, Aggie. It could just as well be someone else."

I felt a pang like a dart to the heart. He'd always called me Aggie in the old days. I gathered myself together and firmly replied, "Somebody else has an interest in Jennifer's missing mother? Not likely."

I don't know why Andrew continued to defend his friend. Who else would be interested in finding her this badly? I needed to find out additional information about Jennifer's mother. There was a link, but what?

"Roy's room is down the hall," Eleanor said.

I struggled to rise, but an alarm sounded and two nurses ran into the room. "You need to stay in bed, Agnes," one said.

"Why?" I asked, already knowing why. My head was swimming as if I were caught in a whirlpool.

"You can't get up without assistance."

"There is no way you or anybody else is going to tell me what

I can and can't do. I can walk just fine," I stubbornly replied as I swung my leg over the side of the bed and tried to stand.

I watched the nurses as they were poised to intercede. I pushed myself up and felt dizzier still as a pain shot up my hip.

I heard Andrew's voice over Eleanor's, through what seemed to be cotton in my ears, say, "Aggie, don't be a fool!"

I sank back down. "Okay, you win. Will someone please find a wheelchair, because a good friend is down the hall, and I intend to see him."

"Chop, chop, get the woman a wheelchair," Eleanor ordered.

They didn't move. *Why are they making this so hard,* I wondered. *Can't they understand how crucial this is?* One of the nurses left the room and returned with a roller walker that only had wheels on the front.

"Oh, no you don't!" I erupted. "There is no way I'm using any walker. I'm fine. I'm just weak," I admitted and saw everyone in the room staring at me, bug-eyed. "You can help me, but if you start counting to three, I'm going to start swinging."

So much was racing through my head, and it all amounted to, *Don't embarrass me in from of Andrew!* The whole standing-on-the-count-of-three thing might be good for some people, but not for me. I know the cute young nurses thought I was a frail, elderly woman, but there was no need to make me look worse than I am.

I allowed them to place a gait belt around my waist, but even that made me feel degraded. They only use a gait belt in case your ass hits the floor. It was a safety requirement of any hospital these days if you happened to be a fall risk. The nurses failed to realize what Eleanor and I realized: that I'm an independent woman, and that was my problem ... the same problem with anyone who got older or became sick. Everyone treated the likes of us as if we were suddenly so damn fragile. I looked down and saw the color-coded bracelet that indicated I was a fall risk. This might be a reality for some, but not for me. "You know, dears, I-I didn't fall. It was the stabbing pain in my hip that caused me to go down."

I stood with their help and moved the walker forward. I felt sore, but I wasn't going to let that hold me back. Eleanor guided me down the hallway and finally into Roy's room. The whole way, Andrew held my arm like he, too, thought me incapable of this simple task. I felt a single tear escape on the side of my face, away from his view.

Roy was ranting at a nurse so loud his face had turned red. "I need to go home, damn it! I have a business to run."

"The doctor will be here soon."

"You have been saying that all goddamn day."

Roy smiled when he saw me, and I sat in a chair next to his bed. "Calm down, Roy." I turned to look at the nurses. "Can you give us some privacy? I promise I'll call when I'm ready to go back to my room."

They nodded, but I knew, what with the way they shuffled toward the door, that they didn't want to.

"I see they got you, too," Roy said.

"No, *they* didn't get me. It's just that my hip is acting up."

He made a fist with his hand. "Once these doctors have you in their clutches, you're doomed."

"Can you walk, Roy?"

"Yes. They claim I'm getting released today, but my doctor is taking his sweet time getting here to sign me out."

I laughed. "Sounds like a doctor." I paused. "Tell me, Roy, why were those men in your shop yesterday?"

"They wanted information." He shrugged and scratched his head and eyed Andrew suspiciously. "Who's that?"

"He's an old friend."

"Can you trust him?"

"Yes, he was the one who found me passed out on the floor at home. The goons came to my house and broke out all the windows on my Mustang."

"Bastards."

"I guess they don't like my meddling."

"You're meddling? No, not you, Agnes." He laughed, but then became serious. "Agnes, they're looking for Stella, and there is no way I can let them find her."

"Stella?"

"She's a woman who moved here ten years ago. Her husband tried to kill her, and she took off; wound up here."

"Hold on, took off?"

"Yeah, fast, leaving her daughter behind."

"Jennifer?"

He nodded. "Stella's husband was into something big, but she never exactly gave me the lowdown. She told me if he ever found her, she would be as good as dead."

"We were told Jennifer came looking for her mother. Did she come to your shop?"

"Yes, and I should've called the police because I think somebody followed her there. I remembered seeing the same black Impala that came to my place yesterday."

"Did you tell Jennifer where to find Stella?"

He nodded. "Yeah, but she never made it to Stella's place."

"You need to tell me where Stella is."

"I can't, Aggie."

"Made promises, eh?"

"They find her, they'll kill her. I know that for sure. Look what they did to me!"

"Jennifer's dad pushed me down, and I see him capable of just about anything." I eyed Andrew and rubbed my hip because it was aching again. "I need to find out who the goons are and who they are working for, and why in the hell they're trying to stop me from poking around. I'm beginning to wonder if Jennifer is even alive."

After I told Roy goodbye, I stood with Andrew's aid and walked back to my room, Eleanor bringing up the rear. If Roy knew where Stella was, his life could be in jeopardy. I wondered how he knew Stella and what other information she had shared with him, and why? It didn't take a brain surgeon to know he was holding back important details.

When I got back to my room, my doctor was waiting for me.

"Hi, Doc," I said.

Dr. Thomas had a reputation as the best doctor around these parts. He stood six foot three and had sandy blond hair and piercing green eyes ... damn good eye candy.

I sat down. "So, what's the verdict?"

"You bruised your hip? Did you fall?"

"I was pushed down yesterday, and afterward, my hip started hurting something fierce. I didn't really fall. I just slipped to the floor, and I couldn't get back up."

Laughter filled the room, and I glared at Eleanor until she stopped. "Sorry ... just pictured you in an ad for Life Alert."

"It's not so funny now that it's happened to me," I said.

"I see. Did you report it to the police?" asked Dr. Thomas. "Being knocked down?"

"Yes, but the trooper who showed up didn't do a damn thing."

"I whopped the sucker over the head," Eleanor added.

Dr. Thomas laughed. "Somehow I can see that, but someone who knocks down a woman needs to be in jail."

I loved that he didn't use the words 'old woman' because I'm not old, not yet. I'm younger than Eleanor. He knew how to talk to his patients, most of whom were older.

"I'd like you to stay here a few more days until you feel a little stronger." He glanced at the clock. "You may want an orthopedic surgeon to look into your hip problems."

"Did the X-rays indicate that?"

"You didn't break anything. That's the important thing." He put his hand on my shoulder. "Be careful, Agnes. I'd sure hate to lose a patient like you." I felt a tingle when he touched me. It felt good.

Dr. Thomas left the room.

"You can quit gawking at him, Aggie. You know very well he's gay," Eleanor scolded.

"He's still damn good eye candy. Let me have my fantasies."

"I think you might want to get one of these little gadgets," Eleanor said, swinging her Lifeline Alert necklace in my face.

I cringed, but I knew she was right. It might be time, but for so long now I had prided myself on dodging AARP, and now this?

"I know of someone who has one of those gizmos hooked up to GPS," Andrew said. "That way if you get into trouble anywhere, I could find you."

Get into trouble? He said it as if predicting I'd get in over my head. I'd be dammed if I'd let him know he might be right. "Sounds great."

"I want one like that, too." Eleanor pouted.

"I think that's an even better idea," Andrew said. "Agnes, you look tired. I'll take Eleanor home so you can get some rest."

Eleanor plopped into the single chair in the room. "I'm not leaving."

"Eleanor, you need to get some rest, too. Besides, when I get sprung, we'll be pretty busy."

Eleanor clapped her hands. "I can't wait."

"Andrew, could you go back to my house and water my plants and feed my cat?

"Your cat?"

"Duchess, yes. Poor dear is probably out of her mind with me gone."

"I can only imagine."

"I don't want all my vegetables and flowers dead when I get out, either."

"As it happens, cats love me, and I have a green thumb, so yeah, I can do that."

Eleanor got off her ass and went willingly with Andrew, winking at me behind his back as if she had won him in a bake-off. They walked out, and I was left to my thoughts, dark thoughts that involved a murder-for-hire plot. I felt certain that I could dig up something about Stella. This remained a small town, so how invisible could she be?

Chapter Twelve

I awoke and felt someone standing over my bed. I snapped my eyes open, and it scared the hell out of me. Sure, I was still at the hospital, but that didn't mean I was safe. Who knew what kind of security they had at St. Luke's hospital in Tawas? It was more of a Band-Aid hospital. I sure as hell knew it couldn't be a nurse, as they loved to flip the light switch on and blast me with the fluorescent light that bored into my eyes like a dagger whenever they entered.

"Shh," I heard a male voice say. "It's Kevin, Jennifer's friend. You're the one asking questions about Jennifer Martin, right?"

"Yes," I whispered.

I heard footsteps walk toward my room and stop outside my door as if listening. I held my breath until they walked away.

"They're looking for me."

"Who?"

"The goons who beat me up."

"They're here?"

"Yes, and I think they want to finish me off."

"Why?"

"Not sure; I'm not sure about anything, anymore."

"Calm down, Kevin."

"I only know one thing," he cryptically replied.

"What's that?"

"If you don't find Jennifer soon—she's done for."

"You don't think she's been kidnapped."

"I think she may be lying low."

"How can you be so sure?"

"Because the goons were looking for her."

"Maybe they work for her dad."

"Not sure. Could be."

"Her dad said you got her pregnant last year. Is that true?"

"That's impossible."

"Last I looked, it's quite possible," I countered.

"No, you don't understand. We never even did it."

"Oh, I see ... well, that is a horse of a different color."

"Horse?" He coughed. "It's not safe for me to stay here."

"How do I know you're really Kevin?"

"You don't."

Footsteps retreated, and by the time I located the light switch, he was gone.

"Who in the hell was that?" I asked the silent room. "And why does he want me to think Jennifer is in hiding?"

* * *

Two days later, I was released from the hospital. Upon arriving home, I strode toward my garden, and just as expected, my plants looked to be about dead.

I frowned in Andrew's direction. "I thought you said you'd water my plants?"

"I thought you meant the ones indoors." He winked.

If he thought putting on the charm would work, he was sadly mistaken. I stared into his eyes without blinking, less than amused with his take on the situation. I spend every free moment maintaining a garden to die for, and he was making a mockery of it.

"Sorry," he muttered.

"Sure." I glared at him. "How were you to know how high-maintenance my plants are?" I frowned. "I'll just have to give them extra lovin', I guess."

I walked to my cute little barn-shaped shed and retrieved a watering can. I had a lattice archway to the right with a bench beneath, as I hoped one day to sit out here in the evenings, but it wouldn't be tolerable enough until August. I kind of hoped Andrew would stick around long enough to join me one night.

Stop it, Agnes. He doesn't even see you in that way.

I filled the watering can with rainwater reserved in a metal tub under my downspout. "My momma always said rainwater is best." I nodded. "That way you know God himself touched your plants." I tried to sound believable without laughing.

"Did God tell you to gather rainwater in buckets?" He smirked.

"God speaks to me in ways you'll never know." *My lip must be dripping blood by now*, I thought, as I'd been biting down hard, trying not to smile. "Just like my mother's words. She kept a yardstick over every door, and the ones she didn't, she kept a hickory switch. I learned fast to always listen to momma. In those days, God spoke to me a lot! More than my sisters and brothers, I can tell you!" Now, I laughed.

His eyes widened for a moment, and I wondered if he had his own memories to reflect upon.

I watered my plants and noticed the empty space reserved for my Mustang.

"Goddamn it, they came back and finished poor Bessie off!"

He raised an eyebrow. "Bessie?"

"My car."

"You named your car Bessie?"

"I always wanted a cow named Bessie, but I named a car that instead." I wrinkled my nose. "I don't really want to clean up cow poop, so I thought the Mustang was the better choice."

Andrew's facial expressions changed back and forth between bemusement and wonder, finally settling on a glare that seemed to say, 'Has she lost it completely?'

"Goddamn it!" I exclaimed.

"Taking the lord's name in vain." He clucked his tongue. "I'm shocked, and what would momma say?"

I wouldn't give him the satisfaction of responding. I opened my door and stopped him when I thought he would follow me inside.

"Where the devil is my car?"

"It's down at the shop getting new windows."

"Thanks. I'm real tired, so you best be going home now."

"I'm being dismissed? If you want me to go, I will, but only after I check out your place."

I opened the door, but I didn't want to. Fluttering in my stomach moved south. I didn't know what to think.

Duchess was in the middle of the living room, playing with a mouse; a mouse that was very much alive. When she saw me, she scrambled away, and the mouse scooted up the hallway.

I knew Andrew had let her out because I'd caught the last mouse Duchess brought in.

"Thanks, Andrew, I so appreciate you looking after my cat. For the record, I don't let her outside. Now, I have another mouse to catch," I said with a scowl.

He didn't respond. Andrew moved through my house and scanned the rooms, and I felt flushed when he walked into my bedroom. I think my bra and panties were still lying on the floor.

He returned and glanced at his watch. "See you later. I'll have the garage drop your car off when it's done."

"Thanks. I really do appreciate all you've done, Andrew."

"No need to thank me, Agnes."

I walked him to the door, and he turned one last time before leaving. "Nice panties."

I slammed the door shut behind him, but I could still hear his laughter through the door.

"I can't let him get the best of me," I said to Duchess. "He somehow manages to make a mockery of everything."

Duchess meowed loudly as if in total agreement. I tried not to smile, but couldn't help myself. I bet he sure wondered why someone who dressed as conservatively as I do would wear such sexy, frilly things.

I wondered that too sometimes.

*　*　*

I drove Eleanor's car to her house. I had two choices: either call Andrew for a ride home later, or have Eleanor drive me home. Only one of the choices was likely to result in a multi-car collision.

I walked inside and saw Eleanor huddled on her kitchen counter. The shattered remains of her sunflower canister set lay broken on the floor, flour and sugar spread out like a white inkblot against the colored tile.

"What the—?"

I saw two green snakes slither by, and I jumped backwards onto the sink. My ass sank into the sink, which happened to be full of soapy dishwater. I dropped my purse and heard the contents scatter across the ceramic tile, setting off my lipstick vibrator. It rumbled across the floor and into the next room as if it were also afraid of the snakes.

Eleanor jerked her head up. "I should have bought one of those."

We both watched in shock, and I began to laugh so hard I snorted while Eleanor laughed so hard I feared she'd fall to the floor.

I wiped the tears gathered in my eyes.

"How in the hell did snakes get inside the house?"

Eleanor was atop the opposite counter on her hands and knees. "It's them squirrels' fault."

Oh, God, I was almost too afraid to ask. "Squirrels?"

"I left the door open, and the furry fellows ran inside." She grinned. "They seemed nice enough outside, but you should have seen them inside. As you can see, Chip 'n' Dale made quite a mess, and they looked a bit rabid." She paused. "I thought if I left the door open all night, they would run outside eventually. The snakes must've slithered in."

"Why didn't you call me?"

"I didn't want to be a bother."

"Eleanor, you're never a bother. You know that."

"But you just got out of the hospital." She frowned. "Now what are we going to do, Aggie?"

Eleanor acted like a child, sometimes. She was prone to getting herself into trouble, and I was inclined to help her out. We really were a pair.

"Where is your phone?" I asked.

"Outside. I got so flustered yesterday that I barricaded myself in my bedroom."

I glanced down and spotted my cell phone lying on the floor next to my purse. The back had come off, but I could see where the battery had landed. "Problem one, as I see it, is that there are snakes inside."

"Problem two?" she asked.

"One of those snakes is slithering inside my purse."

"Figures."

"Go for your phone," I suggested.

"No way I'm hauling my big ass out there to get it. I'm petrified of snakes."

"Wish I knew what kind of snake it was."

"What good'd that do? Even if it's not poisonous, it may bite."

"True, and being bitten by a snake is not on the top of my bucket list," I said. After a minute, I had made a decision.

"I'm going for my cell," I informed Eleanor.

"Are you nuts, Aggie? There's a snake right under you."

"I don't have a choice. I gotta go!"

"Go? As in—"

"Yes, damn it. I hafta peeeee!"

I eased myself out of the sink and kept my eyes peeled on the snake that was inside my bag. I could see its head poking out slightly, enjoying its newfound home. I decided to drop down behind it. When my feet hit the floor, I trembled and waited, making sure the snakes hadn't moved.

I jumped over my purse, gave it a kick, and grabbed my cellphone back and battery, but the snakes came toward me. I froze, and saw Eleanor jump off the counter, intent on belting them with a pancake turner. It was a battle to the finish. The snakes lurched upward, and Eleanor swatted them away.

I jumped back on the counter and dialed Andrew's number.

"Hello, Andrew." I paused and panted. "Please come to Eleanor's house. We've gotten ourselves into a fix." I dropped the phone. "Eleanor, get back on the counter!"

She climbed back on the counter, and the snakes slithered just under her. "They are pissed," she said.

"You think?"

"What did Andrew say?"

"Nothing, I don't think he had the chance. I dropped the phone again."

"Good going, Aggie."

"Don't you have one of those lifelines?"

"I forgot. It's in the bedroom."

Luckily Andrew was staying close by and it only took him five to get here. Andrew ran through the door and scanned the room. I hung onto the handle of a cabinet door, and Eleanor was, yet again, on her hands and knees.

He shook his head and walked outside, returning with a large stick. He wound the snakes around it one at a time and tossed them out the patio door on two trips. He pulled his cellphone out and began to take pictures.

"I'm so putting this on Facebook," he said, and laughed.

I twitched my lip. "Really?"

Finished with taking photos, Andrew helped Eleanor and me down. "I'm not sure what happened in here, and I'm not sure I want to know." He then walked into the living room and picked up something from the floor, ambled back toward me, and handed me the lipstick vibrator. "I think the battery is dead," he smirked. This, atop the panties of earlier, had earned him a smirk.

I got the broom while Eleanor made coffee, but Andrew took the broom from me. "You're all wet. How long were you up there?"

"I jumped into a sink full of water, if you need to know, and now

I need to pee," I said while rushing down the hallway toward the bathroom.

I would have felt mortified, but what was the point? At my age, I cared less and less what people thought, and more about what I wanted for lunch. Aside from having to urinate, I was starved. I prayed Eleanor had something in this house to eat; if not, I was looking at a grocery run.

Chapter Thirteen

I hadn't thought Andrew would show up like some kind of superhero; although, come to think of it, I'd love to see him wearing a Batman outfit.

Stop it, Agnes.

"Thanks, Andrew, I appreciate your gallant efforts, but Eleanor and I need to get groceries today, and I'm sure you have better things to do than hang out with us."

"I'm game," he said, as he winked at me.

"Store will be packed." I tried to dissuade him by making it sound as unpleasant as possible.

"I hope not with gun-toting seniors."

Eleanor beamed at Andrew. "Somebody's got to keep the peace."

Andrew squeezed Eleanor's shoulder. "You can be my backup any day."

"I have to freshen up before we leave," I said while walking to the bathroom.

I straightened my hair and smeared a layer of lipstick on. Then, reaching under my shirt and pulling the girls up, I found myself hoping Andrew would look at me differently for a change. So far, I'd gathered his impression of the mature Agnes was that of an outlandish fool, what with guns, goons, bait shops, and now snakes. What woman my age has things like that happen to them? I chastised myself, thinking, *Andrew doesn't even know I'm alive. Yet he'd shown up when I called, and he did so promptly.* Still, I felt sure he had no designs on me, not like I did on him.

I walked back into the kitchen, picked up my purse, and glanced inside. Not seeing any snake eggs, I put my things back inside and swung it over my shoulder.

Andrew, broom in hand, froze mid-sweep. It surprised me that he knew how to push a broom. Most men my age don't.

"We're really going shopping today?" Eleanor asked.

"Yes, I need some groceries. Do you have anything I can snack on before we leave?"

"Nope, I ate the last of my snacks." Eleanor moved and retrieved her purse with lightning speed. Was she afraid to be left out of anything, no matter how small? Not that I'd call grocery shopping a small thing. It proved the closest thing to a social event in this town.

"I'll drive," Andrew suggested.

We walked outside together.

Although I glared at him, I doubt he noticed my irritation. The "I'll drive" reference irritated me a tad too much, but why did men always want to drive? Men never asked for directions, even if lost, so what gave them the automatic right to drive?

He ignored me and opened the door to his silver Lexus LX.

I moved toward the door, but he cleared his throat.

"Eleanor should sit in front," he said.

Eleanor bee-hived her way to the open door and climbed inside. "Thank you, Andrew," she gushed. "I have never met such a gentleman before."

I grinned, despite wanting to smack Andrew. I didn't understand his sudden pleasant attitude toward Eleanor. What had happened while I was using the bathroom?

I stood outside, fuming, and waited until Andrew climbed inside and flipped the switch to unlock the door. Apparently, he wasn't gentleman enough to open my door. That was fine with me. I could just as well open my own damn door. *He's trying to push my buttons, and he had better stop,* I told myself.

I listened to Eleanor rattle off directions while I slid into the backseat directly behind Andrew, and I gave him a kick through the seat for good measure. I know he felt it, even though he didn't react.

Perhaps Andrew liked to show off his wealth by driving around in fancy cars. I rubbed my hand across the ivory-colored leather seat. It sure felt soft, and my mind wandered a bit more as I caressed it. I imagined how it would feel to have the cool leather against my back while Andrew...

Stop it!

I spotted Andrew's amused eyes reflected in the mirror as he pushed a CD in. Classical music blasted throughout the LX, not one of my favorites. He looked very full of himself today. I felt tempted to push a shopping cart over his foot once we got into the store.

When the box store giant, Walmart, first came to town, the place did not carry food products whatsoever, but once they realized they could turn a coin doing it, they turned all their stores into super shopper centers. Now, there was nothing in the way of food you could not find at Walmart.

It was crowded in East Tawas. The tourist season had begun in unhappy sync with the local schools closing for the summer. The usual hope for more snow days that would result in the school year being extended was a pipe dream. Winter in East Tawas hadn't been vile enough to support snow days this year, drat it!

The parking lot consisted of a fair amount of spaces, with an expanded handicapped section. I never minded the walking for a moment. I preferred it, despite the pain. I never let a little pain get in my way. I'd muddle through somehow. I could always take an Ibuprofen later.

Most of the light pole bases were once painted yellow, but had been scraped down to gray concrete. I think from some of the seniors living in town. I know, on occasion, my own eyesight was tested. Seniors had just as much right to a driver's license as the younger population, although I had noticed through the years that my reaction time *is* much slower.

Andrew parked at a slant. Oh, God forbid someone plow into his expensive LX. Not that I knew how much it cost. I just knew a Lexus can be a bit pricey, as in the cost of a modest home, which always begged the question of how many Lexus owners actually lived in their vehicles.

We strolled inside, and Eleanor found an electrical shopping cart, or buggy as she called it.

"Oh, no, you don't. That's the last one, and it's mine," Dorothy Alton said, running toward her.

Who knew Dorothy could move so quickly?

"I don't see your name on it," Eleanor retorted.

"She was here first," Andrew said.

"Well..." Dorothy froze, her eyes shifting between Eleanor and Andrew. "Who are you?"

"I'm Eleanor's friend, and she was here first." He grinned. "Find yourself another one."

"She won't even fit on it, she's too—"

"Jesus Christ, Dorothy!" Dorothy's husband, Frank, now protested. "Will you leave that woman alone? You want another episode like you had in the ice cream shop?"

Dorothy lowered her shoulder and rubbed her hands together. "Oh, Frank, I don't mean anything by it. I just don't like the way she's looking at you."

Eleanor climbed into the buggy seat while Andrew unplugged it. She backed up and turned it around with ease. She drove the buggy better than she did her car. *Maybe I should buy her an Amigo to get around in. It might just save a life,* I thought.

It was hard to keep miffed at Andrew for long. "Thanks," I whispered into his ear for sticking up for Eleanor the way he had.

"What happened in the ice cream shop?" Andrew frowned, curious.

"You'd have to have been there to believe it. Let's just say Eleanor is a real scrapper."

I selected a cart and made my way toward the grocery area.

Fluorescent lights hung overhead, lighting our way, so blindingly as to resemble a runway strip. So much so, I had to stop and rub my eyes because the light here distorted my vision. I needed to get my eyes checked again, if I could ever find the time.

When we rounded the corner, I saw the store packed with persons of a certain age, commonly referred to as seniors. I hate the word elderly, even more than seniors. "If you are able-bodied enough to make it through this pack, you're not feeble, Andrew, and for it, you deserve a medal," I philosophized in his ear.

"I recall a time when the older generations were treated with respect," mused Andrew, "but given how bloated the population of seniors has grown, you have to agree. A lot of zombies among us!"

I had to admit he had a point as, together, we looked over the obstacle course of 'zombies' ahead of us.

As we went down the aisle, I nodded and said, "Nowadays, the young, they push us around and lock us away!"

Eleanor piped in from her seated position with, "And if we sign the wrong piece of paper, they can throw away the key."

I nodded. "Alzheimer's or dementia is one thing, but most of the older population are of their right mind and capable of making their own decisions."

I saw two young couples laughing and taunting an elderly man using a walker with a basket. The younger people were treating it like some Saturday Night Live skit.

"Move your ass, old man," one said.

"I'm going as fast as I can," he muttered. He shuffled along, moving off to the side, and as the couples moved past him, he pushed his walker out and tripped the one that was yapping the loudest. The young man fell headlong into a display of potato chips. Bags burst open, and it rained barbecue and sour cream dust all over the place!

"That'll teach you, young man." He continued past the surprised couples. "You younger folks need to learn some manners."

"Do you know him?" Andrew asked me.

I nodded. "That is Mr. Wilson. I'm not sure what his first name is. I'm not sure he knows either, but he doesn't put up with any Dennis the Menace types."

Andrew strolled down the aisle and picked up items, placing

them in the grocery cart.

Employees couldn't fill the shelves fast enough. They barely moved away before the customers were on the merchandise like flies on honey. Beginning of the month sales were always the worst, as everyone's social security deposits had automatically landed in their accounts, or so it seemed in East Tawas. It sure beat the old days when you had to wait for a check to arrive in the mail, with all that worry about someone snatching it. Yes, times had changed entirely. It was hard to know if it was for the better, or not.

The busiest aisle in the store always proved to be the pet food section, specifically the cat food area. "This is obviously the most packed aisle."

"How's that?" Andrew asked.

"Most senior citizens in East Tawas must have a cat."

Andrew shrugged. "I don't know one person around our age who doesn't have a pet of some sort. In a way, it's downright therapeutic. Cats are just an easier pick. They're pretty self-sufficient, and as long as you feed them, keep their litter box clean—"

"And rub their fur the right way," I added, "they'll let you think you're in charge."

"Where is Eleanor?" Andrew suddenly asked.

"She's given up on this aisle, I suppose." I turned my cart around to find an easier route, because there was no way I was getting around this pack of shoppers.

I moved down the next aisle and saw Eleanor talking to Mr. Wilson. I moved nearby and picked up their conversation.

"Hello, Eleanor, sweetie. How are you doing?" Mr. Wilson asked, his voice cracking.

"Great."

"You should come over for dinner sometime."

Eleanor blushed. "Oh, that sounds great. What are you fixin'?"

"I don't know." He snickered. "I can make a damn good dessert though, ha!"

She placed her hands on her ample hips, even though the gesture was unnoticeable while she was sitting on the buggy. "If you want dessert, you have to make a girl dinner first."

Mr. Wilson's cheeks turned pink, a hard feat considering how gray his skin looked of late, which was never a good sign. His gaunt face did take to shining as he spoke to Eleanor, though. A longtime resident here, Mr. Wilson was well-known for his tomatoes. They won ribbons at the county fair and were the best around. His system of covering the ground with hard plastic helped to keep the moisture in the ground, thus turning out prize-winning tomatoes.

Even I was a little jealous—not of Eleanor catching his eye, but of his fat and delicious tomatoes.

Wilson wore gray work pants and a long-sleeved shirt. You could almost always find him in the garden or mowing the lawn, even on the hottest of days.

Eleanor fluttered her lashes like a preening bird and said to Wilson, "If you can whip up one of your famous tuna noodle casseroles, I'm game."

Wilson's voice crackled again as he replied. "Okay, then, it's a date, sweet Eleanor. I better get over there and buy some tuna fish. I think they're offering a two for a dollar sale."

He moved his frail body, quickening his pace.

I shook my head. I needed to erase the image of Eleanor and Mr. Wilson in a compromising position out of my head.

"There you are, Eleanor. Wherever have you been?" I asked.

"Just driving around. I should have started putting things in my basket because there is no way I'm going to make it through that pack in the next aisle."

I nodded in agreement. "Maybe you should stalk the stock boys, eh? Get items as they come outta the box!"

"Great idea, Aggie." She darted away, headed for the swinging stockroom door where the young stock boys came and went, a louder whirling coming off her hot-wheel-like buggy. My imagination flashed a scene where there was a fire coming off those wheels.

I was kidding, but no harm if it'd get us out of this store sooner.

Andrew beamed as he walked toward me, carrying four cases of canned goods. He reminded me of a hunter bringing home his kill. Rightly so, if you managed to get anything before the throng of people bought it all.

"What did you catch?"

"I almost caught a cane upside my head. Does that count?" He put the cases in the cart. "I saw Mr. Wilson getting into a fight with Dorothy over tuna fish. I'm not sure what that was all about."

I roared and almost spit out my upper. "Oh, really?"

"What gives?"

"He's making dinner for Eleanor. He said something about dessert, too."

"And it involves tuna fish? I don't think I want to know what he plans for dessert."

"Me either, but I'm pretty sure it will kill him."

We both laughed so hard tears came.

"She's waiting outside the stockroom door. I better get over there before she gets into trouble."

"I'll push the cart," he said.

"Go right ahead; maybe you can make it through the savages easier than I can! Just like a man to want to take charge," I lightly chastised, and when he ignored me, I added, "It's as if a man can't be happy unless he's driving something."

Andrew laughed this off.

I directed him toward the stockroom door, and just as I feared, Eleanor was heatedly waging a battle of words with an employee.

The employee was trying to push his cart past her, but she had blocked his path.

"Can't you see I'm practically an invalid?" Eleanor asked.

"Lady, that describes most of the customers here today."

"I'm not moving until you give me what I want."

Sweat poured from the thin, lanky man's forehead and down his cheeks. His wide eyes watered and were unblinking as if he were facing down a ravenous mountain lion. "Lady, I'm just trying to do my job."

"Let me see what you have on your cart. Maybe I won't want anything."

"If I let you do that, it will violate store policy, not to mention we will start getting attacked at the stockroom door. If I do it for you, everyone will expect it."

I imagined the picture the employee envisioned—a feeding frenzy.

"Eleanor, let the man pass." I winked.

She drove away, but once the poor man had moved ten feet, Eleanor leapt from her seat and started pulling boxes off his cart and handing them to Andrew, who then put them in my cart.

The employee threw his hands into the air as a show of defeat, and stalked back into the stockroom.

"You better hurry!" I said, indicating check out. "I think he's going for reinforcements," I said.

Eleanor pouted for a minute, then smiled before saying, "I hope he doesn't call the police like last time. I sure would hate to be banned from the store again."

"Banned?" Andrew asked.

"Three months ago. I had to come incognito."

We moved away when the manager came out, and by then, the cart was being emptied yet again by another throng of walker-wielding seniors.

The manager clenched his fists and waved them in the air. "I hate the beginning of the month," he very nearly shouted.

"No more than, ahhh, me!" I countered. "Can't the store do something about it? Create kiosks or Disneyland holding areas or something? Maybe create spiraling aisles, I dunno. I mean, with the backup at the registers, I could have gotten a PhD in the time it takes to get through there."

The manager did not look as if he wanted to take me on.

Eleanor added, "And forget about the handicapped register! It's even longer."

The manager, having had multiple run-ins with the two of us, and especially Eleanor, proved the virtue of retreat to fight another day.

"Did you get anything good?" Andrew asked Eleanor.

"I sure did. Plenty of baked beans, green beans, tuna fish, and Ramen noodles. I even found a date."

"I heard! So what is Mr. Wilson's first name?"

"Beats me," she chuckled. "He's really a nice fellow when you get to know him, and his lips are so soft."

"Too much information on register five," I quipped.

"Oh, quit being such a sour puss. I'm old, not dead." She smiled at Andrew. "Isn't that right, Andrew?"

"Just because we're older doesn't mean we can't still have fun." He smiled suggestively at me.

Chapter Fourteen

I picked up a Snickers bar and examined it, as if half expecting someone to dissuade me from making a random purchase.

"Don't do it, Aggie," Eleanor said, eying up the offending bar of chocolate. "They get extra points when you pick things up at the register."

"Points?"

"Sure. Why else would they load all this extra merchandise close by the registers?"

"For add-on sales."

She eyed me, looking serious. "You don't want the cashiers getting points the easy way. They need to earn them the old-fashioned way."

"How would that be?"

"You know dang well they are gonna try and get us to buy something at the register, like always. They love to try and squeeze more sales outta us before we leave the line." She grinned. "They do that and I'm paying in pennies."

"You do that and I'm leaving you here," I volunteered.

We straggled through the line when it was finally Eleanor's turn.

The frazzled cashier looked up and rolled her eyes. Yes, they all knew Eleanor, and from the looks many of them threw her way, they'd rather she not be taking up space in their checkout line. I imagined that there was a wanted poster in the back with her picture displayed.

Trying not to glance up, the pretty blonde scanned Eleanor's items with the speed of a gazelle.

"Aren't you gonna ask me if I found everything I wanted?" Eleanor asked.

Still not looking up, she shrugged.

"You're supposed to ask me if I found everything I wanted!" Eleanor demanded.

"Fine," the cashier said and looked up. "Did you find what you were looking for?"

"What if I said no?"

"Please..." The girl looked across the aisle where a man in a suit stood with a clipboard. "Don't make trouble for me."

"Eleanor," I whispered, "stop harassing the girl."

We paid for our goods without further incident, and the three of us made our way into the parking lot, Andrew leading the way to his LX. Eleanor, still in her riding buggy, followed close on Andrew's heels, occasionally hitting the back of his shoe. I walked slower. My eyes focused on two black Impalas that crawled into the parking lot.

I tried not to let my mind work overtime, but I couldn't help it. Black cars always worry me. The only people known to drive black sedan-type cars were government men or crooks. I had seen my fair share of crooks in my day, but I also knew I possessed an overactive imagination; still, that same imagination seemed right more often than wrong. Perhaps it was because I had married a state trooper, or the fact that I had little else in my life to focus on.

I was so absorbed in my thoughts, I bumped into Andrew.

"What are you looking at, Aggie?"

I turned my head and eyeballed him. "Hurry up and get the groceries loaded."

He didn't say another word. Within minutes, he had both the groceries and us loaded into his LX.

I sat on the edge of my seat as we made our way through the lot. Right before he pulled back onto the road, I heard what sounded like firecrackers, followed by a series of loud bangs.

"Get down!" Andrew shouted.

The car shut down as the glass breakage sensor chimed. He

picked up his cell and dialed 911. The two Impalas raced past, and I was sure I saw the barrel of a gun.

I glanced over my shoulder, noticing the shattered rear window, too close to my head for comfort. I shuddered involuntarily, as if I had no control over my body.

"Oh, my!" Eleanor cried out.

"It was those damn goons!" I shouted.

Andrew looked at his broken window, less than amused, and a maybe-I'd-best-take-this-seriously look on his face. Maybe now he was on his way to believing what I'd tried to tell him earlier.

Two State Police cruisers ripped into the parking lot, followed by the sheriff. We exited when they approached the car. Their game faces appeared more serious than ever, and why not? Tawas wasn't the sort of town to have a shooting, and in the Walmart parking lot, no less.

I noticed a crowd forming, and they all stood there gawking. I couldn't blame them. After all, this was the most exciting event to happen all year in Tawas.

Glass littered the ground, and something red splattered up onto the remains of the back window—most likely chili beans and tomatoes.

Trooper Sales led the way. He ripped his dark sunglasses off when he saw me.

"Oh, thank God you're here!" Eleanor gushed. "Someone blasted our back window out." She shuddered. "What kind of town are you running here?"

He grimaced and didn't immediately speak, as if struggling for words. I knew what he really wanted to do was run us out of town like a John Wayne character in a western film.

"Did you see who fired at you?" he asked.

I exhaled. "I saw two black Impalas that looked similar to the ones we saw at Roy's Bait & Tackle."

Eleanor nodded so hard her head looked ready to topple off. "It was those same goons."

"Goons?" the trooper asked.

"Yeah, the same ones that roughed up Roy, duh," Eleanor said.

Trooper Sales shifted his eyes to me. "Is there anyone who'd want to harm any of you?"

I didn't want to answer, because I had no idea who would go to this extreme to stop me from investigating Jennifer's disappearance.

"That list could be mighty long," Sheriff Peterson began. "Agnes is a meddler, and folks don't like meddlers."

Trooper Sales jerked his head toward Sheriff Peterson. "I think we can handle it from here, Sheriff," he said.

Peterson glared at me as he walked away. He was still glaring as he jumped into his car and sped away. I didn't know what his beef with me was, and I couldn't care less. "He'll see what a pain I can be at the next election," I muttered to Eleanor, and Andrew, overhearing me, erupted with a chuckle.

Sheriff Peterson had won office only by default when embarrassing photos had surfaced of his opponent on the eve of the election. Personally, I always thought it was odd because his opponent was a happily married man with three children. He claimed the photos were false, but the voters didn't see that. They just saw another sheriff who they figured would bring more grief than this impoverished community needed. It didn't matter to me if he liked men. I still thought he'd be a better sheriff on his worst day than Peterson on his best.

"I think the sheriff is partially right. I think someone is trying to stop me from poking around into Jennifer Martin's disappearance." I looked down and gathered my thoughts. "I know you think I'm just a silly old woman, Trooper, but in part, it has more to do with the disappearance of my granddaughter, Sophia, last year. Maybe I wanted to hope that if I found Jennifer, I'd find Sophia too, but that seems less likely all the time."

"I know about your granddaughter. I understand your husband was a state trooper, too, but you need to let us handle this investigation. Like I said before, I'd hate to have a woman of your status in the community end up harmed or ... dead."

The troopers asked Andrew to open the back of his car, and when he did, it looked like a bad batch of chili. There were busted cans sprayed all over. I swallowed hard when I saw a bullet lodged into the back of my seat. It must have missed hitting me by inches.

"I'm sorry about your LX," I said to Andrew.

"The important thing is that we are all okay."

I grinned. He really was one of a kind. I hoped he'd see the possibility that William could be behind this sudden rash of violence. I knew it was not easy to admit someone close could do something so horrific.

I wondered if Jennifer was hiding. There were only two reasons I could think of that would make her do so. Either she was protecting someone, or she felt her own life was in danger. Regardless, I needed to find the truth, and soon, because now I had become a target.

"Did Sheriff Peterson turn over the backpack that belonged to Jennifer Martin?"

"What backpack?" Trooper Sales asked.

"Kevin, the boy she was seeing, gave it to me."

Trooper Sales gave me the most peculiar look. It was obvious he had no idea what I was talking about. That damn sheriff was covering for someone, but why? I smelled a rat, and he wore the uniform of someone sworn to protect us. What hope did we have with him as sheriff? I had a mind to begin a recall. Better yet, I needed to find out what he was really up to.

"I gave the sheriff a backpack that Kevin Marks gave me. He told me that it belonged to Jennifer Martin."

"Who is Kevin?"

"He's someone I questioned about Jennifer. I think the two may have been involved romantically. Her father indicated that to be the case, too." I could tell Trooper Sales wasn't happy when his face tensed up. "He was staying in a cabin close to where Jennifer went missing. I went back to talk to him the other day, but I couldn't speak to him because someone had beaten him up. An ambulance took him to the hospital."

Trooper Sales looked down and scribbled into his notebook. "I see." He glanced up. "Anything else you can tell me?"

"Well, no, that's all I know." I couldn't possibly tell him about Kevin having visited me at the hospital, or the fact Jennifer may be lying low and not kidnapped at all. I had no idea if it was true. I had to know for sure before I could share that information.

"I will again stress to you that you need to stay out of this. It's apparent this shooting may be directly related to your recent activities." He swatted a mosquito from his arm. "Agnes, Mrs. Barton, I'm only going to say this once. Butt out unless you have a private investigator's license."

I smiled. "I don't need a license."

He cocked an eyebrow up. "How do you figure that?"

"Because I'm not charging a fee, nor will I accept any rewards."

"Nobody likes a know-it-all."

"And nobody likes a cocky trooper, so I guess that makes us even."

"Fine. If you insist on doing this, at least get a concealed weapon permit." He laughed.

"Fine, I will."

"I'll do my best to look into who's trying to blow your head off, and we'll be asking the sheriff some hard questions." Trooper Sales then said to Andrew, "You can pick up the police report tomorrow morning at the post."

I heard the troopers snicker when they walked away. "A concealed gun permit," one laughed. "That should keep her busy for a few months."

I ground my teeth and frowned.

I'd show them.

"You better quit doing that, Aggie! You're gonna get nasty frown lines."

"Don't look so smug, Eleanor. You're coming with me. Who knows, maybe you'll learn how to be a better shot."

"What's that supposed to mean? I shot one of the goons in the ass."

"Yeah, via ricochet off a metal tub. I'm lucky to be alive."

Eleanor was quick to change the subject. "Can we really get a concealed gun permit? How do we do that, Aggie?"

She sounded like an excited child being offered her favorite toy, but a gun was no toy. It was dangerous to begin with, but in Eleanor's hands, oh my!

"We have to take a pistol safety training class."

"I can't wait to see this," Andrew said. He walked to his LX, and his face reddened when he saw all the beans the bullets had splattered in the back.

"That's enough gas to fuel your LX for a year," Eleanor observed with a laugh.

I tried not to laugh. "It's not going to be easy to clean up."

"I hope the scotch guard works." He rolled his eyes. "Not to worry, we'll do it together."

We got back into the LX, tooled over to the car wash, and rinsed off the cans. Andrew flipped up the backseat and assembled the groceries there. He then drove Eleanor home before taking me home right after.

When he pulled into my driveway, I saw my Mustang parked in its usual spot. Smiling, I brought my groceries into the house and waved at Andrew as he left. I had the distinct impression he could not get out of there fast enough.

I unpacked my groceries, put them away, and noticed my answering machine blinking. I pushed the button and listened to the message as I snapped the tab on a diet coke.

I took a huge swig and coughed when I heard the message.

"Agnes, this is Trooper Sales. I'm starting a gun safety course at the range on Old Creek Road. If you're interested, give me a jingle."

He didn't leave his number, but I had his card, given to me months ago. Okay, not actually given to me. Trooper Sales was known to give his card out to women at the bars in town or leave them on a woman's windshield, if they told him where they worked. Most women might think that a little creepy, but Bill was anything but creepy. I had picked up his card from a table, discarded by a woman he had briefly spoken with. He had scribbled the note, "Call me." If he wanted to score, he had better up his game, but he's the type of guy that I describe as "chillin", because nothing seemed to ruffle his feathers.

Trooper Sales could be a ladies' man if he lightened up a little. He owned a Harley Davidson, and I had seen him blazing up and down US 23 on many occasions. His taste in women included anyone between the ages of thirty and fifty. Maybe he liked them older because the more experience the woman had, the better the ride. That way, he didn't have to worry about accidentally hooking up with a minor.

There were women who would like nothing better than to screw up a man's life, especially a trooper.

My cat, Duchess, looked longingly in my direction as she sat perched on the edge of the chair. I grabbed the phone and sat next to her. She crawled into my lap, and I scratched her under her head as she purred.

"I sure wish cats could put the groceries away," I said.

Chapter Fifteen

Light blasted my eyes when I opened them; way too much light, streaming from my lacy curtains. I rolled over and glanced at my alarm clock, which I had used more often as a time clock than alarm clock for the last ten years. The large digital numbers twinkled half past six, a bit late for me. I recalled that I needed to haul my ass down to meet Trooper Sales at the shooting range. *Lord knows how that's gonna go,* I counseled myself, and truth be known, as Eleanor isn't the sharpest shot around, I'd rather her not be armed.

I stood, ignoring my aching limbs that centered around that damn nagging hip again. Maybe I would think about surgery after this case, but that was not on my mind today.

I padded into the kitchen and started the coffee, drinking three cups before I was finished, and then feared it was a bit too much, considering I planned on going to the shooting range. I held out my hand, but it barely shook. I let out a breath that sounded like a motorboat: An annoying sound to others, but I have done it for years, and no one but Eleanor has ever 'called me' on it. Either no one notices, or they just don't care.

I had called Trooper Sales the night before to arrange to meet him at ten this morning. Andrew was going with me. He was picking up Eleanor first, and then picking me up on the way.

I hoped this would work out okay today. I thought long and hard before retiring last night and decided to find my private investigator license, if only I could remember where in the hell I had put it. I'd had one for years and kept it active; you just never know when it might be useful. Ever since the old days, I haven't worked a case, but there was something about the Martin case that was enough to pull me out of retirement. Oh, I admit I have a suspicious nature, but until these past two years with two disappearances, I had never had a reason to take that suspicion beyond the second look.

I shuffled through every cupboard, drawer, nook, and cranny for the license. I wanted to show that upstart trooper just who he was dealing with.

Smiling, Duchess watched me with wide eyes.

"Stop watching me, would you?" I said to Duchess. She had seen this happen before. I picked up my phonebook, and an envelope slid onto the floor. When I bent over, I saw it was my PI license. "Why do I always find what I'm looking for in the last place I look?" I asked the cat.

Andrew honked the horn right then, and I gave Duchess a careful pat and hobbled out the door, changing my gait once outside. I didn't want anyone to worry about me. I try to maintain the image that I'm strong, even when I feel like crap.

Eleanor sat in the front, but that was fine with me. I know it would be hard for her to fit in the backseat. Plus, had she been there yesterday, that bullet may have very well found its mark. That would be the death of me. I counted on her as much as she did me.

I noticed the back window was intact. "You sure got your window fixed fast."

"Yup, I got connections."

"I'm well aware of the kind of connections you have," I said with a smile.

I rattled off the address, and Andrew found it with little prompting from me.

I tried to act nonchalant. "How well do you know the area?" I asked him.

"Well enough. I brought my wife to the East Tawas area on vacation for most of our marriage."

"Hmm, I think this is the first time you've ever mentioned your wife. Why, back in the old days—"

He glanced in the mirror with a stern look. "Like you were interested in my wife."

"I think this is the first time you've ever mentioned her, is all. When I worked for you in Saginaw, you never said a word about her. I always wondered why."

Andrew remained silent. Apparently, he had decided not to take the bait.

I gulped. *Shut up, Agnes,* I lectured myself, but I couldn't stop the words that tumbled out of my mouth like a vile brew. "It's almost like she didn't exist."

I earned his glare. "Jeez, Agnes, do you think I'm the deceptive type?"

"We can be deceptive if we want to be—any of us!"

Andrew didn't look in the mirror again, which I was grateful for. I had pushed too far.

Could it be that he had been somewhat attracted to me back then? Not that it would have mattered at the time, since he was married and off the market.

I glanced at the mirror and saw Andrew looking back at me again. Maybe he still wasn't over her death. How could he ever get past the fact that she's gone? I know I still mourned my Tom to this very day.

Tom Barton had been one of the good guys. We had had a great life filled with love and laughter, and I missed him even now, even as I flirted with Andrew. But time was the cure, and I'd moved on— or had I? All these years later, I'm still alone. Not that there weren't men along the way, there were, but none of them could touch Tom's memory. This was a real problem for widows. They put their late husband on a pedestal so high that no other man could ever measure up. Who needed that kind of grief?

"Are you okay, Aggie?" Andrew asked, having noticed me wiping my eye.

That rattled me. Why was he acting so concerned when I'd just acted like a shrew? I rubbed the tears away. I hadn't noticed they had formed, but he had. "I'm fine. Just a little lost in thought, I guess."

He smiled, a weak effort at best. I felt his pain. We had a common link, now. We'd both lost a beloved partner in life.

Andrew made a turn down a gravel drive that led to the gun range, a twelve-mile drive from East Tawas. The parking lot consisted of a clearing, empty except for a Harley Davidson and two tables. I knew the Harley belonged to Trooper Sales.

I expected him to be in uniform, but he wasn't. His black jeans were molded to his slim frame, and a white T-shirt with a Michigan State Police emblem and black biker boots complemented him well. His dark, slicked-back hair had the sheen of a raven.

We exited the LX, and Eleanor led the way. She seemed so eager to fire her weapon. "I hope there're no birds flying near," I muttered to Andrew, who half-kiddingly whispered back, "Maybe we should've brought bulletproof vests!"

"Thank you, Trooper Sales, for helping us out on such short notice." I handed him my PI license, and he glanced at it for minute, his mouth inviting flies in.

"I figured you might be pulling my leg yesterday. I did some checking around and found out you were once, ahhh, properly licensed. Otherwise, we might have had a problem."

I put my hand into the air. "I swear everything is on the up-and-up now. Scout's honor."

"They had scouts way back when?" He said it with a smile, so I let it go, taking my license back in hand.

"Sure did. I miss the price of gas back then, among other things. But most of all, I miss the standard of law enforcement we had back in the good old days."

He smiled and seemed more relaxed than ever. He may have potential after all. I'd hate to have a trooper of his stature leave the area. I knew him to be an honest and fair trooper, more than we could count on from the local sheriff, that's for sure. Maybe I was too hard on Peterson. I could be a tad judgmental at times, something I'd only admit to myself. If you tell folks something like that in a small town, they might give you a key to the city.

"At this point, I won't turn away any extra help on this case because all I'm turning up are dead ends," he said. "Just don't tell Peterson or he'll call my sergeant and create all kinds of havoc."

"I have a few leads that I'll tell you about if they pan out. Deal?"

"Sounds good."

He motioned us each to a table. "I wasn't sure if either of you had a handgun yet, but…

Eleanor and I each pulled out our Pink Lady .38 specials and set them on the table. Andrew cocked an eyebrow toward the trooper as if sharing a subliminal message.

"They aren't loaded yet, are they?"

"Of course not, Officer," Eleanor said. Her face took on a serious tone, and suddenly, I wondered if I knew her at all. "Stop looking at me so, Aggie. I can be serious, you know."

I hadn't known, I really hadn't. I smiled and pulled out the bullets and loaded them into the chamber of my revolver, making sure not to point the gun at anyone. I placed it back on the table and prepared to wait for Eleanor, only to discover that she had hers back on the table before I did.

"I'm a pretty fast loader," Eleanor said, with the same sheepish smile that fooled no one.

"I see," Trooper Sales said. "Do you know how to shoot?"

"Oh, she knows how to shoot, all right," I replied for Eleanor. "She just can't hit the broad side of a barn."

Eleanor glared at me.

"Always remember these simple rules: Point your gun in a safe direction, preferably away from me. Don't load the gun until ready to use. Keep your finger off the trigger until ready to fire." Trooper Sales now spoke like a high school English teacher would to his slowest student. "And finally, never pull a gun unless you're going to use it."

"How good is it for self-defense if it's not loaded?" Eleanor asked.

"You can't have your gun loaded and carry it with you unless you have a concealed pistol license," Trooper Sales informed her.

"Okay, Eleanor, you can start first," continued Sales, who was being quite the 'trooper' here. "Do you know how to hold the gun in a proper firing position?"

Eleanor shrugged, and I pulled the trooper back as she turned in a circle. She planted her feet shoulder-width apart, and raised her arms, locking them into position. She banged off five rounds. I heard the bullets skim over the target, and a seagull fell to the ground.

"Eleanor," I said. "You know seagulls are protected."

"I wasn't aiming for the damn seagull."

"You weren't aiming at the target either."

Andrew, a scowl on his face now, said, "You weren't aiming at all, Eleanor. Your eyes!"

"What about my eyes?" She batted her fake eyelashes at Andrew.

"Your eyes were closed the whole time you were firing!" Andrew replied.

"Reload and try again, but you must steady your arm, and definitely keep your eyes open," Trooper Sales patiently suggested.

Eleanor snapped more bullets into the chamber of her gun, and when she began to fire, we hit the deck. This time, she skimmed the edge of the target. More bullets were put in, and she shot again.

And missed. Again.

She panted. "Shooting is hard work. I think I need to take a break."

"I think I'll keep your pistol license and your gun, Eleanor, until you can pass this safety course," Trooper Sales said.

Eleanor pouted and looked to me for support and pity from Andrew, neither of which she got. All this before she stuck her tongue out at Sales. She stepped forward and loaded her gun with the last of her bullets for one last try. This time, she not only hit the target, but all five bullets hit the mark. I wouldn't say with the best precision, but after three tries, she had finally proven that not only could she shoot, but her smoking aim could find her target. And in the bargain, she'd only killed one seagull, leaving the rest of us alive, even if shaken.

"I told you I could shoot," Eleanor said. "I was just nervous."

"Perfectly understandable, dear, under the circumstances," I reassured her, nodding toward the men. Having Andrew and a state trooper looking on might make anyone nervous. And now it was my turn.

I loaded my gun and, lifting it up, I closed one eye with menacing intent. I cracked off my rounds and hit the target.

"Showoff," Eleanor said.

"My husband, Tom, taught me to shoot when we were first married."

"Smart man," Andrew said. "I'm not so sure I'd give my wife a weapon, though."

"And, why not?" I asked, staring intently as I waited for an answer.

"Afraid she'd use it against me!" He slapped Sales on the back, and the two men laughed as if that were funny.

Andrew added, "I happened to have had a somewhat, ahhh—"

"My Tom was a real good guy, model husband. Got it." As soon as I cut Andrew off, I was angry at myself. He was about to reveal something about his relationship with his wife, and I had stupidly interrupted.

I cocked my head and watched Andrew walk away. What in the hell had gotten into him?

Eleanor and I signed the paperwork for the license, and Eleanor scoffed a bit when he told her that it would take forty-five days for the permit to clear. He told us the sheriff's department already had our fingerprints on file. "Which will facilitate things a good deal," he ended.

"Facilitate? Facilitate—how very efficient of them!" Eleanor fumed and stalked off.

I was busy trying to recall how they had our fingerprints on file. Then I remembered it might have had something to do with volunteering at a local school. Nowadays, anyone coming into contact with children or working in healthcare was mandated to have a background check, which included fingerprints.

"Thanks, Trooper Sales, for caring enough to come down here and take time with two old broads."

He nodded. "I'm officially off duty the rest of the day. You can call me Bill."

I shook his hand. "Thanks, Bill."

"You two just be careful, and don't forget our pact, Agnes."

With that, I rushed to catch up to Eleanor and the brooding Andrew. Watching him, I feared I had bruised him more deeply than I knew.

Chapter Sixteen

All things considered, things at the shooting range had gone fairly well. I always considered it a great day when I wasn't shot by a stray bullet. Eleanor had even managed to hit the target. Perhaps now I could stop worrying about her carrying a pistol in that monstrosity she calls a purse.

We made our way from the driving range toward Andrew's LX, where Eleanor and I climbed in and waited for Andrew to say something. He turned and stared at me, his eyes warm and inviting like a blanket on a cold night.

"Are you hungry?"

"Sure, why?"

"Me, too." He turned and tore out of the drive.

I sat there wondering what was bothering him. He had gone from Mr. Nice Guy to a stranger in a matter of minutes and back again, all without an explanation. I needed to think. What did I really know about Andrew? I hadn't seen him in twenty years, and he could well have changed. I needed to remember that. I needed to keep my guard up. I didn't need to get blind-sided or hurt. In the disappearance of this young girl, no one was above suspicion, not even Andrew. *Then again*, I wondered, *what kind of a way is that to live?* Trusting no one. At times, I felt like a character in Steinbeck's *Of Mice and Men* for being so naturally suspicious.

I saw the trees flash by my window and enjoyed the refreshing blast of the air-conditioning. The sound of Eleanor and Andrew talking in what I thought were hushed tones in the background lulled me into closing my eyes and meditating. There were days I couldn't hear well, while on other days, the sound of my hair scratching across my pillow kept me awake all night.

My mind was simply elsewhere at that moment. All I could think about was finding Jennifer's mother. Who could I ask, and why would they tell me anything?

I rubbed my head as it started to pound. I needed a pill of some sort, but my mouth already felt stuffed with cotton. When I saw where Andrew turned, I knew it would only get worse.

The white farmhouse was known to me—and just about every other person in the state. Andrew stopped his LX, and we piled out without prompting or thought. I noticed three other cars in the drive and didn't have to guess why they were here, although I did wonder why we were.

The washed-out siding of the farmhouse with dirty windows greeted us with overgrown rose bushes. I had the urge to find some pruning shears next fall and trim the bushes myself.

We followed the dirt drive into the backyard and joined the circle of seniors who were sitting in lawn chairs. Rosa Lee Hill sat in her chair casually, dressed in a mustard-colored T-shirt and brown crop pants, her thin, straight brown hair hanging loose. Her lawn chair had seen better days, but it was, by now, perfectly molded to her body. It might be because she spent so much time outside in it rolling fatties.

When I say fatties, I'm talking Mary Jane, marijuana, and funky flower. You didn't have to smoke anything. The contact buzz alone would knock you on your ass.

Andrew gave her a hug. He'd been here before. No surprise there. As I watched the fatty being passed, I saw Jack Winston sitting with yet another twenty-something girl. He was smoking a hookah filled with marijuana. Everywhere I looked, marijuana.

I nudged Eleanor. "Look, your boyfriend, Jack, is here."

Eleanor gasped. "Not even on a bad day would I go near the likes of him."

"Seems like he has a steady supply of young women to traipse around with."

Eleanor added, "Yeah. Does he own a Hooters or something?"

It was no surprise Jack would be here. Jack and Rosa Lee Hill go way back. I think, at one point, she had rented him a room when he left his wife back in the day, or so Eleanor had told me.

We walked past him, hoping to avoid another battle of words like the one we had at Roy's Bait & Tackle the other day.

I smiled at Rosa Lee. She was one of the most laid-back women I had ever met, and now I know why. None of these people needed to smoke for medicinal purposes that I knew of.

I wanted to leave, because the last thing I needed was to be here if she got busted. Goodbye, concealed pistol license; goodbye, PI license. It wouldn't be worth it.

I ignored most of the crowd, focusing all my attention on Rosa Lee. I waved at her and smiled briefly. "I was wondering if you knew about anyone who might've moved here to Tawas, say about ten years ago? Possibly by the name of Stella? I think Roy may have—"

"Oh, my God, Agnes, I told you just drop this," Roy cried out sternly through gritted teeth as he was rounding the grill.

"I can't," I said.

"Do you realize what's at stake here?"

"I know. Believe me, I know." I looked around. "We were shot at yesterday at Walmart."

Gasps split the air from the group.

"The goons are on to you, then?" Roy asked.

"They're trying to scare me off, and if there's something you *can't* do, it's scare me off."

"It always has to be your way, doesn't it?" Roy sneered. "Agnes Barton's way."

"Well, look, Roy—"

"Isn't that just the way it is?" he continued to sneer.

"Yup."

"No matter what happens or who gets hurt?"

"Oh, Roy, I don't have a choice. I need to find Jennifer before the goons get her."

His eyes became round saucers, and the whites of his eyes filled with bulging blood vessels. "Who says the goons want her?"

"Why else are they here in Tawas?"

Roy rubbed his hand over his face, making a loud noise as sweat popped out of his pores. "I don't know, but I'm not giving up Stella, I tell you that."

I pointed my finger in his face. "I wasn't asking you to."

"Come on, you two, lighten up," Rosa Lee said. Her eyes were dilated, and she had one of those smiles you couldn't help but recognize as the happy results of drugs at play in her head.

I sat, waited, and watched a fatty passed to Andrew, who took a toke and promptly began coughing and sputtering.

"Oh, city boy! Can't hack the good stuff, eh?" I teased.

He handed it to me. "No, I don't want any." My jaw tightened and felt locked. I rubbed it to loosen it up.

"Over here, Andrew," Eleanor leapt in. "I'll take it."

"You can't," I protested.

"Why the hell not?"

"Because we're on duty."

"On duty. Are you joshing me? I don't see any damn time clock."

I wanted to shout out the list of reasons why it was a bad idea, but I didn't want to give her the satisfaction; I just wished that my partner in crime would straighten up. "You wanted to help. You said you did, and I'm the boss."

Eleanor's lips twisted into a snarl as she walked toward the grill.

A picnic table next to the grill was piled with paper plates and every salad imaginable, complete with potato chips. On the grill, hot dogs and hamburgers were smoldering to perfection, the aroma wonderful enough to enchant the squirrels in the trees all around.

Manning the grill, Roy filled Eleanor's plate with hotdogs placed neatly into buns. Andrew followed suit and loaded a plate. They sat and munched as I waited for Rosa Lee to respond to my questions.

"Oh, Agnes, I know you don't expect me to remember someone that I may have met from ten years ago. Heavens, I have trouble remembering this morning."

I frowned. I had no idea where to go from here. I should have known that Andrew had brought us to the wrong place.

"Eleanor, is that a roach?" Jack Winston asked. Holding a hookah between his legs as if it were an extension of himself, he sneered at me as the twenty-something girl next to him giggled.

Eleanor flung her plate up and food flew into the air, barely missing Andrew. Then, she started running around, hollering, "Where's the roach? I don't see any damn roach."

No one made a move, as if seeing food flying and old women screaming happened every day.

Eleanor walked over to Jack. "Hi, Jack," she purred. "I didn't see you over here."

He rolled his eyes upward. They were bloodshot and bulging like a bullfrog in ill health.

I sat back on a lawn chair. This might just loosen up the crowd enough to get them to start talking.

"Well, now, Jack, who's your new friend?" Eleanor asked, eyeing the woman up and down like the stripper she may have been.

"This is Stacy." He glanced toward his companion. "Stacy, this is tuna lady." He began to laugh, not realizing how close Eleanor was to him.

"And this is Jack falling down," Eleanor said. She pushed the top of his lawn chair, and he toppled over the back.

It rather resembled a somersault.

"Oh, my! Oh, my! Watch Jack do a flip. Oh, watch Jack get so mad. Look and see him get so mad," Eleanor began to taunt him.

Jack was tangled in the lawn chair, and somehow, it had managed to shut with him inside. His face turned bright red, and I could almost see smoke rise from his ears.

I glanced at Andrew. "Don't just stand there. Help him, before he turns purple."

"I'm not sure that will be safe for Eleanor."

"You don't look so damn smug now, do you?" Eleanor said. She looked down and found a small medicine bottle and snatched it up, shoving it into her pocket.

Jack disentangled himself from the chair and tried to stand, yelling, "Oh, God, will somebody help me get up?"

I whistled innocently and thought, *No, not me.*

"Let me guess. You have fallen and can't get up," Eleanor continued to harass the man.

"Old Biddy."

"Old Rooster!"

"When I get up..."

"You won't be doing that tonight," she taunted.

Rosa Lee laughed so hard that tears fell from her eyes. What a sight. A lawn full of laughing seniors who didn't seem to mind so much that they were on the ground.

I yanked Eleanor's arm and shoved her toward Andrew's LX. Pushing her inside, I jumped in, too.

"What in the hell are you trying to do, Eleanor? Kill him?"

"Nope, but it was nice to finally get back at him."

I rolled my eyes as she snickered.

"He's not going to have a very good night tonight."

I flashed her a look. "What did you do?"

"Oh, nothing..." She jiggled a bottle of pills.

"What is that?"

"His Viagra."

My jaw dropped open. "His Viagra?"

"I could use that myself," Andrew said. He turned and winked.

I glanced out the window and saw Jack running toward us. I couldn't speak, but my face did.

"What are you looking at?" Andrew asked.

He turned and saw Jack lunge for Eleanor's door. Andrew pounded his foot on the gas pedal, and we were off and away from the enraged man. I knew this wasn't over by a long shot.

Eleanor laughed.

"It's not funny, Eleanor. He's going to kill you the next time he sees you."

"I'd like to see him try. I'd give him a one-two-three kick and bring him to his knees."

As if it would be that easy. I had seen that man in action before, and he was strong as an ox. Eleanor didn't have a clue what he may be capable of or what he might do to her.

Roy was waiting in Eleanor's driveway when we arrived, and I jumped out of the LX. How Roy managed to slip away and get ahead of us I don't know, but here he stood with a sad look on his face. In addition, the man was white as a ghost, his usual ruddy complexion absent.

"Aggie, I went to check on Stella, but she's gone." He began to sob.

I tilted my head sideways. "What do you mean, gone?"

"Follow me and I'll show you."

We piled back into the LX as Roy directed us up US 23 and down a pathway that led to an old cabin deep in the woods. It looked dark—even the sun had trouble breaking through the canopy of leaves.

Roy leapt from the vehicle, and we were hard pressed to catch up to him. When we made our way around back, we spotted a woman's nude body on the ground. Her red hair cascaded around her, making her look like a broken doll. She wasn't young, forties perhaps. Her red hair almost concealed the blood that matted her hair to her head like a helmet. A bloody claw hammer lay next to her body.

Her torn clothes were also next to her, and all I could think about was the Robinson murders all those years ago. This didn't speak to me of the goons or William Martin, although he could very well be responsible. I wasn't about to rule anyone out yet, though. Not yet.

She looked familiar, and I couldn't help but think that I knew her from somewhere. I could remember what my favorite toy was as a child, but remembering what I just did or with whom, this sometimes proved impossible. More times than I could remember, I would simply forget something but not remember what it was I'd forgotten! Usually and eventually, I could remember what it was. It just took me a while before I did. If there is a book on aging—they forgot to give me a copy.

Andrew called 911 while I huddled close to Eleanor. Poor dear looked scared half to death. I so wanted to dig around the scene, take pictures even, but I certainly would've hated to disrupt the crime scene. Finding Stella's body automatically complicated matters.

Chapter Seventeen

I kneaded my hands together, trying to body-block the sight of Stella's body from Eleanor's startled eyes. She quivered involuntarily every few minutes.

"Keep it together, El. We-We'll be out of here soon," I assured her.

She bobbed her head, her version of a nod.

I heard state police cruisers blaze up the path with sirens blaring. The many faces that were suddenly upon us were not entirely unfamiliar to me. I saw tense, determined people on the edge. They came from the surrounding counties, including Saginaw, where I had lived. As a result, I knew most of them.

We stayed where we did, not want to damage the crime scene further. Roy cried, and Eleanor's eyes were cast to the ground. Even Andrew's face appeared ashen. This wasn't old potatoes for any of us. I'm damn sure none of us had ever seen a dead body before. Not outside a funeral home, that is.

Even so, as hard as it was to do so, I tried to memorize the scene.

I took in the cabin behind the body. It was more of a shack really, its door hanging by one hinge. Obviously, a struggle had transpired. Trash was strewn across the back, and I wrinkled my nose because it smelled of uncooked meat left in the sun over a goodly amount of time.

Dressed in plain clothes, Trooper Sales walked onto the murder scene. That's the type of trooper he was. Even on his day off he had shown up, but murders don't happen every day, or at all, around these parts.

His eyes met mine as he walked toward me.

"Tell me none of you touched the body."

"Of course not. We watch *Criminal Minds*," I said, trying to lighten the mood. Sales glared at me, which prompted, "We know better than that. Look, Roy here was waiting for us when we returned to Eleanor's house, and he told us something bad had happened to Stella," I said.

Roy cried. "Stella, my poor baby. You can't tell my wife. Swear to me you won't."

Trooper Sales looked into Roy's eyes. "I can't promise you anything, Roy, you know that. What do you mean by your baby?"

"I had an affair forty-some years ago, and she's my daughter." He shakily pointed to the dead woman. "My wife will leave me if she finds out."

I found myself patting Roy on the back and said, "One of the reasons you two kept it quiet, eh, Roy?"

He rubbed his eyes with his meaty hands. "She moved here ten years ago. She had left her husband, and claimed he had tried to have her killed. I never knew if it was true or not."

"Jennifer Martin is Stella's daughter," I added for the benefit of Sales.

Trooper Sales looked down at the victim. "I knew her, but she didn't go by the name of Stella. I knew her as Hannah O'Hara."

I saw by the look in his eyes that he knew her well. I exhaled sharply, and it made my chest throb. I couldn't think straight. I felt the hot, stale air that smelled of death. I wondered if her killer could still be lurking in the woods, watching and waiting.

Roy, choking back tears, stuttered, "S-She took t-to hiding out here w-when the goons came to town looking for her."

"Did she tell you who they could be?" Trooper Sales asked.

"She had no idea. After her daughter went missing, she kind of went loco."

"Understandable," I assured Roy.

"S-She started calling people, people from her past who all had thought her long-dead... and now, now she's been killed!"

"Take it easy, Roy." I held firmly onto his arm. He looked as if he might keel over from a heart attack, but leaning against the stoop now, he went on. "I wish she hadn't done that—called people about Jen. It's the worst thing she could've done."

"I'm sure she just wanted to find her daughter," I added for him.

He looked deep into my eyes and, tightening his grip on me, said, "Stella, she was a good mom. She didn't have a choice but to leave Jennifer behind. Her husband is a powerful man with plenty of connections, and she didn't stand a chance."

"I don't see William doing anything like this," Andrew quickly put in. "He only wanted to find his daughter. That's the only reason he's come here, and it's consumed him since she went missing."

"Really? I didn't see that," I countered. "I mean, the man became enraged just because I asked him about his marriage, about Stella here, and now she's dead!"

Andrew fixed me with a glare. "I tell you, this has been hard on him. His nerves, his judgment ...it's all off. He's not himself."

"Or he's showing his true colors!" My emotions got the better of me. "Look, when my granddaughter went missing last year, just like Jen now, I would have done anything to find her, anything. And you know what I got? Nothing. They could have asked me anything!"

Andrew tore his gaze from me. I knew he was angry that I still blamed William for any part of this, but who else did we have to suspect?

"I think you all need to go home now, and let us do our job," Trooper Sales sternly suggested.

Roy staggered back to the car as Eleanor, Andrew, and I followed. I glanced back at the knotty pine cabin, a mere shadow amongst the crime scene that would now put this sleepy community on edge, and change it forever.

I knew one thing: The Robinson's cold case had to be reopened, because this felt too similar. Mrs. Robinson had been raped, and then she and her family were killed in the end by a madman wielding a claw hammer.

I had no idea who the goons were or who they worked for. I did not know if they had done this, or if someone else had killed Stella. I did not know if the crime scene was staged in copycat fashion or not, staged to throw police off the trail of the missing person's case, but common sense and what my eyes had witnessed at the scene told me one thing was for certain: whoever had killed Stella, he, she, or they knew about the Robinson murders in detail.

We traveled back to Eleanor's house in silence. I knew after our heated debate earlier that I might never see Andrew again, and that saddened me, but in a way, I knew maybe that's the way it should be.

Andrew pulled into Eleanor's drive, and we all exited the vehicle, Andrew, too. We walked through the darkened house and onto the deck. We watched the sun sink lower in the sky, which was painted in blood orange streaks that seemed to reach to infinity.

Eleanor brought beers out for everyone, and we all drank.

"I'm sorry that you think me wrong for defending my friend," Andrew said, breaking an awkward silence between us, "but it could be the lawyer in me that says he's innocent until proven guilty. And in my experience, appearance is often not reality."

"I'm not sure if William or the goons did this," I said, raising my beer to his and tapping out a truce. "But I do know one thing: Stella was killed just like Mrs. Robinson was in 1968."

"They never found her killer?"

"Nope."

"Did they have a suspect list?"

"I'm not sure, but we need to find out. I plan on getting those files and looking them over. I think they could have missed something. I always felt the person responsible for the Robinson murders is still in the Tadium area, possibly closer than we know. And now, with all the women going missing in the area, I'm certain of it. I hate to think this person killed my granddaughter, but I must be open-minded."

"I'm sorry about that, Agnes, and I hope somehow or some way you are able to find her."

I nodded. "Me, too, but as more and more time goes by, I realize it's highly unlikely."

Eleanor gasped. "Don't you dare think that."

"Eleanor, I need to be realistic. I can't keep holding out hope for something that'll never happen. Besides, now we have another young woman in danger. I just feel it, so I need to focus on the case at hand."

"You always held out hope for me. Most people would have let me rot in a nursing home, but not you. I don't want to hear any more talk about you giving up, you hear?" Eleanor tried to reassure me.

I drank my beer, but I didn't enjoy it, because I hated beer. I always had, and why I was drinking it was beyond me. I wanted to dull my senses enough to get the image of my granddaughter, lying out there somewhere, dead, out of my head.

We kept drinking until the sun disappeared behind the blue lake, which, under the cover of darkness, turned the color of purple below a sky that finished off with softer shades of orange, pink, and gray.

After this, we began mixing drinks as Eleanor trotted out wine, vodka, and gin. I so wanted to forget the images this day had left in my head that I failed to heed my better judgment on this and followed Eleanor's lead instead.

Chapter Eighteen

I slept like the dead. I felt the bed beneath me and knew it as mine. Still, I opened my eyes with a jolt.

How did I get home, and what was that hard mass behind me? Well, part of it anyway. It felt warm and ... naked! I jerked around and found Andrew's amused face looking back at me. His lips curved into a smile, and I felt my nakedness in that instant.

"What in the hell happened?"

"I think we made love," he calmly stated. "Don't tell me you don't remember?"

I wasn't about to respond.

That can't be, I thought. The last thing I recalled was ... *oh my, it can't be, but I think he's right.*

I felt enraged. How dare he!

After all, I'd been intoxicated and hadn't been aware of what I was doing and oh, God, at last? I hated the thought and yet, I felt a tremor ripple through my body. Why, I certainly never thought Andrew and I would ever really do ... that.

I sat up, pulling most of the blankets with me, exposing more of him than I cared to remember, but I did recall ... every detail. God help me. I hated to think that I had enjoyed it, but it wasn't my fault. I was drunk. I think that gives a person a pass. You can't be responsible if you're drunk. At least, that's what I've always told myself.

I quickly stood up, and instead of a dignified retreat, I fell face forward. The only thing that saved me from harm was the blanket. I landed with my legs splayed apart. I slid my body to a sitting position, and I couldn't face him, not yet. He roared in laughter, causing me to feel flushed and hot all at the same time.

"Agnes, are you okay?" Andrew asked as his laughter subsided. He sounded concerned, but was he, really?

I felt angry and turned my head, staring into his bemused face. "I'll be fine when you leave."

"Leave? So you're going to have your way with me and just throw me out like used goods?" He laughed more.

I continued to hold the blanket against my skin as I stood, but it slid to the floor. I felt the cold air blast my bare skin, and I felt ashamed for feeling so turned on, like some kind of schoolgirl. Me, a seventy-two-year-old woman. Women my age shouldn't be feeling like this, but looking at his amused face, I saw that he felt it, too.

I spun, only to turn the other cheek, so to speak, and then I walked, with as much grace as I could muster, into the bathroom. I barely made it there before my bladder exploded. Have they invented Depends for lovers? I don't wear them usually, but I felt as if I could use a pair, because I was wet in places that I had not been in years.

Perhaps tomorrow I will find the humor in the situation, but not today. I relieved myself in a way I hadn't ever before, and I'm not just talking about peeing.

I stood and ran the shower until it was hot, but what I really needed was a cold shower. Jumping in, I enjoyed the feel of the hot spray. II suddenly felt cold, and noticed Andrew had crawled into the shower with me.

"Get out of this shower now!" I couldn't help but let my eyes wander down, and that brought a smile to Andrew's lips.

"Not happening. Let me wash your back."

He motioned for me to turn around, which I did, only because I couldn't think straight. My mind was jumbled, and for once, words failed me.

He loaded soap on the loofah sponge and rubbed my back.

I hated to admit it, but it felt terrific. It had been years since a man had put his hands on me, and I hated to admit how much I missed that. Not the sexual stuff, but the simple gestures, like someone holding my hand or giving me a hug—or this.

After Tom died, I shut had myself off from men, except for a few brief encounters. One of them was Dr. Maxwell Nobel. He was a bit older than I was, but I had been taken aback by his voice. He sounded just like Jimmy Stewart, cute, quivering stutter and all.

I turned and rinsed, moving out of the shower since the water felt lukewarm now.

Andrew immediately complained in complementary fashion with, "Hey, it's all cold in here without you."

"It's even colder out here ... without you," I countered, and waited a few minutes for his reaction, thinking, *Agnes, this should be good.*

He yanked his soapy head from behind the shower curtain. "Yikes, it's freezing."

"You better just suck it up! It's only going to get colder." I wasn't sure if I meant the water or me.

I dried off and wiggled into my clothes before he stepped out. I had decided to wear tan pants and a white button-up shirt because I planned to go to the state police post, among other places.

I had just brushed my hair when I saw him step out of the shower. I felt safer now that he was shriveled down to size. It's not the best look for any man.

Suddenly, a hissing Duchess ran forward and pawed Andrew, scratching his ankle.

"Jesus." Andrew jumped back. "What in the hell is that, a cougar?"

I laughed. "She thinks she is. I think she's an assassin. She's Russian."

"I sure wish I had clean clothes to wear," he whined.

"I can wash your clothes. I think I have something that you can put on."

"That'd be great." He wrapped a towel around his waist and followed me into the bedroom.

I smiled and pulled out my frilliest pink bathrobe. "It's chenille and has plenty of ruffles, too. It's perfect for you!"

"You got to be kidding?" He cocked his head to the side. "You have to have something else."

"Sorry, that's all I have."

I scooped his clothes up and walked to the door. I swung around for one glance in his direction as he stood contemplating himself in the mirror, wrapped in my robe. Seeing how amused I was, he quickly turned from the mirror and, instead, moved to where I stood.

"You better hurry, Andrew. House rule: my guest makes breakfast."

His eyes narrowed, but he walked into the kitchen while I detoured into the laundry room and started the washer. When I glided into the kitchen, I made coffee and saw him making himself at home by rummaging through the refrigerator.

He wiggled his butt and I grinned. I was enjoying this too much. He stood up with an armful of bacon, eggs, and butter. He set them down on the counter, and he looked through my knotty pine cupboards. He seemed to find what he needed without any prompting from me.

"Coffee?" I asked.

"Yes, please."

I pulled two cups out and poured, asking, "Cream or sugar?"

He raised an eyebrow. "I think you know the way I like it."

"I should. I sure had enough cups ready and waiting for you when you came to the office all those years ago."

"Why did you do that?"

I froze. Was it possible he really didn't know? I felt my heart drop a little with the confirmation that I had gone unnoticed to that degree. I retrieved the creamer and nestled it in my hands, thinking about pouring it on his head.

I shrugged, fiddled with the creamer a bit more, poured an additional splash into my cup, and handed his cup to him. I felt the tears burning in the back of my eyes, but I refused to let them escape.

My brain screamed, *If he's clueless, then he doesn't deserve to know.*

I opened the curtains, and Duchess nearly broke a leg dashing into the window. Her head low, she softly meowed, followed by a series of noises that only she understood. But it didn't sound like an apology to Andrew.

"Oh, my God," Andrew said.

I turned and saw a mouse scurrying across the living room floor. "Some cat."

"She brought that one in the last time you were here."

He turned to Duchess. "Hey, you, cat! Get the mouse, cat." He pointed to the mouse, but Duchess only turned her lazy head and looked at it with a stone face. Not interested. She snapped her head back to the window, nearly diving through the screen. Perched outside was one of the fattest, juiciest mourning doves yet. The dove turned its head as if to say, "You know you can't get me, you stupid cat."

I had to pull Duchess from the screen, which was hard because she'd dug her claws deep. Andrew helped me remove her one claw at a time, and she hissed at him again. I shut the window, and Duchess dove for it, smacking her face into the glass.

Andrew clucked his tongue. "Not very bright, is she?"

"You better watch out or she's going to get her revenge on you."

I looked over at the frying pan. "Make my eggs over hard, but don't let them get crispy," I ordered as if I were in a restaurant.

He rolled his eyes, but I walked off to place his clothes in the dryer. When I returned, I relaxed, sitting at the table.

A few minutes later, he brought two plates to the table.

"You need to start eating healthy," he said.

"I do. It's a perfect mix of protein with more protein, and no carbs."

"Eating like that will land you in the hospital. That's what Dr. Atkins died from, a heart attack."

"I'll have you know that my blood pressure and cholesterol levels are fine."

"That's what a friend of mine thought when she had her heart attack last year." He shoved a mouthful of bacon in his mouth.

"I have heard of that happening."

"Have ya, now?"

"I wasn't being flip, Andrew. I had a friend who ended up making several trips to the ER before they found she had a heart problem. She ended up with a quadruple bypass."

"Oh, I am sorry to hear it," he said after swallowing a mouthful of coffee.

"Thank you. Anita acted as if the world had ended, and maybe it does feel that way when you have major surgery. I hope that doesn't happen to me. I have been lucky enough to have had no major health problems."

I forked my breakfast into my mouth. I wondered what Andrew had done to make the eggs taste so good. I rolled my eyes toward the clock and saw it was almost ten. I needed to get moving, and soon, but I first needed to tend to my plants.

"There's another rule around here. If you cook, you don't have to do the dishes."

He smiled like a kid who loved the sound of getting out of distasteful chores. "Sounds good to me, but don't you have a dishwasher?"

"Oh, that thing? I don't use it much." I yawned. "I never have that many dishes."

I cleared the table and washed the dishes. As I wiped my hands, I turned and saw that Andrew was now dressed.

I stood there, uncertain what to say.

"I have to get going pretty soon," he said.

"Great. I mean, me, too. First I need to water my plants, though."

I busied myself watering my indoor plants, and then ran outside to water the garden.

I turned to see Andrew standing behind me. "What are your plans today?" he asked.

"I'm going to ask about the Robinsons' files, and after that, I plan to question William. I'm counting on you to have him ready to answer some questions."

He scratched his head with a disgruntled expression. "You are?"

"Sure. I'm sure you knew that I'd ask him more questions, eventually."

His face looked tense as if he was angry. "I suppose you have to do what you think best, Aggie."

"Yes, and it's nothing personal. I don't even hold a grudge against him, considering our last encounter."

"I don't know why he did that." He rubbed his neck. "It's the sort of thing that will land you in trouble. Treat the man with the same respect you would any man that has a daughter missing. That's all I ask."

"I'll try my best. I did try to be civil to the man, but he went all gaga when I asked him a simple question."

He placed a hand on my arm, gently turned me from my hosing down the garden, and looked me in the eye. "Remember, you are not the law."

I blew out a breath. "I know."

Andrew gave me a wave goodbye, and as I watched him walk to his car, I wondered if I had gone too far. This seemed like it was a problem between us, yet it need not be. I promised myself that I would try to question Andrew's friend more gently next time, but damn it, that wasn't how I got the information I wanted out of people. I needed to press and push. It was the only way I ever gained useful information.

I turned from watching the last of Andrew leave my driveway, hoping it was not a sign of his going out of my life. Then I realized that I'd left the hose running, and my poor garden looked like Noah's flood had hit.

Chapter Nineteen

After Andrew finally left and I calmed my nerves a bit, I gathered my purse and jumped into my Mustang. It had been so long since I had driven my car. Poor baby was raring to go, too. Today, I planned to be a lead foot and burn all the carbon off just like my father always preached was good for getting the 'gunk' out—whatever gunk is. I inhaled deeply and took in an unusual fragrance. I figured it was Andrew's cologne, since he might have been the last person in my car.

Air conditioning on full blast, pedal to the metal, I was in Mustang heaven. One of the reasons I had purchased my muscle car was that I felt like a hotsy-totsy driving it.

I roared into Eleanor's driveway, scattering stones at her house. She was waiting just inside and came out when she saw me. In a matter of minutes, I had swapped my car for hers, and, together, we left. I tried not to look at my all-knowing, busybody best friend, doing all I could to glance at anything but her prying eyes.

"What?" I asked finally.

Her eyes became large. "So, how was it?"

I tried to act like I had no idea what she was talking about. I really would rather she not know what'd happened between me and Andrew. "How was what?"

Eleanor nudged me. "Oh, you know." She winked.

How could she know what happened between the two of us?

"I know you more than you think. It's written all over your face." She giggled, and the sound grated on my last nerve. I think I only had one nerve left, so it was easy for someone to get on it.

"I don't know what you could possibly be referring to." I tried to keep my eyes on the road.

"Did you do it?" She grinned. "Was it good?"

"Eleanor, I have no damn idea what you are referring to."

"Oh, come on, you two were all over each other before you left my house. I thought you were gonna do it on the deck. Even Roy thought so."

I was mortified. "He did?"

"Sure."

Oh, God, I feared it would be all over East Tawas by now if Roy had the story. I managed a weak grin. I hoped it wasn't the talk of the town, but knowing Roy and Eleanor the way I did, I could not help but believe it would be. Then, I decided, to hell with it. We were, after all, two consenting adults.

"Eleanor, how many people have you called and told?"

"Oh, come on, Aggie! We're buddies. I wouldn't do that. Not to you. Some people I know, yes, but not you." She toyed with a tissue she held. "But I don't know what Roy might say. He can be a gossip at times, and with something this juicy ... who knows?" She shrugged as if it were nothing to worry about.

I gulped hard, feeling a lump in my throat. "If I were Roy, I wouldn't go around talking about anyone else," I said.

"That was something, wasn't it? I had no idea Roy could be that sneaky."

I scoffed. "Uh, he flirts with everything that has tits."

"Well, now, Aggie, that's not true. He flirts with Connie at the bank, and she doesn't have any at all."

I gripped the steering wheel tighter. I hoped the wheel would fly away and take me with it.

I pulled into the parking lot of a small, simple brick building that housed the State Police Post. We walked inside and were met by Trooper Sales.

"I'm in a hurry, ladies, but I have some of the files on the Robinson case for you."

"I'm in my own hurry," I shot back. "Where are the files?"

"Just ask at the desk. The sergeant on duty is expecting you. I figured you would want to take a peek because of the hammer."

I looked at him expectantly. "So, you think it could be related to the Robinson case?"

"That, or someone went to an awful lot of trouble to make us think so. I'll be investigating the murder, and you can go over the files, but you need to keep them on the premises. That's the deal."

I nodded, and watched the trooper dash to his car. He tore out of the lot with sirens blazing. I never knew the rationale behind them putting the sirens on unless they really had a call. I had seen them, on occasion, snap them on just to pass someone. Not that it would bother most folks for them to do that. In fact, most people would probably prefer that because it was extremely nerve-racking to have a cop tailing you. There was a fix for that, however. A driver just goes so slow the cops'll pass on by—not an easy task on US 23 sometimes, unless one has a burning desire to be run off the road by some old coot. Senior citizens around these parts didn't have much patience, or driving skills. Perhaps it was just Eleanor I was thinking about, though.

I went to the desk sergeant's counter, designed to make appear like a dwarf, where I craned my neck and explained who I was and that Trooper Sales had sent me for files. I was handed a packet containing files, and we were directed to a room where I saw ten additional boxes.

"It's going to be a long day," I said to Eleanor, whose face had dropped.

Eleanor rubbed her hands together. "I'll be at the beach if you need me."

She ran out the door. I shook my head and started going though the paperwork until I saw a name that popped out at me. Billy Chambers.

Billy Chambers had worked as a handyman for the Robinson family, and he was long thought to be a potential suspect in their murder. He hadn't had an airtight alibi, but his uncle worked for the governor, and as folks know, governors can be boneheads and can be bribed or blackmailed, or both. At any rate, Chambers was never charged. Just because he worked for them didn't mean he killed them, though.

The sheriff had searched his property, but they didn't find incriminating evidence.

He had no reason to kill them. In fact, he lost his job after their deaths, and from what I'd heard, Billy Chambers left town shortly thereafter.

Sheriff Peterson walked into the room. I expected him to be angry that I was allowed access to the files, but he seemed quite calm.

"Hi, Agnes. I'm sorry about the misunderstanding we had about the backpack. Truth is, I didn't get a chance to bring it here, is all."

I nodded. "The only thing that is important is finding Jennifer." I continued to look at the file I held.

"I agree." He turned to leave.

I glanced up. "One question, if you please."

He whipped around to face me.

"Has Billy Chambers ever come back to the area since he left town?"

A strange look passed over Sheriff Peterson's features, and he shook his head. "He never left town."

"No? That's strange. It's in the notes that he did." I showed him the file, and he shook his head again.

"That's not true. I know he never left town. I'll have to check his exact location, but I'm sure he never left. Hell, I saw him just last week."

"Where?"

He pulled his shirt from his neck as if it suddenly felt tight. "After the Robinsons were murdered, he was all but ostracized by the community. Everyone thought he had done it, even though he was never arrested for the crime."

"That doesn't sound fair, but who could blame them? Folks were probably afraid. They needed someone to blame."

"Yes, but that doesn't give them the right to ruin the man's life."

The sheriff almost sounded like he was taking up for Billy.

"He could have left town," I volunteered.

"And went where?"

"Hell if I know, but he could have gone somewhere," I insisted.

"He wasn't the brightest man, you know. He was a little on the slow side. That job was all he had."

"Thanks, Sheriff."

"I sure hope you find out something, Agnes. Fresh pair of eyes on a case never hurt."

He walked away, and I wondered about the sudden turn-around in his attitude. I was always one with a suspicious nature. I began to wonder if putting me in a room with a load of files was a conspiracy to get me out of his and Sales' hair.

I took the files back to the front desk and watched as the clerk, Melinda, locked them inside a cabinet. Unlike the now-invisible desk sergeant with whom I'd never had dealings, I knew something about Melinda, who was a bit older than I am and twice as mean. Her relatives' name for her was Sis and Sissy, and you didn't want to mess with her. I had heard she had been a trooper at one time, and they had given her a desk job. By her attitude, it was something she hated. Or, perhaps, she just hated people.

She stared across the counter at me, her eyes like narrow slits. Not only did that baffle me, but it also made me mad. Who did she think she was?

Her gray skirt and white shirt didn't complement her skin. I had never seen her smile, and I wondered if she ever did. I wanted to know what had gone so wrong in her life that it made her so positively sour and dour.

I drove over to the dock's parking lot, which charged money on the weekend but not during the week. There should have been a big banner waving here that read, in bold print, *Tourist Trap*.

I walked through the crowd that was moving in unison toward the dock. Parents with excited children, snobbish boat owners, and barely dressed teenagers milled around. Plenty of boats docked at East Tawas during the summer, most considered yachts. I noticed one of them making its way in. It sported a foolish-looking, less-than-classy pirate flag with the words, *Arrr want your booty*. I think it's one of those double meanings. I'm sure the booty they were referring to had nothing to do with treasure, but then again, one man's treasure could well be someone else's booty. My mental quip had me flashing back to Andrew's booty wrapped in my frilly robe.

Shaking off that distracting thought, I walked beyond the boardwalk and onto the beach, where the sand immediately compacted into the sandals I wore. It felt like a thousand shards of glass to my sensitive feet. It burned my skin, because it was near ninety-five today. The wind coming from Lake Huron was brisk, and it helped with the heat somewhat, creating one-foot waves as it arrived. I saw children jumping into the waves, and the sounds of their excitement drifted to me.

As I walked along the beach, I searched for Eleanor. I stopped, perplexed, and then I heard a cackle of hard giggles that I knew could only have come from El.

I walked up into the part of the park that had picnic tables and playground equipment. Just on the other side was an area where the camper park was situated.

I strolled toward Eleanor and saw Rose Hamilton sitting on a lawn chair with a blanket covering the length of her body. Her ever-watchful daughter, Laurel, busied herself filling plates with potato salad, baked beans, and freshly grilled hot dogs.

I smiled. "Hi, Rose."

She looked up, and I noticed her reddened face. I knew it wasn't from the sun. She had been ill for quite some time now.

Something large was bulging beneath the blanket.

"Is that your knee?" I asked her.

Looking down at the spot, she snapped her eyes upward. "I think it's somebody's empty head."

I took a step back. "Like whose?"

"Well, it's not mine," she insisted.

I hid a smile, wondering if she was being serious.

My face felt hot as if I were having a hot flash, although it had been years since I had had one of those. She was talking about me. The idea played about inside my head like a drum. Not an unpleasant beat, but a drum nonetheless.

I had never known Rose to say a bad word about anyone, and yet, she said one to me. It had to be the Vicodin talking. It had to be, because I liked Rose.

I watched the hint of a smile that played about her mouth grow. I knew she had me. She had me totally fooled into believing she was serious.

I added. "I see you're up to your old tricks, Rose."

She shrugged. "Not much else going on. So, I hear you hooked up with the former hotshot lawyer, Andrew Hart."

"Who told you that?"

Eleanor's head was glued upward as if she hadn't said a word. She finally looked at me. "Sorry."

"It's pretty good gossip to find out the most uptight woman in Tadium actually let a man touch her," Rose said.

"Uptight, am I? And what are you?"

"I'm too sick to do something like that. But believe me, if I could, I would."

I shut my mouth. I couldn't argue with that. I looked at her mousey daughter, Laurel, and wondered what would happen to her when Rose died. She had completely wrapped her entire existence around caring for her mother. At times, I wanted to cry out to Laurel that she might never get over the fact she'd let her own life slip away from her. I respected Laurel more than any woman I had ever known for being such a diligent daughter. Still, I worried about who or what she would become once that role was finished, once she had to step off that stage.

"Lunch is ready," Laurel said.

We all sat and enjoyed the fare of burnt hot dogs, hot dogs

smothered in ketchup for those of us who didn't care for hot dogs burnt to a crisp.

We dove right in and gobbled the food. Thankfully, no words were exchanged. I watched the sailboats in the distance moving along quite nicely. It prompted me to observe, "What a magnificent day for sailing."

Eleanor burped and replied, "Are you kidding? You may be able to stomach all that moving and swaying, but just thinking about it makes my stomach roll as if it's doing a somersault!"

I waved the comment off, Rose and Laurel laughing, and it was such a wonderful moment under the sun that I wasn't even bothered by the pesky seagulls. The birds were desperately trying to steal our food. How people kept from pulling out their guns to shoot the beggars down, was beyond me. However, I was familiar with the fact that seagulls had somehow become a protected species.

Chapter Twenty

Upon finishing our picnic fare, my stomach protested, and I hoped nothing would decide to erupt. Just then, Eleanor let one rip.

"Oops," she said as she giggled. "Oh, come on, Aggie, it's not like a body can hold gas inside. It's unhealthy."

"Better out than in," Rose piped in.

Eleanor grabbed ahold of my hand and pulled my finger as if she would somehow deflate me, and right on cue, I let one go. It was one of those giant bubble farts that seemed to go on for minutes.

Laughter surrounded me, and not just from the girls. A small child shouted, "Daddy, what is that smell?" Her round cheeks flushed with the exclamation.

Her father moved her along toward the beach, laughing so hard that there were tears rolling down his cheeks. "Th–That's not very nice, Amy. Hurry, before it's too late to go swimming," said the father, attempting to distract his child. It didn't help, of course, as the small child glanced over her shoulder, waving off the odor as if she'd smelled a skunk close by.

My so-called friends were, by now, rolling on the ground laughing.

Eleanor patted me on the back. "I always knew you were full of hot air, but dang, Aggie."

I stomped over to the picnic table and sat down. "I ate beans, duh?" I tried to change the subject. "Rose, dear, how are the treatments going?"

Laurel shook her head. "She had a reaction to the chemo so—"

Rose added, "I'm sending money to that man on TV."

I was almost afraid to ask. "What man?"

"Reverend Franklin Brooks."

"The televangelist?" I didn't mean to shout, but I couldn't help it.

"He cured Frances Meyer," Eleanor affirmed.

I gasped. "You mean that old hag he travels around the country with?"

"Aggie," Eleanor interrupted. Her eyes darted to the right as if hoping to silence me.

"Believe what you girls want to, but he's living high off the hog on you." I left the picnic area, and Eleanor begrudgingly followed behind me.

"Aggie, I wanted to stay."

"I couldn't after Rose said she was sending money to a televangelist."

"What's wrong with that? I send money to him, too."

I whirled around. "Are you just plain crazy? There's no way they can cure that woman. She's in God's hands now."

Eleanor stood with hands on hips, tapping her foot. "How do you know? She may live far longer than you think."

"If they can no longer treat Rose, what possible prognosis is there?"

Eleanor nodded. "Faith. The televangelists will cure Rose, you'll see."

"I don't believe much in faith healers or anything else these days. Seniors are just easy targets." I softened my tone. "Rose is a good woman and doesn't deserve to be sick. One of the reasons my faith has been tested—as you know."

I had seen too many people put through the grinder labeled cancer. I'd witnessed too much suffering for far too long. It didn't seem right. And furthermore, it certainly wasn't right that any charlatan offering a miracle should ever profit from such suffering! Meanwhile, it broke my heart to see Rose this way. A tear leapt to my eye.

We proceeded to the car, but on the edge of the parking lot, I saw Dorothy and Frank Alton making their way toward the dock. I glanced over and noticed that Eleanor had a snarl on her face.

"Ignore them, Eleanor."

"Humph."

"Hello, Aggie," called Dorothy. "I hear you found yourself a man. About time, too."

I had no idea if she meant it in a good or bad way. My face reddened, because I now knew the gossip mill was in full swing. Thanks to Eleanor, no doubt.

She grinned. "We're going out on Maxwell Nobel's yacht today."

She obviously knew about Maxwell and me, but how?

Dorothy continued. "I heard you were quite the wild one, back in the day."

I stared at her without blinking. Perhaps, I was shocked speechless.

"Maxwell just used you, though. He said you were a horrible lay, like a dead fish." She smirked.

I leapt forward, intending to rip the smug look from Dorothy's face. I pulled her hair, but this time she wasn't wearing a wig, and her head yanked backward. In response, she clawed at me with her jagged nails, and as a reflex, I head-butted her, sending her flying to the ground. Okay, so that was a bit much, but watching the woman scurry away like a frightened rabbit was worth it.

I looked at her disheveled appearance as she retreated, squared my shoulders, and walked away with my dignity intact, pleased that I had defended my own honor.

This time, it had been Eleanor who tried in vain to hold me back from hurting Dorothy beyond reparation, and now Eleanor pulled me to the car, laughing the whole way. "I love you, kiddo! You got her good!" she said between laughs.

We left East Tawas without further incident. Once on the road, Eleanor whistled like a longshoreman and said, "Damn, Aggie, and you talk about me."

"She had it coming, and she better not mess with me again."

"Oh, my, what will the girls at the card party say tonight?"

"Card party?" Then it hit me, of course. "I forgot all about it!" It was our monthly card party at Elsie Bradford's house. "I really don't want to go, but I know it might be a good opportunity to question Elsie."

"Question Elsie about the case?"

"Come on, she's the only person who knows more about local gossip than you, Eleanor!"

Eleanor nodded in agreement. "Tadium does have quite a dark history."

"One that, so far, has stayed under the radar. They say if you don't want to be suspected of anything in this life, keep it under the radar."

"You mean in the closet?"

"Yeah. That was what you had to do in the past with an unwanted pregnancy. Even theses days, you're often judged by how you conduct your life."

"Yup. If you have ever had trouble with the law, the authorities will look at you first," began Eleanor, speaking from experience in a sad tone. "I've known a number of people in my life wrongfully charged and proven innocent later, but by then, lives are already destroyed. The simple sorry is not enough for the pain the wrongfully accused go through."

I added, "I have, at times, been labeled a bad apple, and at the time, I really believed it to be true. But who's got the right to label or judge anyone?"

"Damn straight!"

"I am, by nature, a very passionate woman and have been known to be a little emotional at times. That doesn't make me bad. It makes me a caring person." I glanced at my watch. "I have, through the years, learned to take it with a grain of salt."

Eleanor chuckled as she said, "If you sift your fingers through the salt, you may find something useful, but usually, you only find salt."

"Nobody knows who you really are unless you expose yourself. I've learned not to tell anyone anything unless I want it to be repeated, because, in a small town, it will be repeated no matter how trusted the person!"

At this, Eleanor's face became red as I didn't hold back the glare I sent her way, making sure she knew I was talking about her. Her reaction was silence as she promptly turned to glance out the window.

I shouldn't have been mad at Eleanor because she can't help herself. What else did she have to look forward to except for our crazy outings and her gossip?

I drove to Robinson's Manor, and we made our way inside. I led the way, walking up the stairs, admiring the crystal chandelier in the foyer. I moved slowly, waiting for Eleanor. Stairs were not only dangerous, but also downright treacherous at our age.

"Where are we going?" Eleanor asked.

"To William Martin's room."

Her eyes became large. "You mean ... the room?"

I nodded, and we made our way down the hallway. I was soon tapping on William Martin's door.

Andrew swung the door open and moved aside so we could enter. I didn't know what to expect. I saw William gazing out the powder blue gauze curtains, possibly deep in thought, trying to prepare for my barrage of questions. He knew by now just how persistent I can be.

Eleanor's pallor changed as we entered the room, and her knuckles tightly gripped her black bag. Her gaze darted around, as did mine. I looked at the four-poster bed with a blue quilted bedspread, the kind you'd expect to see used during the summer. I gazed at what looked to be a European Tudor cabinet. I gulped, recognizing it as the one from the Robinson crime scene photos. *I wonder how they got the blood off?*

William was dressed in black pants and a white shirt. He turned and gave me a somber look, his eyes red and puffy. He walked over to a chair and sat, massaging his temples as if they ached.

He looked up. "I'm sorry about the other day. I just don't like to be touched."

"I'm sorry, too. I shouldn't have touched you. I don't like to be touched much, either." I flashed my eyes toward Andrew, expecting a reaction, but I was disappointed when he only leaned against the bed. I decided he was trying to be strong for his friend, admirable under the circumstances.

At least Andrew put in, "I informed William about Stella's murder."

"Well, all right then. Was Stella your wife, sir?" I wondered if I'd get the same story Andrew funneled me.

"Ex-wife. She left me years ago."

I scanned his face for any sign of deception. "And?"

He shrugged. "I had no clue what really happened to her after she left me."

"She just disappeared into thin air?" I countered. "Did you report her missing?"

"There was no need," he insisted. "She left a note."

"Let me see if I have your story right. She left you for no apparent reason, but left a note. Leaving her child, Jennifer, behind, and it never occurred you to call the authorities?"

Andrew's face became tense. "What in the hell are you hinting at, Aggie?"

"In my experience, women just don't leave their own flesh and blood behind like that, especially a child."

"Some do," Andrew insisted. "You oughta remember that after working with me all those years."

I continued, dismissing Andrew's comments. "What can you tell me about your life with Stella?"

"She was a great wife and mother, but..." He shook his head. "She started acting strange and out of character a while before she left."

"In what way?"

"She started getting a babysitter for Jennifer, and on a few occasions, I was home before her."

"Did she explain her absences?"

"No, but she was acting very nervous. Whenever we went out, she appeared to be looking over her shoulder as if she thought someone would pop out of the bushes."

"Did you press her for answers?"

"No, I just thought she was upset because I was at work so much. She complained for years that I was a workaholic, and she was right, but I thought we could weather the storm." He sighed. "All marriages go through ups and down, and I thought that was all it was."

"I see. So, you had no idea why she was upset, other than your strained relationship?"

"I was sure one day I saw her with a strange man. At least, I thought it was her. She wore a red scarf over her head, and she seemed to be having a heated discussion him. When I questioned her that night, she not only denied it, but also became irate. She accused me of having her followed, and of ruining her life. I wondered if Jennifer was even my daughter, and I when I asked her about it, she told me she wasn't.."

I gasped. "Is that true?"

His eyes were red. "I have no idea, but it killed me to think that the woman I loved would betray me. I couldn't believe it was true, because Jennifer looks just like me. She even has the same birthmark as I do—and that was the clincher for me."

"What happened after that?"

"Her behavior became more erratic. One night, she didn't come home at all, and when she finally showed up the following morning, she had bruises on her arms."

"Bruises?"

"She looked bad enough to seek medical attention, but she told me if I made her go, she'd tell them I did it to her!"

"Is there anyone you can think of who would've wanted to hurt your wife at the time?"

"Hell, no, but I wish I knew because I'd have killed anyone who tried. I loved her that much." William wiped tears from his eyes.

"The next day, she left and never returned. I found a note saying she was leaving and not coming back, and to keep the bastard child." He stood and began pacing. "Poor Jennifer. I still can't believe Stella would leave Jennifer behind. I mean, what kind of mother does that?"

"I can't imagine a mother doing anything like that. Does mental illness run in her family?"

"I can't say because Stella was adopted."

I stared at William. His story seemed very genuine. Still, I wondered how Roy had known for sure that Stella was his daughter if she had been adopted.

"Thanks, William. I'm sorry about Stella. I had really hoped finding Stella would bring us closer to finding Jennifer."

"Me, too."

"Did you have anything to do with Kevin's beating or the goons in town who roughed up Roy?"

"They shot out Andrew's car window," Eleanor piped up.

"What?" William looked at Andrew. "Is this true?"

"Yes, but I think they were aiming for Agnes."

"I have no idea who would do anything like that. Sure, I was mad at Kevin and blamed him because he was the last person to be seen with Jennifer, but I know he'd never harm her. I had hoped to question him myself."

"I'm continuing to work on this case, and believe me when I tell you that I won't rest until we find out what has happened to Jennifer."

I walked out the door, trailed by Eleanor and Andrew.

"You're getting to be a dangerous woman to be involved with," Andrew said.

"You weren't too worried last night."

He scratched his head and smiled. "Maybe I should stay there tonight to make sure you, ahhh, stay safe."

"There's nothing safe about having you stay at my place." I walked away. "Stop worrying about me, and instead keep an eye on William. He needs a friend today."

We made our way outside, and I saw a hint of dark clouds. Unfortunately, we didn't make it to the car before a torrential downpour caught up with us.

We leapt into the car, panting as if we'd run a marathon. "Jeez," Eleanor gasped. "I just had my hair done yesterday, and look at it now."

I couldn't help but laugh, because Eleanor's hair was plastered to her head and face.

She shook her head at me. "I wouldn't laugh if I were you, miss fancy britches."

I gazed into my mirror and saw that my own hair looked equally atrocious.

"Do you think William seemed a little too upset about his ex-wife's death?" Eleanor asked.

"I was thinking that, but perhaps he's telling the truth."

Eleanor shuddered. "Horse's behind that he is. I just don't trust him."

"I'm just not sure what to believe."

"Don't let his tears fool you, Aggie. I smell a rat."

"Even if he's lying, Andrew won't believe it, I'm afraid. Not without hard facts."

After a time, when the rain had let up some, I drove back to Eleanor's house, where we changed clothes. I spent at least thirty additional minutes trying to make our hair presentable. Lucky for me, I had kept a fresh pair of clothes at El's place.

Eleanor smiled. "Are you ready?"

"Ready as I'm gonna be."

Eleanor clapped her hands. "Oh, goodie. I just love Elsie's card parties."

"Yeah, you just never know who might be there." I laughed as we rolled back into Eleanor's car and roared up US 23. The dark clouds had moved past and the sun peeked out, displaying a wonderful, transparent rainbow.

Chapter Twenty-One

I gripped the steering wheel and popped a glance over at Eleanor as I drove to Elsie Bradford's house for the card party. "Please, don't tell Elsie about Andrew."

"Oh, my, Aggie, the whole world doesn't revolve around you like you think it does."

"I don't think that at all," I spat out. "I just know how you—"

She glared at me. "You know, most women our age would kill to find themselves a man, any man." She huffed. "From the way they keep dropping off like flies, it's a wonder you can find one at all."

I shut my trap, thinking, *What's the point?* Eleanor was gonna do just what she pleased, as always. It didn't matter what I said.

I drove up Elsie Bradford's paved driveway and saw three other cars, parked haphazardly, all of which displayed scrapes and dents.

I parked near an elm tree, well out of striking distance. What would Eleanor do if her beloved car got any more dents? I simply could not risk any more damage to it or we'd be shit out of a roomy ride.

I pounded on the door, knowing that a light tap would hardly be heard over the ruckus of the goings on inside. Elsie yanked the stout door open, and I heard a sizzle that I knew was oxygen funneling through tubes that led to all the senior noses in the room. Oxygen tubes crisscrossed the floor, and it reminded me of trip wires. If there was a fire, there was no way anyone would escape in time.

I prayed no one had a match.

Eleanor and I cautiously made our way across the room, careful not to trip. With the ease in which we did so, you'd think we were on an episode of *Mission: Impossible*.

Inside, everything was floral white, even the furniture in the dining room. Even the tables and chairs. Most of the seniors' complexions allowed them, like chameleons, to blend in perfectly.

Abstract art hung on the living room walls, which were painted in pastel colors. White vases filled with red roses sat on the end tables. The interior resembled a funeral home. The only thing missing was a casket, and I feared I might find one in another room.

Elsie wore a powder blue outfit that highlighted her complexion and baby blue eyes. Her cheeks were a bit more rosy than usual, and I saw why when we entered the room.

Mr. Wilson sat on a chair, sipping what looked to be punch. I knew it had to be spiked, a staple at every card party held here.

Eleanor strutted over to where Mr. Wilson sat, acting like a bitch in heat. I knew it spelled trouble, but before I could intervene, Bill and Marjory Hays were waving me over, a welcome distraction.

They were the cutest couple in town and had been married for over sixty years. In fact, they'd been together so long they'd begun to resemble one another, and played it up to the hilt, dressing in the same color. Marjory had put on weight over the years, but was dressed respectfully in a matching lavender pantsuit alongside Bill.

Bill stood six foot, and I could tell from his clothing they had been golfing earlier in the day. He still wore the standard trousers and polo shirt that he always wore while golfing. I pictured how he must've stood out on the golf course, even among all the pastels, dressed as he was, all in lavender.

"Hello, Agnes, it's been way too long," Bill said. He flashed me a huge smile.

Marjory pursed her lips for a second, in disapproval perhaps.

I had seen them at last month's card party, but I doubt they remembered. "Yes, it's good to see you two."

Marjory leaned on Bill's arm like she was marking her territory. "I heard you were in the hospital recently," she said.

I nodded. "Yes, that's true. My hip has been acting up."

"Mine, too, and it hasn't been right since my last surgery," she declared.

I asked, "How is your health otherwise?"

"I had rectal surgery last month, and I don't need to tell you what a pain in the ass that was."

She said it with a straight face, and I wondered if she meant it as a joke. I bit my lower lip to make sure I didn't smile. She always looked so serious that it was nearly impossible to judge. Too much information was standard fare with seniors, who were ever so happy to share each minute detail about their every medical condition.

"Are your bowel movements regular?" Elsie asked Marjory.

"They are, but sometimes I have trouble, and the stool softeners don't seem to help much."

"Milk of Magnesia always works for me," I added, just to carry on the pretense that I was one of them. When you get to be my age, you had fewer and fewer places to go where everybody knew your name, so you sacrificed, pretending small talk of this sort was welcome. Soon, they'd be talking about folding towels.

"That doesn't do a damn thing for me." Elsie countered my Milk of Magnesia remark.

"I like prune juice," Bill stated, with a huge, toothy grin.

"You have a colostomy, you twit. It's not the same thing," Marjory added.

"You try carrying around a bag-a-shit everywhere you go," Bill fired back at Marjory.

"It would be better than trying to shit your colon out," she retorted.

"Have you ever tried a brown cow?" I asked, trying to move the conversation forward.

"No," everyone said.

"It's Milk of Magnesia and prune juice mixed together. All you have to do is heat the prune juice before you mix them."

"I thought they called that the bomb," Elsie said.

"No, to make the bomb you need to add coffee, too," Eleanor yelled from across the room.

I laughed. "I'm pretty sure if you drink it, you'd drop a bomb."

It never ceased to amaze me how the main topic of conversation for anyone over the age of sixty was bowel movements.

We strayed away from the conversation, and right away, I noticed Eleanor and Mr. Wilson had gone missing. Maybe she was helping him to the bathroom. I decided I'd rather not know.

I sat at the card table laden with enough of the wrong kind of snacks to make blood pressure and sugar levels skyrocket. Most of us had too much bulk on us already, but we still dove into the cheddar crackers, potato chips, puffed popcorn, and chocolate bon bons. I swilled down punch that I knew to be spiked with whiskey, more than my taste buds could handle, but I drank it. I needed a stiff drink.

With Eleanor still missing, we shuffled the cards and began to play Euchre, not my favorite game. In truth, I was lousy at anything other than five-card stud, and from the way Elsie peeked over her hand, I knew she would rather have a different partner.

An hour later, I excused myself to go in search of Eleanor. I listened through the bathroom door and heard heavy breathing. I didn't want to open the door, but what if one or both of them needed medical assistance? I feared, at their age, it could well be an emergency.

I opened the door for a peek and then quickly slammed it shut. *That's what I get for being so damn snoopy.*

Stumbling back into the dining room, I sat down and ended up losing four more games of Euchre before Eleanor surfaced with a smiling Mr. Wilson. I gave a thought to how most old folks, men in particular, take a long time to seal the deal, and I had a new respect for Andrew.

"What do you think of the recent murder in town?" I asked Elsie.

"Kind of strange that the person responsible waited all these years to reoffend," Elsie said.

I nodded, glad I was able to bring the subject up. "I heard the Robinsons' former handyman never left town." I looked over my glass of punch, sipping.

Elsie scoffed. "That simpleton couldn't hurt a fly. He's in a wheelchair these days and hardly speaks a word."

"Where does he live?"

"In a cabin, two miles away from here. The Robinson murders destroyed his life."

I patted her hand. "Not a good suspect then, is he, dear?"

Elsie met my eyes head on. "I can't see Billy hurting anyone. Hardly the type to rape and murder anyone, much less an entire family!"

"Do you know the exact location where he lives?" I cleared my throat. "I'd like to clear up any suspicion the police may have."

"Aggie, it's not like you're the law," Eleanor jabbered, straightening several errant curls dangling over her brow.

Elsie ignored Eleanor and volunteered, "I can show you on a map."

Elsie stood and pulled out a map, and I glanced at it. Realizing I knew the area she pinpointed, I hoped Billy was still around.

I stood and thanked everyone for a lovely night and pulled Eleanor outside. She blew kisses to Mr. Wilson, and it left the bitter taste of bile in my mouth.

The image of Eleanor with a man the likes of him was too much for me, and while I tried my best to forget what I had seen in the bathroom, it appeared that the image was burned into the back of my eyelids for eternity.

We barely made it outside before I lit into her. "What were you thinking, Eleanor?"

"Damn, Aggie, what are you hollering about? You were doing that and more last night with Andrew."

"That is none of your business."

"And Mr. Wilson is none of yours." She smiled. "At my age, the pickings are mighty slim. I have to get what I can get."

"I wish I had never opened that door."

"Humph! That makes two of us. You broke our rhythm, girl!"

She faced the window and ignored me until we pulled into her driveway. "Aggie, you know, we really are a pair." She fidgeted with her keys as she slid out.

Eleanor rounded the car and gave me an odd look. "Maybe you should stay at my place That punch was extra strong tonight," Eleanor suggested. "Are you sure you're gonna be able to—"

"I'll be fine. I made if here, didn't I?" I insisted, yelling it from my open window. Although, I wondered as my head spun a bit. Eleanor presented herself, leaning in the window. "What!"

"Oh, Aggie, don't be such a sour puss." She pouted. "You're not gonna stay mad at me, are you?"

"No. Now, please let me leave before it gets much later."

"Fine, but I think it would be a safer bet to stay the night," she said over her shoulder as she trounced away.

I exchanged Eleanor's Cadillac for my Mustang, and I pulled onto US 23, thinking I should have really stayed the night as Eleanor suggested.

As I drove toward home, two images struggled for prominence in my head. One, I really detested: Eleanor with Wilson. The other was the idea of confronting decrepit Billy out in the middle of the woods, to figure out if he was or was not a multiple murderer, as Elsie, though smart about cards, was no judge of character.

Chapter Twenty-Two

I journeyed home, enjoying the breeze from my open window. "Lord knows the breeze might help me think straight," I muttered, just to hear myself. First thing tomorrow, I planned on locating Billy Chambers, the original suspect in the Robinson case. I'd find Billy if my life depended on it, though I kind of hoped it wouldn't come to that. But with goons in town, who really knew what might happen?

I had a hankering for munchies. Anything of the salty potato chips and chocolate variety would really hit the spot right about now. It didn't take much arm-wrestling to make the decision, so I pulled into Quick Stop for a late night snack, although I reckoned it wasn't much past eight. I'd have gone to Taco Bell, but I thought it prudent not to drive any more than necessary.

I concentrated hard on not stumbling as I made my way inside, where I grabbed a bag of Better Made sweet barbecue chips, ripping the bag open and shoving chips into my mouth while I made my way toward the register. I wouldn't normally have been so ravenous, but drinking had that effect on me.

When I set the bag on the counter, chips pooled out. I started cramming them into my mouth like I hadn't eaten in a week, but the teen working the cash register barely glanced up. Her eyes were glued to the pages of what appeared to be a Japanese anime book. She looked just like the illustration on the cover, too, pink hair all but covering her face. She glanced at me over the top of the book like I'd interrupted her from performing brain surgery. Only one eye was even visible. Still, with that single eye, she managed to stare a hole through me with this oddly blank, dazed look for a moment.

After this awkward moment, in which I felt like a fugitive being featured on *America's Most Wanted*, the clerk gave my opened bag of chips, barbeque-stained face, and equally stained hands a careful inspection only a girl of her age would do. When she rolled that one visible eye, she resembled a Cyclops. Yes, the elderly were supposed to be seen and not heard, and tucked in bed long before six.

A grin formed on the girl's lips. "You stoned?"

I was taken aback by the assumption and spat out, "No!" I squared my shoulders. "Why don't you cut that pink hair of yours before you get cross-eyed," I snapped, grinning at her. "Last time I checked, you need two eyes to make proper change, and perhaps see things properly."

She leaned toward me. "Last time I checked, old hags like you were home eating cat food long before now."

I narrowed my eyes. "You oughta mind your elders."

The girl scoffed. "You sound just like my parents." She rolled her eye again.

There was no use in arguing with this kid, so I started counting pennies to pay the girl for my purchase.

"You got to be kidding me?" the girl exclaimed, slapping her head with one hand.

She never said a word after that. I'm betting even she knew arguing was pointless. As I trounced out the door, she shouted aloud, "Y'all don't come back, now!"

I made my way to my car, pulled my keys out, and sat inside. I laid my head back for a minute and that was all it took.

* * *

I jerked my head up and smacked it on the steering wheel when someone rapped on my Mustang window. I turned my head and saw Sheriff Peterson shining his flashlight through the window, directly into my eyes. It felt like a laser searing into my pupils, but ignoring the pain, I powered down my window.

"Oh, thank god! I thought you were dead," Sheriff Peterson said. "Are you okay?"

"Yes, I just have a headache."

He rocked back on his heels. "Have you been drinking?"

I shook my head. "Of course not!"

"You smell kind of strange."

"It might be the barbeque chips." I held up the bag and offered him some.

"It might be spiked punch. Weren't you at Elsie's card party?"

"Yes, why?"

"Then you have been drinking, because everyone in town knows what you older folks do at those parties."

I started laughing. "No, I don't think you do." Visions of Eleanor and Mr. Wilson rushed in to haunt me.

"Were you driving?"

"No, I flew here. A big bird carried me and my car and placed us here."

"Agnes, please step out of the car."

"What for?"

"A sobriety test."

"You have to be kidding, because there's no way I'm doing that."

"You'll leave me no choice but to place you under arrest."

I sighed, pushed open the door, and struggled out of the car, not an easy task considering how long I may have spent asleep in this parking lot.

"Walk a straight line, Agnes."

I know he wanted to get back at me, but this was a bit too much. Walking a straight line is not the easiest of tasks for anyone my age, and with my hip trouble, I imagined this could go south real quick.

I put my hands out and struggled to walk a straight line, but I swayed numerous times. I frowned.

"This is hardly fair! I have problems with my hip."

He frowned as if lost in thought. "Say your ABCs backwards."

"You have to be kidding!" I shouted. "I'm lucky if I can say them frontwards."

"You leave me no choice but to place you under arrest, pending the outcome of a blood test."

"Did your mother drop you when you were a child, because you are making less and less sense all the time!"

"Turn around."

"You turn around and haul your ass home. I wasn't even driving. Is there some law against sleeping in your car?"

Two state police cruisers pulled into the parking lot, and Trooper Sales walked forward. He shifted back on his hip when he saw me. "What's going on here?"

"I asked her—"

"I got a little drowsy and pulled over. I must have fallen asleep. The sheriff woke me up and accused me of drinking and driving."

"Were the keys in the ignition?"

"Nope."

Trooper Sales stared at the sheriff. "She doesn't seem drunk to me."

"She was at Elsie Bradford's card party. Jeez, it's well-known that all those old coots get lit up when they go there."

"Old coots? Well, I oughta..."

"You have no idea what medication she's on, and we may be keeping her from her nighttime pills. Go home, Agnes. I'll follow you there," Trooper Sales said.

I smiled at the sheriff and twitched my nose at him. What an idiot.

I got into my car and drove home, while the trooper followed me from a safe distance. When I got home, I waved to the trooper and walked inside.

Duchess was lying on the couch. She stretched once, meowed, and curled back up where she was lying. I noticed her bowl was still full of food, but one of my beloved plants lay broken on the floor. I knew leaving Duchess alone all day wasn't good for her disposition, or my plants. I would try to transplant it later, but orchids are hard enough to keep alive under the best of care.

I crawled into my bed with my clothes and shoes still on. I couldn't care less. If it hadn't been for the trooper, I'd be rotting in a jail cell tonight because the punch at Elsie's party was that strong. I still felt a little drunk, and the room spun. I could deal with a little buzz, but not the spinning or jail fine. I was on a fixed income!

I still couldn't believe Eleanor had put anything of Mr. Wilson's anywhere near her lips. Perhaps it wasn't that shocking for Eleanor, but why at the card party?

"It's so not on my to-do list," I confided to Duchess.

She was busy at her food dish and didn't care to reply with her mouth full.

"Now Andrew, Duchess, he's another story. His lips are firm yet gentle. His body's muscular, not a bag of bones like Mr. Wilson's."

I fell asleep hoping I'd remember that I owed the trooper, and I'd find a way to pay him back for helping me out tonight.

* * *

I fell out of bed when I heard someone pounding on my door. I stumbled towards the noise, stepping over Duchess.

I yanked it open and saw Rosa Lee Hill standing there. "I'm sorry I woke ya. I was kinda hoping I could use your oven." She walked in with a plastic bag loaded with who-knows-what. "It's the bake sale today. Remember?"

"Why can't you bake at home?"

"It's already full, if you need to know. You know my brownies always sell well."

I remembered. I made coffee and readied myself for the day, pouring a cup for both of us.

"I heard you had a great time at Elsie's last night."

I jerked my head up. "I suppose."

"That is something about Elsie, don't you think?"

"Elsie?"

"Yes, her son was one of the main suspects in the Robinson

murders. Now he's a suspect in Stella's murder too. They are tearing up the woods looking for him."

It dawned on me how Elsie knew so much about Billy Chambers. I'd had no idea he was her son, not that I'd blame her for failing to tell anyone.

"Sheriff Peterson?"

"No, the good ole boys."

"Your boys?"

"Yup, I tried to tell 'em to leave it alone, but you know how boys can be." She shrugged.

Rosa Lee's boys, Curt and Chris, were what I'd call a menace. They had spent most of their lives in and out of juvenile hall when young, and jail cells once they were of age. They were repeat offenders, but had thus far eluded any charges that would keep them behind bars.

I loved Rosa Lee to death, but her boys made me want to hold my purse closer and keep my doors locked. I had heard tell they were part of the militia hereabouts, but I had no way to tell if this was true or not.

"That's not a good idea. Billy Chambers has never been officially charged in that case."

"I know, I know! But you know my boys."

I waited for Rosa Lee to finish and leave. Once she had, I raced over to Eleanor's and got her ass in gear. We jumped into Eleanor's car and headed off down US 23. When we arrived, we followed a pathway that led to a shack in the woods that consisted of boards nailed together with enough gaps between them to, as Mark Twain would say, "throw a cat through." I couldn't see anyone living here in the winter.

We walked around and noticed firewood was scattered, and clothing strewn across the yard. I noticed a clothesline with a blanket strung over it. A silhouette appeared from behind. Sure looked like someone was standing back there, but I had to be sure.

I peeked on the other side and saw a man I didn't recognize. He looked dirty, and his clothes had a stench about them. The clothesline was wrapped around the man's neck, and his eyes and mouth were gaping open. I observed a bug crawl out of his mouth, and I tore into my purse, retrieved a handy wipe, and spit out the vomit that filled my mouth.

I knew he had been dead for quite awhile, three hours at least.

I jerked my head away. I couldn't look anymore, and Eleanor's lips quivered.

"I'm so tired of finding dead people," Eleanor said.

"Me, too." First Stella, now this In a town the size of Tadium, it was enough to call it a crime spree.

"Who is he?"

I pulled my cell phone out, dialed 911, and alerted them that we had found a body. The dispatcher took my name and location, assured herself I was in no danger, and told me police were on the way in the unit of time she called a jiffy.

"I think it might be Billy Chambers," I told Eleanor once I'd hung up on the 911 lady who kept shouting, "Stay on the line!"

"The one you were asking Elsie about?"

"Yeah, while you were playing footsie with Mr. Wilson."

"I'll have you know, I played with more than his feet!"

I breathed in such a gasp of air at this, I feared I might hyperventilate. Then I got back to the problem at hand, saying, "Chambers here worked as a handyman for the Robinsons."

"Why kill him? I know he couldn't have killed Stella." Eleanor pointed toward the cabin.

I looked in and saw a wheelchair lying on its side with one of the wheels spinning ever so slightly with the breeze.

Minutes later, we heard cars pulling up, and I knew help had arrived.

Trooper Sales raced forward, followed by three other troopers and Sheriff Peterson.

"I'm not sure, but I think this might be Billy Chambers." My voice trembled when I spoke to Sheriff Peterson. "I heard tell somebody might have come after him. I think they thought he killed Stella, but

I don't think he did it."

"Why is that?" Sheriff Peterson asked.

"For one thing, he was confined to a wheelchair, and that's proof enough for me."

"I'm not so convinced."

If it were up to the sheriff, he would close this case, but I knew this wasn't as clear-cut as it appeared.

I watched the troopers haul the man off the clothesline and lower him to the ground.

Trooper Sales strolled over to where I stood. "Why are you here?"

"I heard the Hill boys might be coming after Chambers."

"Chris and Curt Hill?" He scratched his head. "Who told you that?"

"Their mother, Rosa Lee Hill."

"I see. You two need to leave before the medical examiner gets here, else he'll chew my ass up and spit it out."

"It's getting awfully discouraging when everyone I want to question keeps ending up dead."

"I second that," the trooper said as he walked away.

We left, and I noticed an ambulance heading in with a black sedan labeled medical examiner on the side. I tasted bile again, and I heard my stomach gurgle.

I felt horrible.

In a span of just a few days, I had seen more death than I cared to. It made me think that finding Jennifer alive was becoming less and less likely.

"What now? Where to next?" asked Eleanor, still in shock.

"We do have a bake sale to get to, remember?" With that, we piled into El's car and got out of there.

Chapter Twenty-Three

I intermittently trembled as I drove toward the fundraiser. When I glanced over toward Eleanor, I noted her white face. We were both rattled. Finding Billy's body was an unexpected turn of events. Here I was worried about questioning him, all the while worried that he really was a psycho killer, and now—dead!

I patted Eleanor's hand. "You okay, El?"

"Sure thing, Aggie." She tore into her purse and retrieved her inhaler. Taking a puff, she said, "I like finding dead people."

"You do?"

"Not so much." She smiled. "Why can't we just see them at the funeral home like everybody else?"

"'Cause, El, we're not like everybody else."

"Damn straight we're not!" She flashed me those wicked eyes I knew all too well. "Do we have to do the fundraiser today?"

"Yup. How else are the old folks at the nursing home gonna go on all those fancy trips?"

Eleanor scoffed. "Fancy trips? I'd hardly call taking them to McDonald's a fancy trip. I have half a mind to take them on a real trip, like to the zoo in Saginaw."

"That would be a trip."

"Trying to pry them off the carousel would be priceless." Her expression soured. "That nursing home just makes me nervous."

"You afraid they're gonna give you a room, eh, El?"

"That's no joke Aggie! Hell, that nearly happened."

I remembered all too well all the paper work I had to file, plus the two months of waiting before they released Eleanor. Hardest part was convincing El to stay put until it was legal.

My mind was elsewhere, but no point in worrying about who may have killed Billy Chambers. Life had to go on, and if I was lucky, I'd get an idea of where to go from here ... somehow.

I drove into the parking lot of the County Medical Facility, or nursing home to most of us, dreading the next step. It's a modern brick building with extensive gardening beds, an outdoor fountain, patio, and it possessed over half a mile of pathways that led through the park and woodland setting. If I ever ended up in a nursing home, the CMF was precisely where I'd want to be.

When Eleanor and I walked up, we saw a large line already forming. They had two bake sales a year, the summer one being the most attended. All proceeds paid for trips for the residents. Insurance certainly didn't pay for that.

Long tables were set up along two of the walls, with the receptionist desk to the left of the entrance. Directly behind the receptionist desk, and through a closed door, was the administrator's office. All the other couches and chairs had been removed for the event. All things considered, it was quite spacious. They even allowed the residents to participate.

Rosa Lee smiled at us when she saw us come in. She appeared to be having the time of her life. She winked at me from across the room. She was wrapping up brownies that I knew contained specialty herbs from her garden. Not just any brownies, but hashish brownies.

When I saw the administrator buy one, I hoped it would loosen the bitch up a bit, because she always walked around acting like something unpleasant had been shoved up her ass.

Melanie Paxton had been appointed administrator some years ago, and although she was fair, she could be a royal pain in the ass. I knew people who had worked here, and they never lasted more than a year. Melanie would tell them that at orientation, too, taking pride in running good people off. What a hard-ass. I know state inspections can be a real pain, but it failed to excuse her for running off all the good staff; the ones who actually cared about the residents. As my dear, departed father always said, "You can have a box of apples, and maybe they all look shiny, red and great, but there are a few bad ones in every bushel." Melanie treated all employees as bad apples, and that simply was not right, as well as short-sighted on her part.

I watched her so intently that I hadn't noticed Mr. Wilson walking up. I should have known by the squeaky wheels of his rolling walker. It was like fingernails across a chalkboard.

"Hello, sweet Eleanor," he said. "What you selling?"

His gray eyes made him look like the Grim Reaper. I gave him a dirty look and glanced away.

"What I'm selling, I can't give you here," Eleanor teased, to which I rolled my eyes and turned my back.

"Agnes, you are looking so fetching today."

"I don't give a damn—" I looked up into Andrew's smiling eyes. "Oh, I-I'm so sorry. I didn't see it was you."

He nodded. "I'll be right back. I'd hate to miss out on the brownies. I hear good things about them."

He ran over, and Rosa Lee pressed one into his hand, winking at him. For some reason, that bothered me, but I tossed it off as irritation because nobody wanted to buy what we were selling. When I looked down, though, I was reminded that we were selling chocolate chip cookies that were burnt near black!

"What?" Eleanor asked. "It was the best I could do on short notice."

"You could've picked up something from Rogers' bakery."

"I tried, but they were all sold out. Look around the room!"

I did so and realized why Rogers' bakery was sold out. I frowned, but as with every frown these days, I fretted over developing deeper wrinkles, so I admonished myself to stop it at once.

"Want a brownie?" Andrew asked, holding one out to me.

I shoved it into my mouth. I figured I might as well, because just about everyone else was eating them, including a few residents. Had all these people gone loco? These people were on all kinds of medications, and who knew what, so the last thing they needed was something that may interact with their meds.

Mr. Wilson had a brownie in one hand, and his walker in the other, rocking to the music that obviously was only playing in his head. I rolled my eyes, remembering not to frown when I noticed a few residents had joined in.

"Hell, no, I'm not gonna go," they chanted.

I looked around and saw two nursing assistants trying to bring the residents back through the double doors. They ran around the lobby like scurrying squirrels, with the workers in pursuit. It was at least entertaining. I was impressed by the residents' agility today. Perhaps it could be the brownies.

"Stay away, you hear," one of the residents named Jenny said. She had a large cane, and I knew she wasn't afraid to use it. She intended to use it as a lance, judging by the way she swung it, and I almost pitied anyone she used it on.

"Come on, Jenny," encouraged a nursing assistant. "Let's go back inside."

Why that crazy nursing assistant put her face so close to Jenny was beyond me. Jenny grabbed the woman by the hair and proceeded to knock her on the head. Melanie, always the effective administrator, ran to help her, but Jenny caught her just under the chin with the cane. Melanie flew backward onto a table. It wobbled a few times, then fell straight down, taking Melanie with it. A banana cream pie flew into the air and planted itself atop her head.

She lay there for a few moments, shaken, but when she stood, her face looked as red as a fire engine. She raised her head a notch and limped to her office, obviously too enraged for words.

I knew she wanted to kill Jenny, but that was just not possible, and she should have known how this particular resident was. Rule number one: never get close enough for Jenny to grab ahold of you. Rule number two: leave her alone until she calms down.

They finally herded Jenny through the double doors, distracting her with an offer of ice cream. Seconds later, she had forgotten all about the encounter.

I saw the crowd step over the broken parts of the tables and continue to buy the brownies. After eating them, even our burnt cookies looked good. I didn't have the heart to charge for them, though. I planned to give a donation before I left.

Andrew hung around until the bake sale ended to help with the clean up. It really was our mess, after all, but I blamed the brownies. I noticed Eleanor had gone missing again, so I waited outside with Andrew.

It could have been the brownie, but he looked more fetching than before, dressed in Bermuda shorts and a clinging gray T-shirt that displayed his well-muscled frame.

"I found another body today," I said.

"Who?"

"Nobody you would know. It was someone I wanted to question about the Robinson case."

"You're still stuck on that?"

"Yes, of course. Stella's murder was so similar."

"And so copycat."

"I think that too, but what else do I have to go on?"

"Maybe you should just forget about it altogether."

I gasped. "There is no way I'm doing that."

"Do you hate William that much, or are you hoping it will somehow bring your granddaughter back from the dead?"

"Hold on! Just who do you think you are?"

"I think someone needs to tell it to you straight. You have no evidence about William, and your granddaughter is most likely dead."

"How do you know for sure?"

"It makes perfect sense. It would be better if you just faced the facts."

"Faced the facts? There are no facts in Sophia's case, and unless they find her decomposing body somewhere, I refuse to believe she's dead."

"I can understand why you'd want to hold out hope, but Aggie, you're just not being realistic."

"You are a complete ass, and I have no idea what I ever saw in you."

I walked away and tried to still the tears that were now pouring from my eyes. He didn't know. He couldn't know she was dead. I believed against all reason that she remained alive. She was out there somewhere. She had to be, because that is all I had lived for this last year. I had promised my daughter I'd find her. *And I will, somehow,* I told myself again. I knew I was all out of leads, but something had to turn up. It always did.

Eleanor joined me at the car, and I was so distraught that I asked her to drive. With any luck, a truck would kill us on the way home. But it didn't happen, and I just sat in the car when we got to Eleanor's house.

El asked, "Do you want to talk about it, Aggie?"

I shook my head. It hurt too much to think about, let alone speak about. I still couldn't believe Andrew would be that harsh. Obviously, William meant more to Andrew than what we shared. I willed myself to quit thinking about Sophia lying dead somewhere, but how could I not entertain the notion? It was hopeless. Instead of mulling it over further, I gazed at Eleanor as she sat next to me like a trusty sidekick.

I gave my anger five more minutes and then joined Eleanor inside.

Chapter Twenty-Four

As I walked through the open door Eleanor held, I finally spoke. "Okay, I suppose you think I'm acting like a child for sitting in the car so long."

Eleanor shrugged. "Since you don't want to talk about it, not much I can say."

I trounced through Eleanor's house and whipped open the patio door and whirled around. "Andrew seems to think my granddaughter is dead."

Eleanor stood back, looking puzzled. "He said that?"

I slumped into a chair on the deck. I saw Eleanor out the corner of my eye, but I ignored her. I felt depressed and pissed at Andrew for making me see things I just wasn't willing to accept, but I had to talk to someone. "Sophia is out there somewhere, El, possibly with Jennifer. Will I ever find either of them?"

"I don't rightly know, but you can't beat yourself up. We'll uncover the truth somehow." Eleanor slid the patio door back open and moved back inside. After a long moment, she returned with two dishes of ice cream.

Eleanor pushed a dish of ice cream covered with hot fudge, whipped cream, and nuts toward me. I ate without looking at her. I stared at the lake instead, watching the sun go down. It cast a finger of orange, pointing to a shadow on the beach. It looked like a young woman, but when I raced down to the lake, she was gone. When I found no one, at first, I questioned my sanity, but as soon as I discarded that foolish notion, I said to the trees, "I saw a woman. I know I did. I can't give up hope."

I walked along the shore, hoping to catch a glimpse of the young woman I'd seen, but it looked like she was long gone. Maybe I had imagined it. The sunset had that effect on me sometimes.

Eleanor waited on the deck and looked worried.

As I strolled up the ramp to the deck, I explained, "I thought I saw a young woman down there, El."

"Maybe the sun is playing tricks with your eyes."

"No." I shook my head. "I'm sure I saw someone down there. I even walked up the beach."

"Aggie, you're upset. There's no telling what you thought you saw. It just wasn't real."

"You didn't see her! If you had, you wouldn't be arguing with me. I know what I saw."

I was pissed again, this time at Eleanor. I knew I had seen someone standing down there, but where had she gone? All the other cabins looked empty, but I wondered. What if Jennifer and Sophia were being held against their will?

I thought of calling Trooper Sales, but walked through El's house and out the front door, making my way toward the cabins nearby instead. I pounded on all the doors. Five cabins and not one door opened.

I realized only then that Eleanor had followed me. I frowned when Eleanor looked at me with concern. That was supposed to be my job.

"I guess nobody's home," Eleanor said.

I let out a sad, long sigh. "I guess not."

"That, or they don't want to open their door to some half-baked old crone who looks like she just flew in on a broom."

I jerked my head up and glared at her.

"Seriously, you should look at yourself in the mirror," Eleanor said.

"And maybe you should follow your own advice! You have lipstick on your cheek."

Eleanor wiped it off with the back of her hand and followed me back to her house. She waited for me to enter first. I had a sneaking suspicion she didn't trust me.

Once settled in at my place on an overstuffed sofa, Eleanor said, "I'm making you a cup of tea, Aggie."

I sat mulling over what to do next, and drank the tea down in a few swigs as Eleanor always made it on the lukewarm side.

"What kind of tea is this? It tastes kind of bitter."

"Oh, does it?" Eleanor asked. She spared me her glaring eyes, looking everywhere but at me.

I knew what she'd done, and I'd kill her if I could get up from the sofa. I closed my eyes and felt Eleanor cover me with a blanket.

"Good night, Aggie."

I woke up with a raging headache, and it took me a moment to realize where I was. I saw Eleanor busying herself in the kitchen and heard something snapping in the frying pan: bacon. The aroma had infiltrated Eleanor's entire house. She needed to turn the burner down before—

Eleanor cried out, "Ouch."

"You need to turn the burner down."

"It's done now. I guess it had to have the last word."

I smiled and made the eggs while she ran her hand under cold water. She showed me her finger, but it didn't look too serious. I slathered butter on it. I had no idea if that helped, but it's what I always did, one of those old wives' tales that gets passed down through the generations.

I put plates on the table, and we sat and ate breakfast while watching the sunrise.

"What did you drug me for?" I asked her.

"I can't let you wake up half of Tadium."

"It was only nine."

"What person our age, that you know, stays up past nine?"

I knew she was right. If it were up to me, I'd be in bed by eight every night. I had mixed feelings about what Andrew had said last night, and I wondered if I would ever talk to him again.

I knew it didn't make any sense to hold a grudge at my age, but it was easy for him to say those things. It wasn't his granddaughter who had gone missing. I said to Eleanor, "I'll face it, El. The real reason I can't let this go is Sophia."

Eleanor leapt to her feet when someone rapped on the door, and she waddled over to open it.

Trooper Sales stood just outside the door. "May I come in, please?"

Eleanor waved him in, and I stood to greet him.

"What's going on, Sales?" I asked.

"I just wanted to tell you that the Hill boys both have an alibi for the time of Billy Chambers' murder."

"That isn't possible," I replied.

The trooper pressed on. "How did you know where Billy was hiding out in the first place?"

"You mean living?" Eleanor added.

"He was only a suspect in the Robinson murders. He was never charged, so he really wasn't 'hiding out,'" I said.

The trooper looked more serious than ever. "You're the main suspect in the murders of Stella and Billy."

"You have to be joshing," Eleanor said. "Aggie is no more a suspect than I am ... I mean, I am just as guilty. If she's a suspect, what am I, chopped liver?"

Trooper Sales shuffled his feet. "I know. You're both suspects, and the sheriff thinks I should arrest you both!"

I nodded and said, "All adds up nice and tidy in that small brain of his ... yeah, figures. I see how this works."

"That lame-brained sheriff is telling you stories," Eleanor said.

The trooper turned to me. "You searched through the Robinson files."

"You gave me permission, or did you forget?"

"I know, but I'm just trying to do my job."

"Elsie Bradford drew me a map to where Billy was living. I had no idea that he was her son."

"Who said that?"

"One of the girls, Rosa Lee Hill."

"I see. And you said Roy told you about Stella."

I nodded. "Ask Andrew if you don't believe me. He was there."

"Yup, is he a suspect, too, Trooper?" Eleanor asked.

"No, but ladies, I need to find out who was responsible for their murders before someone else gets killed."

I stood there with a puzzled look. "In all honesty, I can't imagine who that might be as I don't have any more leads."

We watched the trooper leave, and I felt fit to be tied. "Of all the nerve! That crooked sheriff is trying to set us up." I quickly got myself together, although I had only the clothes I had slept in to wear. "Get ready, Eleanor, we're going to pay that sheriff a visit."

Eleanor threw her arms up. "You're going to get us arrested."

I smiled. "Perhaps."

Eleanor suggested, "Maybe we should bring Andrew. He's a lawyer, after all."

"No, I'd rather not." I then gave it some thought and resigned myself to the fact that I needed his help. "Maybe you're right, El."

We drove to the Robinson Manor, and I made my way inside with the ever-present Eleanor in tow. When we walked through the dining area, I spotted Andrew and William eating breakfast.

I lifted my head a notch and bravely approached the pair. "I'm sorry to bother you, Andrew, but I need your help," I said. I hated that I had to ask for help, especially from him, but sometimes it was necessary. I simply could not let the sheriff pin those murders on Eleanor or me, or the two of us together.

Andrew looked up between bites of runny eggs dripping off toast. "What do you need?"

I eyed William then. "Well, they're blaming me for Stella and Billy's murders. Me and El both, in fact! How's that for lunacy?"

"The way I hear it, Stella may've been raped before she was killed," commented William, "and Billy was strung up by his own clothesline." He chuckled loudly enough to draw attention. "The law actually thinks two old ladies could possibly do something like that?"

"Yes. Crazy, huh?"

Andrew wiped his face. "I'll drive," he said as he walked toward the exit, with us following to his LX.

"I feel bad enough that your LX was damaged the last time. We're taking Eleanor's car." I led the way to the Cadillac. "You can't hurt it worse than it already is."

"I don't think I like the sound of that," Eleanor said.

"Oh, fiddle-sticks, you know it's true."

"You don't have to be rude about it," Eleanor huffed.

I retorted, "Eleanor, you need to chill out."

El, never the one to be silenced when she was offended, replied, "You need to—"

An explosion from a gun pierced the air, and Eleanor's windshield exploded into deadly shards of glass that rained down on us like stinging pebbles.

I gasped, jerked around, and scanned the area. Bushes hugged the property line, and although I had the feeling we were being watched, I could see no one. Whoever cracked a shot at us had done it from the woods.

"I guess we'll be taking the LX after all," Eleanor said. "Agnes, in the future, it might be a good idea not to suggest that my car can't look any worse."

"Good point," I said.

"I think someone wants you both dead," Andrew said in my ear, and it was only then that I realized he was shielding my body with his.

I dusted myself off, and smiled. "Dead? Like that would scare me. We're not far from death as it is." I turned my head and saw faces pressed against the glass at Robinson's Manor dining area. The real old folks were trying to see what all the excitement was about, and who could blame them? I'd have been the first one at the window if I were in their shoes.

Andrew called 911, and we waited for Trooper Sales to arrive.

The trooper frowned when he saw the Caddy's windshield.

"I suppose I did that, too," I said.

"Did you see where the shot came from?"

"No!"

"If I had seen it coming, I would have ducked," Eleanor exclaimed.

"I should have known it's not safe to go anywhere with you two," muttered Andrew. "Hell, we hadn't even gotten out of the parking lot!"

While all three of us victims were shaken, I managed to realize that Trooper Sales also appeared shaken. I imagined he was suppressing the urge to kill us. He raised an eyebrow. "Maybe I should place you two into protective custody."

I glared at him. "Let me guess, in a jail cell?"

"It might keep you two out of trouble and alive ... if that is in any way possible."

Andrew laughed. "Nope, I don't think it is."

The trooper gave us the go ahead to leave, adding that we could pick up a copy of the police report later. It amounted to the basic same-o jargon the cops tell victims right before they head out. We piled into the LX and left for East Tawas.

"I'm hungry. Let's stop at KFC," Eleanor suggested.

"Hungry? We just had breakfast," I said.

"That was hours ago. It's noon, already."

I had forgotten how time flew when I was nowhere having fun. I enjoyed Andrew's company despite yesterday's harsh words, and from the look on his face, I felt reassured that he felt the same about me.

We drove into the KFC parking lot, and Eleanor lit out so fast I thought she was in a race.

"What's up with her?" Andrew asked.

I shrugged. "Maybe she thinks they might be out of chicken, or that we might want to be alone."

He smiled at this. "Thoughtful dear, isn't she?"

"As a matter of fact, yes, she is."

We made our way inside just as a loud commotion was in progress.

"Lady, you forgot my biscuits," a young man standing at the counter shouted at the cashier, Ella Bates.

"I did not forget any damn biscuits, child! I don't ever forget anything!" Ella's voice shook the room.

She was well-known as the biscuit Nazi, and that was not being mean, as it was the truth. Her large body was always pressed into a KFC uniform barely her size. She typically swept her gray hair into a bun covered with a hairnet.

She usually worked in the back, so to see her out front manning the counter wasn't good for anyone.

"There aren't any biscuits in the bag, you old hag!" the kid continued to shout.

My mouth gaped open. He didn't just insult Ella. He called her an old hag. "He's plumb crazy," I said to Andrew. "He obviously doesn't know to whom he's speaking."

She came toward the counter, a menacing look on her face. "So, not only are you calling me a liar, but now you're calling me old and a hag!"

I nodded, thinking, *Old as the hills and ornery as shit.*

"Yes, an old hag. Old people just don't have any business working in fast food. If there's one thing a senior can't do, it's move fast." He looked around him, trying to rally support, but the crowd backed up. "You know I'm right. You probably never had a job your entire life and were married to someone who never worked, either. If you don't pay in any social security, you can't collect any, you old bitch."

I shook, my temper rising with every word he spoke, but it was like watching a car wreck. I couldn't look away.

"You probably lived on welfare all your life. That's it. Give me my damn biscuits, now!"

"Oh, you want biscuits, I'll give you some damn biscuits." She picked up biscuits and began throwing them at the young man. One hit him in the eye.

"Ouch! Hey, stop it, you old bitch," he hollered.

She threw them harder still, and they seemed hard as hockey pucks the way the pimply-faced kid reacted when they hit him, raising his arms, trying to fend off the attack.

"You want some chicken with that?" She reached in the warmer, pulled chicken out, and threw that at him, too. I'd never seen anyone throw so hard, or someone trying to dodge just as fast. He slipped and fell, but jumped up and ran out the door when he heard police sirens.

I was so mad that I followed him. I knew it wasn't a wise decision, but I couldn't help myself. I told myself to stop, but I kept walking toward him.

"Hey, you!" I shouted. "How dare you say something like that to Ella? How dare you presume to know anything about her? She and her husband have worked their whole lives. They paid in plenty of social security, and she spends the majority of the money she gets on medication."

He flipped me off, and I was ready to give him the smack his mother obviously never had, but I was pulled backward. I whipped around and stared into Trooper Sales' eyes. He didn't look happy or amused. In fact, he looked pissed.

"What do you think you're doing confronting that man out here?"

"He said some things to Ella that I just couldn't let go."

He laughed. "I see, but from what I heard from dispatch, she kind of fueled his fire."

"He called her an old bitch and suggested things about her that weren't true."

"Maybe, but she made up for it when she pelted him with chicken and biscuits."

"It sure is a waste of chicken and biscuits, if you ask me," Andrew said, followed by a pouting Eleanor.

"They said it'd be twenty minutes before more chicken will be ready," Eleanor whined.

"For some reason, El, I think I've lost my taste for chicken or biscuits today. What about you, Andrew?"

Andrew readily agreed, saying, "Tacos, anyone?"

Chapter Twenty-Five

Andrew dropped Eleanor off and then took me home. I'd had enough for the day, what with having Eleanor's window being shot out and the fiasco at KFC. I was ready for some down time. Jennifer Martin's disappearance was never far from my thoughts, but at my age, there is only so much one can accomplish in a day before a body plain out gets worn down to the quick.

When I walked through the door, Duchess began to wail, and I decided to feed her a can of tuna to make up for my neglect of late. I had forgotten I had spent the night at Eleanor's. I was so absorbed in worrying about Duchess that I failed to notice Andrew had followed me inside and parked his butt on my sofa; that is, until I turned around. It wasn't that I felt unhappy he'd followed me in and made himself at home. No, it was just that I didn't trust myself to be alone with him. Not anymore.

Duchess scratched at the door, and I opened it, letting her out. What's the worst that she could do? I'd become used to the mice by now. We had an understanding. If I leave them some cheese—they stay out of my bedroom.

Andrew patted the couch. I retrieved a beer for him and a Hard Mike's Lemonade for me from the fridge, and I settled next to him on the couch. I felt as nervous as a schoolgirl with my first boyfriend, which wasn't much of a stretch since Andrew was the first man I had let past the front door since I had lost my husband.

I flipped the television on and watched the news report warning the public not to leave their doors unlocked. "In this reporter's opinion, it may also be best not to tell anyone you are old, because at

KFC, there was an incident that will go down in the record books." The newscasters laughed as cellphone footage of the incident was being run.

Looking back, it didn't seem so funny now. Even a biscuit Nazi had rights.

Ella used to spend her days at the dock fishing after she retired, but since her husband fell ill, she was forced to get a job to help pay for their mounting medical bills. She obviously missed fishing and took her job a little too seriously.

I wouldn't call her friendly, more of a brute, the kind of person you never messed with. One look from her could turn even the friendliest of people to stone.

Andrew scooted himself closer, and I felt the urge to move away, but this was my house. I felt warm, but he made me feel hot.

I turned to tell Andrew to leave, but as I faced him, his lips met mine. I welcomed his tongue inside and got lost in the taste of him. Next thing I knew, clothes were being ripped off, and we did it right there on the couch.

I felt something poking me on the ass, and when I pulled it out, I saw what I thought was one of Duchess's cat toys.

Hell, no!

I jumped up and heard a mouse screech at me, before it crawled back under the cushion. I yanked the cushion up, only to discover a nest of baby mice beneath it.

That goddamn cat needed to go. "Some cat I have," I said.

"I kind of like it," Andrew said, grinning. "Puts a little adventure into the foreplay."

We walked into the bedroom, where we made love like two starving beasts, and I fell asleep in Andrew's arms. Nothing could hurt me; I felt completely safe.

* * *

I sat up and walked into the bathroom. I had no idea what time it might be. I hardly noticed Andrew missing until I encountered a man standing in my bathroom.

"Hey there, remember me? You shot me in the ass." The man was tall and thin, and his dark skin and swarthy look made him appear menacing, or it could have been the gun he held in his right hand.

"No, no, that wasn't me, actually." I tried to stand my ground.

"You know what I like about old bats like you?" he asked, laughing. "Nothing. I usually frown upon killing someone old like you, but I'll make an exception for you." He pointed the gun at my forehead. "Even my mother wouldn't blame me."

I inched forward, picked up my denture cup that was full of Efferdent, and threw the contents into his eyes.

He screamed and shrank back.

I limped into the bedroom and retrieved my fully-loaded, Pink Lady .38 from the bureau drawer. I saw a dark shape enter my bedroom, and I pulled the trigger. I saw Andrew's face, a tad too late. He slumped to the floor. Behind him, the man from the bathroom came lunging at me. I fired the gun, not once, but four more times, emptying the weapon.

I flipped the lights on and saw I had hit Andrew in the arm. "You could have just told me I was that bad of a lay. You didn't have to shoot me," he said.

I knelt down. "Oh, Andrew, I'm so sorry."

He didn't say a word. He had passed out, and here I was holding the bag. I stepped over the other man, who I hoped was dead, but then again, I hoped he wasn't, because Trooper Sales already thought me capable of murder.

I never intended to kill anyone, I fretted.

I called 911 for the second time in one day, and when the trooper showed up, I realized I had seen him a total of three times that day.

I stood waiting at the door, and as they approached, I stuttered, "I-I-I'm afraid I shot two men, one of them by accident."

I led the way to my bedroom. "Is he dead?" I asked, of the stranger.

Sales checked his pulse. "Yup."

I stepped over him. "I think I winged Andrew. I thought he was the other guy—the intruder!"

Trooper Sales rolled his eyes, taking in the fact that Andrew was quite naked. The sheet I had thrown over him didn't hide the fact.

"Was he that bad in bed?" Sales asked with a shake of his head.

"That's not near as funny as you think it is! The man I killed came here to off me. Andrew was on me! Well ... not at the time of the shooting." I struggled to take a breath, feeling flustered. "No, but he came for revenge! He said I shot him in the ass, but it wasn't me, it was Eleanor."

"I'm afraid to ask."

"It happened at Roy's bait shop, the-the day they worked Roy over. I assume they were there to get a lead on where Stella was."

"Why in hell didn't you tell me about this sooner?"

"I-I just didn't want to get Eleanor into trouble."

"I see arming the two of you may have been a mistake."

"Poo, if I hadn't had that gun, I'd be the one being taken out in a body bag!"

Trooper Sales rubbed his head like it hurt, and I knew I wasn't helping his headache a bit.

"I'm sorry, is all I can say," I said, trying to placate him. "Maybe I should stay home tomorrow."

"I'd put my money on the fact that you won't."

I didn't smile. I just moved aside when the paramedics loaded Andrew onto a stretcher. I felt horrible that I had shot him, and hoped he would be okay. The medical examiner picked up the body, and I saw that I had quite the mess to clean up.

Blood had pooled onto the wood floor, and I hoped this would be the last time. I dreaded thinking this may be the beginning of something much bigger. I felt a chain reaction coming, and I didn't look forward to the outcome.

* * *

As soon as all the commotion was out of my driveway, I threw on some clothes. I was on my way out the door when I saw Duchess far up a tree. I tried coaxing her down, but she wouldn't budge. I didn't have time for her antics and left her tree-bound.

I drove to the hospital, hoping I hadn't injured Andrew too badly. I didn't know anything about gunshot wounds, but it couldn't be good. If I had learned anything, it was not to shoot until you are damn sure precisely whom you are shooting at. I should've flipped the light on, but I hadn't wanted to make it too easy for the assailant.

I arrived at the hospital, dialed William's number, and told him only that Andrew had been taken to the hospital.

I informed the nurse I was there, and I nervously alternated between pacing and sitting in the waiting room until William arrived.

William ran toward me, a frantic look on his face. "What happened?"

"It was sort of an accident. An intruder broke into my house, and I went for my gun, and I shot Andrew by accident. Actually, the jerk used Andrew as a human shield, but it was so dark ... I just fired, and I'm so sorry!"

"What happened to the intruder?"

I shrugged. "I killed him. I had no choice. He came there to kill me."

"Did they identify him? Did you know the man?"

"He's one of the goons who roughed up Roy at his bait shop a while ago. I guess he wanted revenge."

My eyes shot up when a nurse approached. "You can come in now," she said.

We followed her into the emergency room, and I saw Andrew sitting on the edge of the examining table. He was laughing at something Dr. Thomas had said.

"Lucky for Andrew, you're not that good a shot," Dr. Thomas said.

"Thank God for that," Andrew agreed.

"You just grazed his arm. He can go home. I'll get the papers signed." He nudged Andrew. "Be more careful, Andrew. Personally, women with guns scare the hell out of me."

Andrew smiled. "It's okay, Aggie, I know you didn't mean to shoot me. The guy had me at gunpoint and used me to get at you."

"The intruder was one of the goons who jumped Roy at his bait shop, Andrew, and he left me no choice. I put four slugs into him."

"I suppose he's dead then?"

"You bet, but I had no choice. He would've killed us both."

With his one good arm, Andrew pulled me into him for a hug. "Pretty obvious someone wants you dead, my girl."

"Will everyone quit saying that? I know someone wants me dead. They want me off this case, but I'm not about to quit."

"Yes, you are," Andrew said.

"No, I'm not, and it's too late now. I do wonder how they know where I live. I mean, if they aren't from the area."

"I wondered that myself."

"Somebody must be supplying them with information," William suggested and then said to me, "I'm glad to hear you haven't given up on finding Jennifer."

"Have you received any suspicious phone calls?" I asked William.

"No, I wish I had. It's like there's not a trace of her anywhere."

"Something will turn up. I know it will."

We helped Andrew off the table and outside.

William, who'd closely shadowed us, piped in with, "Andrew, if you'd like, I could check out her place to make sure nobody is lurking around."

"That sounds good," I replied. Turning toward Andrew, I asked, "Where do you want to go?"

"Back to your house."

"Really? Even after I shot a hole through you?"

"It's not safe for you to be there alone."

I waited for a slow-moving Andrew to climb into the LX before settling myself in the driver's seat.

"About the house," I started. "It's kind of a mess right now."

"What?"

"There's blood on the floor, for one thing. If you kill someone in your home, the police leave the mess for you to clean up. It's one of those things folks don't know about until it happens to them."

"I see. Maybe you should come back to Robinson's Manor."

"I can't. Duchess is up a tree, and I can't just leave her outside like that. Who knows what trouble she'd get into."

William followed us back to my house, and he helped Andrew inside once we were there. William checked out the inside of the house while I extracted Duchess from the tree. We met in the living room, where Andrew had decided to lie down across the couch, mice and all.

"Your bathroom window is busted out," began William, "and the screen has been cut. That appears to be how the assailant got in. Do you have any plywood? I could board it up for you before I leave."

"That would be great."

I led him to the shed, and he found what he needed and pulled out the plywood, hammer, and nails. I supervised his work, and he seemed to know what he was doing.

"You sure are handy with boards and nails."

"Surprised, are you? My dad was a contractor, and I helped him build houses during the summers when I was a kid." He smiled. "One of the reasons I don't do that now is that it's backbreaking work, and I decided long ago I wasn't following in his footsteps."

"I bet he didn't take that well."

"Nope, you got that right."

I showed William to the door. "Thanks, William. I see now why Andrew holds you in such regard."

"Take care of the old fellow, okay? He's the best friend a guy like me can have. I don't trust many people."

"Well, you can trust me to take care of Andrew. I've reloaded my gun already." I smiled and closed the door, and when I returned to the living room, I saw that Andrew had fallen asleep. I pulled out my mop bucket and cleaned up the blood. It made me feel a bit queasy, and I could have done without the smell, but I had to get it done. Vinegar water, just like my mother and her mother before her used; it cut through the odor perfectly.

Duchess peeked in at the doorway, sniffing. I said to her, "I sure hope I don't have to shoot anyone again, at least not in our home, honey."

Duchess nodded. I swear she did. She then softly purred, her eyes now watching the mop move back and forth.

"I should feel awful that I ended a man's life tonight," I continued, talking to myself and my cat. "But I don't. I simply had no choice. It's not my time to die, not yet anyway."

My house would never feel like the safe cozy cabin in the woods again until I found Jennifer, and until all the goons were in custody. There was nothing about this whole business that felt coincidental, not to me, anyway. There was a direct relation to Jennifer's disappearance and the goons coming into town. I just hadn't, as yet, been able to find out what that connection might be.

Swish-swish-swish. Slowly but surely, the blood was disappearing from my floor.

Chapter Twenty-Six

I stared out my kitchen window and noticed that, yet again, thick fog surrounded my house. With the way in which events happened of late, I was half expecting someone to emerge from it. I wondered what I could do to feel secure. Electric fencing and vicious guard dogs, perhaps? Woods surrounded my house, just like the locations where Stella and Billy's bodies had been found.

Stella certainly had reason to be concerned for her safety, but what about Billy Chambers? I felt relatively sure that he never saw it coming. Since the Robinson family murders, he had lived in obscurity. It wouldn't matter much to folks that he was never arrested for the crimes. Public opinion could be quite vicious. I'm sure the people in this town felt justified in destroying the man's life. Since Billy's death had gone public, I felt sure many folks thought themselves safer now. Few would consider it cold-blooded murder as I did. But I knew with certainty that he was not guilty of Stella's murder.

Andrew shuffled out of the bedroom, and I poured him a cup of fresh coffee, placing a fresh biscuit layered in butter in front of him. I whimpered at the sight of his arm in that sling.

He sat and looked up at me with a half smile. "Did you bake this morning?"

I nodded. "It's what I do when I get nervous." I walked away because his hard stare unnerved me, and I still felt terribly guilty over having shot him.

His hair was sticking up, but he still looked attractive. I had other thoughts, but they'd have to be put on hold until he was up to par.

After having gathered my courage and swallowing my guilt, I

joined him at the kitchen table. "How are you feeling?" I asked.

"Sore," he said, rubbing his arm. "What are you planning to do today?"

"I haven't given it much thought. Eleanor's car is still at Robinson's Manor with a broken windshield, and my car is too small for her to sit in comfortably."

"If you feel the need to gallivant, feel free to use my Lexus."

"I'm not sure I want to do that. I mean, what if something were to happen to it—again. Why, I'd be mortified!"

"The back window has already been shot to pieces. What more can happen?"

I didn't want to contemplate what more could happen or that it might get worse. One thing I knew for certain: Things could always get worse. It was an illusion to think they would get better.

Duchess walked into the living room and stretched. She looked at me like I should know what she wanted without her having to communicate with me via a meow. When I didn't respond, she meowed.

"I know you want your breakfast, too," I said.

I filled her dish with dry cat food, and she looked at me as if saying, "You expect me to eat this?"

I answered as if I had read her mind. "That's all you're getting."

Duchess walked over and wound herself around Andrew's leg and purred, sounding like a motorboat.

"She has taken a liking to you, Andrew."

"Lucky for me, she doesn't know I hate cats." He smiled.

"That's not what you said yesterday."

"I'm glad you're not the type of woman who has fifty cats."

The gears inside my head started to turn, and I thought of somewhere I could go today.

"Thanks." I kissed him. "You just gave me a great idea."

I skipped into the next room and returned dressed in blue jeans and a yellow top with a picture of a cat covering my bosom.

"Where are you going dressed like that?" Andrew asked sternly.

"I'm going to Cat Lady's house," I said. I kissed him on the cheek, then ran out the door, jumped into the Lexus, and drove to Eleanor's house.

Once at El's house, I walked through the house and out to the deck, and there I found her. She didn't see me at first, and I stared in silence, watching as she worked out, kicking her heels up when she suddenly stopped to stare out into the fog over the lake.

"Hi, what you looking at?" I asked.

She didn't even turn to greet me, her full attention on the lake. "I thought I saw a ship moving through the fog. I know that seems odd." She looked serious for a moment. "Maybe it's a ghost ship."

"You really watch too much TV," I said, then added, "But I think you might try to clean your glasses. I don't see how you can see a damn thing through them."

She snickered. "Oh, that must be it."

She walked inside and turned on the kitchen faucet, running her spectacles under warm water and then drying them with a tissue. "Are we going somewhere?"

"Yup."

"Do I want to know where?"

Without batting an eyelash, I replied, "Cat Lady's house."

She raised an eyebrow. "Let me slip something on that is cat hair proof."

Eleanor returned five minutes later wearing a denim outfit, pants and shirt. It looked rough, like the stiff jeans you used to buy that had to be washed twenty times before they were soft enough to wear comfortably.

"Who's afraid of cat hair? Not me," Eleanor said, as she locked up and we went for the car. On seeing the Lexus, she asked, "Where is Andrew?"

"I'll explain it to you on the way." Even as I said this, I wondered how I was going to explain having shot Andrew and killed a man overnight.

We piled into the Lexus and drove to Crooked Creek Road. It

was more of a local street and made of packed dirt, or a dirt road, as we referred to it around these parts. As we followed Crooked Creek Road, I decided that I had no idea how it could ever be referred to as a road. It had huge ruts large enough for the LX to be buried in, with us inside as helpless victims. We'd never be found! I maneuvered my way along like a pro, averting any serious damage to Andrew's precious LX, or us.

"If I tell you something, El, you are not allowed to make a joke out of it."

"What did you do, kill Andrew for his car?"

"No, but I kind of shot him." I grimaced. "Winged him, to be exact."

Tears broke the surface of Eleanor's eyes. "Was he that bad?"

"I just told you not to make a joke about it."

"Come on, you should know me better than that; it's perfect joke material."

"I killed one of the goons last night. In fact, it was the one you shot in the ass."

El shook for a moment. "Oh, my. I bet you had to do it. I mean, seeing as how you haven't offed anyone before. You must have had your reasons."

"He was in my house and planned to kill me on account of he thought I was you."

"Me!"

"He thought I was the one who shot him. He came for revenge."

Her eyes rolled to the right. "That's awful. I'm glad the goons don't know where I live."

I smiled. "I was thinking maybe I should stay with you for a while."

"You must have gone plain loco. I can't have goons showing up at my house and shooting the place up. I mean, what would my neighbors think?"

"'Crazy old Eleanor is at it again' is what they'd think!"

"It was an accident," Eleanor shouted.

"You're lucky you didn't shoot your damn leg off."

"Oh, look who's talking. You killed someone last night and wounded your lover. I think you are way farther up the crazy meter than I am."

"If I'm crazy ... it comes from hanging out with you."

We stared at each other eye to eye, and we busted into laughter.

"I swear, Aggie, one of these days you're gonna make me pee my pants."

"You already do that." I smirked. "For the record, Andrew is not my lover."

"Of course not, Aggie. What is it those young folks call it these days? He's your friend with benefits, right?" She winked.

"What is Mr. Wilson?"

"He's an acquaintance, and at times, I enjoy his wit."

"Is that what you call it? It looked to me that you were enjoying more than his wit."

"He's just a bit on the freaky side, is all."

"He'd have to be to tangle with the queen of the freaks."

"What does freak even mean?"

"It means strange, and yup that sums up Mr. Wilson and you to a tee."

"You're a real smarty pants."

I had a smug smile on my face. I had won that round.

Was it too much to hope that the crazy old bat out in the boonies would have any clue about the Robinson Murders? There had to be a connection between that cold case and the missing tourist, Jennifer Martin. I felt it in every fiber of my being.

Chapter Twenty-Seven

A dingy white farmhouse came into view. It had seen better days, maybe thirty years ago. Today, the shutters hung downward, and I wondered what held them up. I could see I'd have to wade through the tall weeds that surrounded the property in order to reach the front door.

I yanked the wheel of the Lexus and tore up the Cat Lady's driveway; perhaps I was moving a bit too fast because I found a shotgun leveled at my head when I stepped out.

"Jesus, Aggie. Is that you?"

Cat Lady had a first name I'm sure, but nobody around these parts knew it, including me.

I grinned even though I was about peeing my pants by now. "Yup, of course. Who else is crazy enough to come out here?"

Cat Lady moved her shotgun toward Eleanor. "What did you have to bring her for? You know perfectly well I don't much like Eleanor."

"You don't like anyone much," Eleanor said. "Put that dang shotgun down before you shoot someone by accident."

She moved her firearm down, and her eyes focused on Eleanor with menacing intent. "Wouldn't be no accident," Cat Lady retorted.

She paused, as if deep in thought. When she frowned, her wrinkles formed crevices on her aging face that looked to be filled with dirt. She wore a man's tan shirt and brown trousers with knee high boots. Her straw-like hair was covered with a straw hat. If I didn't know better, I'd say she was a scarecrow and just as stick-like.

I broke the silence and said, "You two behave, or else I'm hunting down a hickory switch."

We followed the Cat Lady through the tall weeds and up the broken steps that led to her dilapidated wraparound porch. Her front door gaped open, and I could see an overstuffed white cat with tiger stripes and spots sitting in the doorway. When she meowed, we covered our ears because it sounded like a lion's roar. It must have been a calling of sorts as cats began to appear out of every nook, cranny, and hole big enough for them to crawl through, until we were surrounded on all sides, much to the amusement of Cat Lady.

I gulped hard and wondered if coming here had been the best choice. We could be eaten alive, and no one would ever come looking for us—not even Andrew or Trooper Sales. Heck, nobody in town would be fool enough to traipse out here.

Cat Lady walked inside, but I hesitated. In truth, I feared following her. I glanced toward Eleanor, and she looked as horrified as I felt.

When I walked inside with Eleanor, she gripped my arm so tight I felt it go numb. Finally, I yanked my arm away, and as I glanced around, I saw there was nothing to be afraid of.

It looked vacant inside, with not even a strip of furnishings.

"What happened to all of your furniture?" I asked.

"It was pretty darn cold last winter, and I had to burn it for firewood."

Noticing a large ash pile in the fireplace, it occurred to me that she might be telling the truth.

When Cat Lady spoke, I noticed she had but one tooth on the bottom. At least she couldn't eat us. She pushed a pipe between her lips and took a drag. It smelled funky as hell, and that worried me, because how I could smell anything over the cat odor was beyond me.

She left the room, and Eleanor nudged me.

"Can we leave, please?" Eleanor's face looked paler than ever, and she trembled. "She must have to clean litter boxes all damn day."

"It wouldn't matter. With this many cats, it'd still stink." I grimaced. "Besides, do you see any litter boxes?"

Cat Lady returned with three glasses. "Here, I brought you two a glass of my moonshine. It's the best you'll ever taste."

We took the glasses, and I noticed they were brown inside and out. I wondered if she ever cleaned them. I knew she didn't have indoor plumbing and just an outhouse out back. I'd pee on myself before I'd use it.

I stared at the brown glass containing liquid that she tried to convince us was moonshine, and maybe it could have been exactly that, but it could as well have been acid for all I knew.

"Down the hatch," I said, downing it. I coughed, sputtered, and spewed. I felt dizzy, maybe a little more dizzy than normal. I felt the floor rise up to meet me, and it jarred me a little when my ass smacked it. "This is good shit."

Eleanor and the Cat Lady clinked glasses and downed theirs, too. We all sat on the floor afterward, intoxicated after just one glass, cats all purring and staring at us.

"You look funny," I said to Cat Lady.

"No, I always look dis way," she slurred. "It kinda reminds me of da old days."

"You know it," Eleanor chimed in. "Like when the Robinson murders happened. You remember that day?"

"Holy shit, was dat a day. Folks were so afraid, they didn't come out for days," the Cat Lady said.

"Who you think did it?" I asked.

"Weren't that half-wit handyman, that's for sure."

"No?" I asked.

"He's afraid of his own shadow, and from what I heard, his plumbing never worked much with the girls."

I stared, open-mouthed. "Are you saying...?"

"He liked boys."

"There's no way he'd rape Mrs. Robinson, then."

"Nope." Cat Lady coughed and choked up something that

resembled a hairball. "I hate when that happens. Those damn cats will be the death of me one day."

I swallowed hard as I imagined her licking her cats clean. "So if the handyman isn't the killer, who is?"

"Beats me, but I heard said Mrs. Robinson had some peculiar interests."

"Such as?"

"Such as she liked to flaunt her ass willy-nilly all over town. She modeled a few times for the Sears catalogue ... thought she was pretty hot to trot."

"You think she was cheating?"

Cat Lady leaned forward, deadly serious. "Now that's where it gets interesting. There were a few fellows who thought they stood a chance."

"Like who?"

"Maxwell Nobel, for one. I heard tell you knew him at one time, Agnes."

I nodded. "Yup, but he was more talk than action, if you know what I mean."

"Aren't they all?" Eleanor giggled, and Cat Lady slapped her on the back and cackled at the joke.

"Eleanor, remember ol' Beer-Belly Peterson?" Cat Lady asked.

"I should, because he was elected sheriff."

I sat, stunned. Maxwell Noble and Sheriff Peterson could be suspects in the Robinson murder? I had to think rationally. This was only a lead.

After clamoring to our feet and saying it was time to go, Cat Lady led us back to the Lexus. We appreciated her guiding us back to the car, as it would have taken us a lot more time to find it. On seeing the LX again, Cat Lady eyed it with suspicion. "Where'd you get this fancy ride?"

"The car belongs to her new fancy ride of a man," Eleanor said.

El and I jumped in, and I backed the LX out before Cat Lady could respond. I wanted to throttle Eleanor, but I needed to thank her instead.

"Good job, El."

"I thought you might need help. I lived here way back when. With me doing the talking, she wouldn't think the questions quite as intrusive as they might be from a stranger."

"Intrusive?"

"Yeah, small-town folks like to keep their dirt to themselves."

"I know a little about that."

"And the Robinson murders are the worst dirt there is in all of Tadium."

We retraced our ride over the rutted road, both delighted when we finally found asphalt.

Chapter Twenty-Eight

I drove to the Iosco County Sheriff's Department. I like to live dangerously. I gripped the steering wheel tightly as my hand felt sweaty. Part of me wanted to turn back around, but the sleuth in me wouldn't allow it.

I whirled into the parking lot, and El and I sneaked out of the Lexus like we had just stolen the vehicle and planned to ditch it here.

I eyeballed El, her face a bit pale. I'm guessing about as pale as I imagined I might look. As we made our way to the front door of the sheriff's department, I confided, "With what we now know, dear, I'm as shaky as a leaf in the wind, so don't think you're alone."

Eleanor nodded and gritted her teeth.

"Come on, El."

She whispered, "You don't actually think the good sheriff is gonna give us any useful information, do you?"

I didn't answer. Instead, I swung open the door and stepped inside, with Eleanor dang near up my backside.

Sheriff Peterson rounded the counter before we stepped much farther, greeting me with a fierce scowl on his face.

He looked down at me, hands on his hips. "What in the hell are you doing here?"

Eleanor started talking, or stuttering rather. "W-Well, a-ah a-ah..."

Sheriff Peterson's eyes narrowed, and his temple began to twitch uncontrollably. I wondered if he was about ready to have a grand mal seizure.

He didn't intimidate me a bit. "I'd like to ask you some questions," I said.

"What kind of questions?"

I glanced around to assure nobody was within earshot. "Questions that you might not want to answer in public."

He nodded and went outside, and we followed from a respectable distance. He led us to a picnic table out back that two deputies vacated when the sheriff sat down. Although he'd not said a word to either deputy, they slunk off like frightened rabbits. He led by intimidation.

I sat down gently, but when Eleanor did, the table tilted.

She stood. "Sorry, this must not be the plus-size table."

Sheriff Peterson's eyes rolled over Eleanor's body like one would survey a prize fish. But she was no fish. She resembled more of a whale, but I'd be damned if anyone should dare say such a thing about her in my presence; they'd have me to deal with. She was, in effect, my spiritual sister, after all.

"What do you know about the Robinson murders?"

"I know that some sick son of a bitch killed them. I believe the handyman did it."

"Did he?"

"Yes, and I'm guessing some vigilante killed him."

"All these guesses all these years later?"

"After Stella's murder, obviously ... well, it stirred folks up. He did it, of course, and even Trooper Sales agrees that much!"

I stared at him with what I knew was doubt displayed on my face. I have never been one to mask my feelings, and what I felt toward this piece of shit excuse for a sheriff was loathing.

"I see you doubt my word."

"Actually, yes, I do."

His eyes narrowed. "And why might that be?"

"Because when I saw Trooper Sales yesterday, he thought I was the one responsible for both murders—Stella's and Billy's."

"He's just grasping at straws. You should know how those state boys are." He softened his tone, "You were married to one. They think they are God's gift to law enforcement."

Inside, I was simmering, and I was about to boil over and blow my top. He was trying to goad me.

"You don't think I'm capable of killing anyone?"

"Not hardly. You may be a snoop, but you don't have it in you to take it to the next level."

Little did he know...

I bobbed my head. "So you're saying if put into a difficult situation, I wouldn't or couldn't use deadly force."

"You're a cupcake. A lightweight snoop."

I stood. "I guess the state boys don't share everything with you, or else you would know that I killed an intruder last night."

He jumped up. "That's not possible!"

"Oh, but it is, and I'm on to you! Don't think I'm not."

"What craziness are you talking about now?"

"I heard you were quite taken with the late Mrs. Robinson, but she didn't return your passions. Did you kill her?"

"Agnes," Eleanor said.

"Who in the hell told you that?" He scratched his head as if lost in confused thought.

I didn't speak. I just turned away.

"Cat Lady."

I cringed inwardly when I heard Eleanor say the name that should never have been spoken. Any credibility I'd once had went out the window as soon as she opened her mouth.

Sheriff Peterson laughed. "Now I know you're both off your rockers. Cat Lady, indeed. She's a crazy old woman who fancies herself a witch. I hope you didn't drink any of her so-called moonshine."

I held my breath. I silently prayed he couldn't smell it on me.

He smirked. "The last person to drink her brew landed in the hospital with certain intestinal difficulties," he informed us suggestively.

"What kind of difficulties?" Eleanor asked.

My stomach lurched suddenly, and I ran toward the sheriff's office, and straight into the bathroom, where I spent who knows how long.

When I raced to the Lexus and sat inside, Eleanor unrolled her window as if trying to suck in fresh air.

"You'll have to come home with me, because I'll be lucky if I make it home before I have to go again!"

"That's strange. It didn't seem to bother me. I guess I'm just used to vile brew that is made by cat people." She cackled. "They say Cat Lady is really a cat herself, one that has been reincarnated into human form."

"I'd like to reincarnate her into a mud puddle."

Silence. Finally. I pulled into my drive and ran into the house. I sprinted toward the bathroom and slammed the door shut.

Duchess was in her litter box, and she froze, her eyes glued to me as if questioning, curious. Her tiny nose sniffed the air, and she bolted into the bathtub and hid behind the shower curtain. She peeked out for a moment but ducked back in.

Chapter Twenty-Nine

Jennifer Martin's case was on hold for the next little while as I spent the majority of time—two days—in the bathroom. Andrew was such a sweetie and didn't even ask me what had happened to bring about such a calamity.

I spooned in chicken soup that Andrew made. I had no idea he was a master chef and could rustle up a meal at the drop of a hat, or that I'd like having a man cook for me. I'm an independent woman. I grinned. I had often been described as a control freak, and it was true, but I couldn't possibly help it, especially now, being so set in my ways. I like to be in charge. I mean, I had gone these years being completely self-sufficient.

Eleanor was still at my house and she walked inside with a fistful of radishes. Strange thing was, I hadn't planted radishes, yet the roots were clearly visible, with fresh dirt clinging to them. Then I recalled how they just keep showing up at the edge of the woods. Eleanor loved the nasty things, and so did Andrew, judging by the way he wolfed them down. They made salad, and if there was anything I was not ready to eat, it was fiber of any sort.

"I think I feel up to going into East Tawas today," I said.

"Are you sure?" Eleanor asked.

"We need to follow up on Maxwell Noble. Not that I believe anything that crazy old Cat Lady said."

"You shouldn't speak about her like that!" Eleanor cautioned. "S-She might just hear you." Eleanor looked over her shoulder as if she believed what she was saying.

"If she's any kind of a witch at all, she'd know, because I have been cursing her for two hellishly damnable days."

Andrew drew his brows together, but he didn't say a word. I think he knew enough not to ask. Perhaps this punishment I was enduring was payback for being so brash, but truthfully, I had no idea why I should be cursed or vexed by Cat Lady.

"Who is Maxwell Nobel?" Andrew asked.

"He's one of Agnes's old flames."

"I'm driving," Andrew said.

I didn't complain, but this would be no social visit.

Once we were settled into the Lexus, Andrew spoke. "What in the hell is that smell in here?"

"I swear I tried to air it out," Eleanor said.

When no one responded further, Andrew dismissed it.

Andrew drove to East Tawas, and we made our way up the dock and found a yacht named *Mystery*.

"What an odd name for a boat," Eleanor said.

I peeked inside the yacht. "Hello! Is anyone on board?" I asked.

Maxwell surfaced from below deck and smiled. His white pants flapped in the wind, as did his white shirt, and he wore white deck shoes to complete his ensemble. He looked like the Pillsbury Dough Boy, complete with potbelly. He may, in fact, have devoured the said doughboy. His hair was a comb-over. I firmly believed that if a man was as bald as Maxwell here, then he might just as well shave his head, but in Max's case, I knew it would do next to nothing to help his appearance.

I was surprised he had let himself go like that. It was bad enough that he had smaller than average equipment, from what I remembered. I snickered to myself.

"Hello, Maxwell," I said. "This is my best friend, Eleanor, and my friend, Andrew."

"I'm her boyfriend," Andrew added.

"Come aboard." He helped Eleanor on, but Andrew jumped aboard and helped me before Maxwell had a thought to.

Men are such control freaks, I thought. He may as well piss on me and mark his territory.

"I'm sorry to disturb you, but I'm investigating the disappearance of Jennifer Martin."

"I can't say I know her."

"You might not, but this investigation is leading me to the Robinson murders."

"That's strange."

"Not really. I don't know how to ask you this without coming right out and saying it, but did you know Mrs. Robinson?"

"Sure did. She was kind of what we used to call a tease."

"Tease?"

"Yes, all she talked about was her modeling gig, although it'd been years since she had done it."

"Were you involved with her?"

"Not the way you're suggesting. As I said, she was a tease. It wasn't just me who thought so, either. There were others. Too many to count, if you ask me."

"Can you think of anyone else I could talk to?"

"Sheriff Peterson."

"I spoke to him already."

"I mean his father."

"You're suggesting Sheriff Peterson's father could be involved?"

"Could be, but I'm not sure you'll get much out of him. He lives in a nursing home."

"The County Medical Center?"

"Yup, one and the same. I'm not sure they'll let you in, though. I heard the bake sale went haywire."

I nodded. "Thanks, Maxwell, I hope one of these leads pans out. I really don't like the idea that a recent murder looks so much like a copycat of the Robinson murders."

"I'll agree with you on that score. Nobody wants that murder case reopened."

We left, and I wondered why anyone would be so concerned

about a murder that happened all those years ago. What was everyone hiding?

* * *

Two hours later, after dropping Andrew off at an appointment, we sat in the County Medical Center parking lot. Andrew had business to conduct with William, and I couldn't have been happier. The last thing I needed was a man to be traipsing around with me everywhere I went. Folks in town had enough to talk about already.

Eleanor peeked from under the visor, pretending invisibility, foolishly thinking that no one would recognize the lady who had destroyed the bake sale. Rosa Lee and her brownies were the true culprits of the fiasco, but Eleanor was the greatest scapegoat who ever lived.

Finally, and without prodding, she confessed, "There's no way we'll get past the front door."

I rolled my eyes but said, "Sure we will."

"How?"

"I have a plan."

"A plan?" Eleanor stared at me with interest. "I can't wait to hear this."

I nodded with menacing intent. "We're going to use a disguise."

Eleanor shook her head. "You better hope the administrator isn't here. She's got radar."

I knew that was true. "I heard she installed cameras in every corridor, the dining room, and the nurses' station." I leaned forward. "I heard tell she can check them from home, too."

"Is it a nursing home or a correctional facility?"

I dared not answer, didn't need to. A correctional facility fit right. "I think it's the perfect time. It's after five. We need to make our move before the administrator can make it home and check the cameras."

"That won't work. They serve dinner at this time."

"Maybe Mr. Peterson eats in his room."

"Oh, no, fancy-dancy administrator won't have that. She herds them in and makes them go down the hall. She makes them wait in line, too."

"What in the hell for?"

"She wants them to think they are going to a restaurant. I bet she hopes that will make them forget where they really are."

"He might be in the feeding room."

"Are we talking about a nursing home or a nursery?" Eleanor puffed out her chest.

"Strange how when you get older, not only do you revert to childhood, you're treated like one, too."

Eleanor shouted. "Residents have rights!"

"Some rights! They lose those when they hit the door." I nodded for emphasis. "Some of them shouldn't leave, though, and I wonder how they ever lived on their own?"

Changing the subject, Eleanor asked, "What kind of disguise did you bring?"

I handed Eleanor a pink wig, and I donned a white one.

"Why do I have to have the pink one?"

"You know pink is so your color, El."

"You should have a blue one, then. I heard blue hair is in these days."

I ignored her taunt, pulled a straw hat over my wig, and adjusted it in the mirror. "In military terms, it is called infiltration."

"I'm not so sure this'll work. Someone's going to catch on and snatch our wigs off, and then what?" El asked. "Oh, no, nobody will ever recognize us." Eleanor taunted.

"El, please, move out the door."

Eleanor sashayed herself from the Lexus to the lobby, and I followed.

Ellen Scott sat behind the receptionist desk and hid a giggle behind her hand. She promptly rolled her eyes. "My, but my glasses are dirty." She took them off to clean them, and we went through the double doors.

"Follow me," I said.

We followed the sound of dishes being rattled and food that smelled so delicious I almost wished I lived here, or maybe just at mealtime.

I passed the open kitchen door and locked eyes with a janitor who was busy hitting on an aide, obvious from the way he was leaning toward her. He turned away and continued his conversation, not paying us a bit of attention.

I let out a sigh, and I pulled Eleanor back as a nurse walked toward us. Eleanor whispered in my ear, "There's nowhere to go. We're busted."

I smiled and led the way. "Hello, can you tell me where I might find Mr. Peterson's room?" I asked the nurse.

Her deeply tanned face gave me a once over. "Peterson? You visitors?" She spoke with an accent, maybe Jamaican.

"Yup, we are real good friends." Eleanor winked.

She hesitated. "Be my guest. He's in room 401 and in quite a mood. Perhaps visitors will calm him a bit."

We walked down the hall, and I heard a commotion in room 401. El and I wisely watched the scene unfold from the doorway.

"I don't want to eat. Don't you tramps get it?" Mr. Peterson stood with his hands on hips, dressed only in a gown displaying a good portion of his backside.

"I believe that's a full moon," Eleanor whispered.

"You're killing me here," I replied.

"You have to eat, Hal, or we'll have to call your son again," said the aide trying to get the older gent to eat.

He walked forward and raised his hand. "Go ahead and call him. Hell, it's the only time he comes to visit is when you snitch on me! I'll tell the son of a bitch what's what when he arrives." He stepped forward, swung his hand, and slapped the aide in front of him while the nurse looked on from a comfortable distance.

I gasped. I couldn't help it. I was shocked. Why in the world did the aide get that close to him if he was that angry? Were they teaching stupid around here?

The trio turned toward us, and I feared for a moment that he'd turn his anger on us, but he didn't. Instead, he smiled.

"Hello, ladies. Are you here to visit me?"

I pushed Eleanor forward.

"Ahhh ... yes, but it looks like, well, you're in the middle of dinner," Eleanor said.

"They just don't have what I like to eat."

The nurse and red-faced aide had scrambled from the room as we'd walked inside.

I turned and closed the door. It might not have been a wise choice, but I didn't want anyone interrupting us.

"Hi, I'm Agnes, and this is Eleanor."

"I called for hookers last week. What took you so long?"

Hal Peterson didn't look a bit like his son. His toothless mouth swung open, and he started licking his lips. His nearly bald head accentuated a scar over his right eye.

"I'd like to ask you a few questions," I said.

"How about one of you asks questions while the other licks my Willie?"

I could taste bile. "If you whip it out, Hal, it'll be the last time you'll see it." I pulled out an ink pen and smacked my hand with it, creating a sting and loud sound.

He sat down. Those aides just needed to show this man they meant business. I knew they dared not speak too harshly to him. If they uttered anything but a normal voice to him, they'd be fired.

"What do you remember about Mrs. Robinson?"

"Mrs. Who?"

"Robinson, the lady who was killed along with her entire family?" I pressed.

He gave it a long moment's thought then said, "Ahhh, yeah, sweet lady, and a married woman, but man did she like to romp around with young men. I think they wrote a song about her."

"I'm talking about the Mrs. Robinson who was raped and murdered back in 1968."

"And her whole family slaughtered, as well," Eleanor added.

He rubbed the whiskers of his chin. He needed a shave, and from the smell, a bath.

"I don't know what you're insinuating here, but I knew her. I won't lie." He stood, whipped out his penis, and pissed in a metal trash can.

I didn't react. I refused to! Because that's what he wanted.

"What other tricks can you do?" Eleanor asked.

"Now, Eleanor, that would be hard to top," I added.

"Who are you again?" he asked. "And why in the hell're you asking questions about the Robinson case?"

I pressed for more information. "Did you like her?"

"I can't say I thought much of her. I saw her naked once, though, but she was dead at the time. Not much time for fornicating then."

"So you wanted to do her?"

"I was the sheriff at the time, you know, like my boy is now. A lot like him, in fact. As to Mrs. Robins—"

"Robinson, sir."

"Yeah, Robinson ... I can't say I had contact with her other than a nod or two."

"What was she like?"

"She liked to flaunt her ass and perky tits all over East Tawas, but that's all. I never knew of anyone who actually got into her bloomers, if that's what you're asking."

"Did you have any suspects?"

"No, except the handyman, but I couldn't imagine Billy doing something like that."

"I heard he didn't much like women. Is that true?"

"Not sure, but there were many men who wanted to be with Mrs. Robinson. What with the way she was strutting around, it could have been anybody."

"That isn't an excuse to rape a woman," Eleanor said.

"Maybe not, but being a tease isn't a smart move. She let a few men cop a feel, but then wouldn't see it through."

"Can you remember the names of any of the men?"

"Maxwell Nobel was one."

"I heard your name mentioned."

"Probably did. Folks weren't happy with the investigation. I did my best, but I just couldn't find any leads."

"I see."

I twirled around when I heard the door pop open and saw Sheriff Peterson's frame fill the doorway.

"What in the hell are you two doing here?" he bellowed, his face red as a beet.

"I'm here visiting your dad, is all."

"Is that it, Pops?"

Hal hung his head.

"Are they harassing you about the Robinson case?"

He nodded without looking up.

"You two come along now," Sheriff Peterson said.

The sheriff escorted us from the building, causing a stir among some of the residents and nurses. Once outside, he turned on us. "You two are under arrest."

I stood with my mouth agape, and I gasped. "You have to be kidding?"

"No, I assure you, I'm quite serious."

He read us our Miranda rights, and Eleanor looked at me with shock.

"Are you gonna frisk us?" Eleanor asked. "Because it's been a real long time since a man has touched me." She smirked. "I think I'd like that."

I was glad we had left our handguns in the Lexus. Plus, a nursing home was hardly a place to take a pistol, and I believed it illegal, even with a concealed gun permit.

"Did you drive here?" he asked once we were in the glare of the sunlight.

"Nope, we walked," I said. I didn't want to see Andrew's Lexus impounded.

We put our hands on the sheriff's car, and the sheriff frisked us. "Hold your hands out. I know you two are old and feeble, so I'll cuff you from the front."

As he slapped the cuffs on us, I repeated for the hundredth time, "What in the hell are you arresting us for? What are the charges?"

"Trespassing."

"I'll have you know this is a public place."

"Melanie Paxton called 911 and reported a disturbance in my dad's room."

"Bull," Eleanor spat. "That happened before we showed up."

I hoped he would come to his senses, but after we were told to sit in the backseat of the sheriff's cruiser, and he closed the door behind us, I knew he had no intention of letting us off the hook.

"I've never been to jail. This is exciting," Eleanor said.

"Yeah, as exciting as a cold sore," I mumbled under my breath as I cursed the sheriff. I knew he had to be hiding something. My head began to pound, and I felt my blood pressure rising, but I couldn't get at my pills with my hands bound by cuffs.

Peterson pulled from the curb and made his way toward his department, fully prepared to book us. I shouted in his ear from the caged back seat. "I can't see these charges sticking, Sheriff."

"I'll make 'em stick! I do have some influence."

"You're obviously just trying to scare me in hopes I'll stop investigating."

"For your own good, yes!"

"Bull hockey!" cried Eleanor.

"She's right. You couldn't give a damn about us, and if you think for one moment that I was determined before, then watch out—"

He reached over his shoulder and closed the small space we were communicating through with a violent shove, effectively cutting off the next word.

Chapter Thirty

We arrived at the county jail in handcuffs a few minutes later. Sheriff Peterson helped us out of the car. We made him put his back into it, too, not exactly resisting the process, just acting as feeble as he pegged us. I smiled when I heard him groan—that's what he gets. If he insisted on treating us as feeble, I'd act the part.

We walked in, and he quickly and urgently shuffled us into the back. What would people think when they found out the sheriff had arrested two such hardened criminals?

They took our fingerprints, which took a while because we weren't cooperating, and Eleanor stuck her tongue out during her mug shot.

Sheriff Peterson led us to a small room, where a female deputy looked less than happy to see us. The small brick room had a bench along one wall and cubby holes that I guessed we'd be using temporarily to put our clothing into.

"Are they under arrest?" the blonde deputy asked. She looked to be twenty-one and had a shocked look on her face. She gulped like something unpleasant was about to go down. She hardly looked the type to be in this line of work, but who was I to judge.

"Yes." Sheriff Peterson smirked when he walked out of the room.

She tightened her ponytail. I judged her to be a tad nervous. "I'm sorry ... oh, my ... I need you to remove your clothing, so I can search you."

"Sure thing," Eleanor said. She pulled her clothing off like she was doing a strip tease while I removed mine in a corner.

The body cavity search was just as I expected, intrusive. I felt sorry for the deputy. She was only doing her job, and now she'd surely have nightmares for at least a month.

We redressed and followed her to a cell with a sliding barred door that she opened. When we walked in, I realized it was a holding cell because we weren't alone. Two rather odd-looking women sat inside. One had muscular arms and a buzz cut, and the other was a skinny blonde with stringy hair. The blonde looked scared out of her mind and was leaning her head on the older woman. Obviously, they knew each other.

The cell consisted of an iron bench affixed to the wall with bolts and a small metal object that seemed too small for either of our asses. I guessed it to be the toilet. Inwardly, I cringed.

"What're you two in here for?" Eleanor asked the large woman.

The woman belched. "I drank a little too much, and they picked me up for nothing, really."

"It didn't have a thing to do with the man she threw through a plate glass window," the skinny woman added.

It sounded like a non-admission of guilt.

"You're lucky I did, too. That man who was soliciting you was a creep. For all you know, if'n you'd gone off with him, your throat'd be cut by now!"

"He was gonna pay me fifty bucks, Momma!"

"Darlene! He tried luring you down the dark alley, you dumb ass."

"Stop calling me that, Momma. He looked clean and spoke with an Italian accent. He said he'd buy me new clothes."

"Sure, and pigs fly."

"They do fly when they walk through a combine," Eleanor said.

I shook my head. Why was El talking to these women? Who knows who they were or what they might do to us. "Eleanor, would you just please leave these poor women alone?"

"What do you mean 'these poor women,' Grandma?"

"Damn, Agnes, shut up. You want them to shank us?" Eleanor

whispered. She turned to the large woman. "I know she's uptight, but ever since the fuzz started finding bones in her backyard, she hasn't been the same. Damn rats we have around these parts."

"I can second that, my friend," the large woman said. "I'm Marge, and this is my daughter, Darlene. We're from Detroit and here on vacation."

"Marge, did you say someone tried to lure your daughter away?" I asked.

"I'm afraid my girl is a bit touched in the head, and I have to watch her all the time."

"I am not." Darlene folded her arms and distanced herself from her mother.

"You are the most gullible girl I know. You can't just leave with the first man who asks you."

Darlene sat and pouted, and I turned my attention to Marge. "You have to watch out. My granddaughter disappeared last year, and I'm searching for another tourist who has recently gone missing."

"Jennifer Martin," Eleanor added.

"That's what the cops are for, isn't it? Missing persons cases and all?" Marge asked.

"Ha! This Podunk sheriff's department? They never even tried finding my granddaughter. I'm thinking the same person could have them both."

"If it's been a year ... most likely she's long gone." Marge tried for all her bulk to look sympathetic.

"You said the man ... was Italian."

"Yes. He's here with three friends, but one of them was recently shot and killed."

I nodded. "I saw that on the news, yes, very recently. Shot by a homeowner during a home invasion. Got what he deserved."

I felt sick. I knew there was a connection, but I couldn't do a damn thing about it, not being locked in cold storage. I banged on the cell. "Hello! Where's my phone call? I get a phone call."

The other three women looked at me as if I'd taken leave of my senses. Eleanor fell to the floor. "Oh, God, I think I'm having a heart attack."

I began to pant. "OMG, I can't breathe. I'm having an asthma attack!" I shouted to add to the bedlam.

The young deputy ran and opened the door. Checking Eleanor's pulse, she tried to reassure El, saying, "Calm down, it's going to be okay."

The door swung open, and Sheriff Peterson walked in. "Couple of drama queens, if you ask me."

"We can't take chances. What if one or the other were to die in our custody, Sheriff?" the deputy asked.

Peterson smiled at this. "My job would be so much easier if only..."

Gasps echoed around the room.

"How can you say that? I'm calling 911," the deputy insisted.

The ambulance showed up minutes later, and Trooper Sales walked in with the attendants.

"What in the hell is going on here?" He narrowed his eyes and glared at Sheriff Peterson. "What kind of jail are you running here?"

"I placed them under arrest."

"What in hell for?"

"Trespassing."

Here we go again. At this point, I felt a real attack coming on, a panic attack.

"Where?"

"County Medical Center."

"Did someone call in a complaint about them?"

"Melanie Paxton called 911 about a commotion. They were harassing my dad."

"From what I hear, your father causes a commotion there every day! Asking him questions does not constitute harassment. I'd like to ask him a few questions myself."

"This is my jail, and you can't just come in here interfering or telling me how to do my job."

"You will drop these bogus charges now, or I'll be on the phone to the governor."

Peterson's eyes narrowed to slits. "Fine, but you'll regret this."

Trooper Sales, not one to be intimidated, replied, "I only see an out-of-control sheriff with a motive that looks a bit questionable at the moment."

"Who do you think you're talking to, state boy?"

"You have done nothing but get in the way since the Martin girl went missing. Are you protecting someone?"

I stood. "Do you know this girl in the cell was being led away by one of those goons who've been shooting up the town?"

"Goons?" Echoed in the room from my cellmates.

"I bet it was one of them from Roy's bait shop," Eleanor said. With the deputy's help, El stood.

"Oh, what a miraculous recovery," Sheriff Peterson pointed out, rolling his eyes.

"Is that true?" Trooper Sales asked Darlene and Marge.

"Yes, I guess so," replied Darlene. "I mean, a man asked me to come with him."

"He promised my daughter fifty bucks and new clothes," Marge said. "But I didn't like his manners or his looks, so I tossed his ass through a window, and then the sheriff here arrested us instead of him!"

"Where did he go?" I asked. "If the sheriff arrested you, he had to have a victim, right?"

"He gave me his information," the sheriff said. "Everyone get out of the cell. I'm dropping all the charges. I see I made a grave error, which I wouldn't have done if Agnes would butt out of this case."

We all followed the sheriff to the front and waited while he shuffled through his paperwork. "Michael Cicero. That's the name he gave."

"Did you take him to the hospital?"

"He went by ambulance, so I can't say for sure if he's there."

"How bad were his injuries?"

"He was bleeding from the head pretty badly, actually."

"Head wounds are good for that," said Sales.

"Let's hope he's still there," I said.

I walked out the door, but forgot that Andrew's Lexus was still at the medical center. My goose was cooked. By the time I got to the hospital, he'd be long gone.

"You want a lift to the hospital?" Trooper Sales asked.

I nodded. "Please."

We sat in the back of his car, and I could barely contain my excitement. Finally, after all this time, we had a lead, a real lead.

Arriving at the hospital, we went inside, and Trooper Sales asked the woman at admitting if a man named Michael Cicero was there. She led us to the room, but the bed was empty. How in the hell had we missed him?

I darted into the hallway and saw a man running away in a hospital gown. I pursued him outside, but he ran across US 23. Before I could do much besides watch, a huge Mac truck barreled toward him. The squealing of brakes sounded like a banshee wail, followed by a horrible crunching thumpity-thump! Unfortunately, the truck had struck the goon, instantly sending Michael Cicero's body sailing through the air like a rag doll. His corpse landed two feet in front of me.

I felt sick. I finally had a lead, and it had just landed dead at my feet. What hope remained that I'd ever find Jennifer Martin alive now?

Chapter Thirty-One

I stood and watched the bubble lights that had nothing to do with Christmas. I turned and shrugged when Trooper Sales walked toward me.

In my most subdued tone, I shakily said, "I-I had no idea he'd run across US 23 like that. Not too smart."

"That's two goons gone, and two to go, and both are connected to you," he added. "Not that I'm placing blame here, just saying."

"Ewwww, it's gonna have to be a closed casket," Eleanor said, "because there is no way they'll ever be able to put him back together again."

I snapped a look at Eleanor. "Please, a man's just died."

She rocked on her heels. "Yup, but clearly a bad man. Maybe the world's a better place now."

Sheriff Peterson met us and cocked his head to one side, giving me an I-know-what-you-did look. How could he? I hadn't done anything; I had no hand in this man's death.

"Should I even ask?" Peterson asked.

Trooper Sales cleared his throat. "When we showed up, he ran. I chased after him, and... "

"Splat," Eleanor added.

"I guess you won't be questioning him," the sheriff said to me dryly.

"Nope, but now I know the goons are here to hunt. We just need to figure out who they're hunting."

"Or what they're hunting for?" added Eleanor.

"It does seem to be an odd spot. You'd think with all the tourists, someone would have seen something," the trooper said. "You might want to be careful. You have been shot at twice, had an intruder at your home, and now this! It must be getting expensive to keep replacing windows."

A half hour later, Eleanor and I sat on a bench rubbing our aching feet when Andrew's Lexus pulled up.

I stood on shaking legs and met Andrew. "How did you know where your LX was?"

"William drove by the County Medical Center, and we saw it was there, but you two weren't. I figured something had to be up."

"Not much of a stretch," the sheriff said and snorted.

Andrew raised an eyebrow. "I heard some half-baked story about you two being arrested, but when I went to the station, a deputy told me you'd be here."

Eleanor grinned. "I got frisked by the sheriff here, but he didn't do that good of a job. I was so disappointed."

"Really?" Andrew asked.

"Yes, I was hoping to be really man-handled but nope. Quite a disappointment after all I've heard," she said saucily.

I stood there with my hand on my hip, because it hurt again. "You'll have to wait for the next card party, I suppose." I curled my lip into a grimace. "I swear, I can't take you anywhere."

Sheriff Peterson and Trooper Sales had remained to oversee the scene of the accidental death, and now Peterson approached us, asking me in a snide tone, "Don't you have two more goons to kill?"

"Not today. I was kind of hoping I could actually catch up with them before they died. It's hard to question a corpse."

We walked toward Andrew's Lexus and got inside. At least Trooper Sales had stood up for us. I always knew he was one of the good guys.

I don't remember dropping Eleanor off. My mind was in a whirl, trying to figure out where in the heck I could go from here.

* * *

I woke up the following morning with something prickly running across my arm. Still half asleep, I figured it must be Duchess. I felt cold, but I didn't even have to check. I knew I was naked, thanks to Andrew, no doubt.

I still couldn't make up my mind if it was a good thing or a bad thing. I felt it wasn't smart to start counting on him to be here. I knew that he'd soon be leaving. He had no real ties with Tadium. I lay there thinking, *When this case is resolved, he'll be gone. I need to accept that and pull back from him before I get hurt.*

I slipped from the blankets and got a soft bite for my efforts. Duchess was too comfortable to be moved. She did miss me so, and I had been so neglectful of late.

I threw on my bathrobe and strolled into the kitchen, guided by the smell of coffee and cooking bacon.

Andrew turned toward me with a cup of steaming coffee in his hand, a warm, kind gesture again.

"Thanks." I took it and poured creamer into the cup. I drank half the cup, dripping some onto my bathrobe. I was eager for the caffeine to revive me.

I grimaced. "What time is it?"

"One."

My eyes widened. "Like one o'clock in the afternoon?"

"Sure. You are quite a snorer. I have Eleanor's Cadillac here."

"I thought the window was still broken."

"I had that taken care of yesterday."

I bit my lower lip. "Are you leaving town soon?"

"Depends on how long it takes to find Jennifer."

I nodded. "I know you're only here to help your friend."

"I like it here, but I have a life in Detroit, too."

My chest tightened. "I'm not quite the idiot you take me for."

He looked confused. "What is that supposed to mean?"

"I was just a lonely widow when I worked for you. But you never gave me more than a passing look."

"I was married, Aggie, so why would I?"

"Maybe you should go back to the bed and breakfast."

"How can you blame me for the past? Is it a crime to be a faithful husband?"

I shook my head. I hurt more than I wanted to admit. I needed to lick my wounds, but it was hard to do with him standing so close, when all I wanted to do was kiss, hold, and make love to him. It was an illusion that I needed to forget. He was someone from my past whom I should never have let into my present or dreams of my future.

"All I am to you is a fling while you're here, and once you're gone, I'll be easily forgotten."

His eyes darkened suddenly. "Is that what you think this is?"

I expelled a breath. I had to push him away before I invested any more of myself, but in truth, what I felt for him was real. I had felt it since I first met him.

"Have your breakfast and go." Tears threatened to surface, but I couldn't let them. "I don't need you or anyone else in my life. Tell William I won't rest until I bring his daughter home."

I stumbled back into my bed and blinked the tears back. *Oh, Tom, how I miss you so,* I thought. If only you hadn't died so young, maybe then Sophia would still be alive. I had at last accepted the fact that she was dead and was never coming back.

I had no idea why I was upset. I had gone all these years without a man, and it never bothered me. At seventy-two, I knew that women my age didn't get their hearts all tangled up over a man.

I heard the front door close and the Lexus tear out of the drive, again taking my heart with it. I grabbed up Duchess and hugged her to me and asked her, "What good is a heart if it's so damn fragile?"

Chapter Thirty-Two

What in all hell was wrong with me? Why had I pushed Andrew away like that? Why had I acted like a twenty-something instead of in the manner of the mature woman I was? I'd moped around for an hour, which was more than enough time to feel sorry for myself. Wasn't that what a younger woman would think?

I put my gardening clothes on, which consisted of worn denim pants and a blue, nearly threadbare man's shirt that I had picked up at a rummage sale. It was not like anybody could see me as my house stood behind a copse of birches and was concealed from the road. I gripped my pink mud gloves and a kneel pad, and made my way outside to water my plants. My tomatoes looked a bit wilted, so I paid extra attention to them. Duchess scampered out the door after me, chasing a butterfly, stalking it. She moved low in the garden, twisting and turning like a cat in the jungle.

I was startled when I heard what sounded like a car tearing into my driveway, the sound of breaking glass, and after a few seconds... an explosion that rocked the earth. I fell to the ground from its intensity and hid amongst the tomato plants.

I looked toward my house and saw a huge fireball. My chest hurt like hell, and my eyes burned as I watched the fire spread from the front of my house, engulfing the entire structure soon after.

Someone must have thrown a Molotov cocktail through my window. If I had been back in my bedroom, I knew there would have been no way I'd have ever gotten out of the house. I would have been trapped. All the other attempts were just that, attempts to scare me, but this time I knew with certainty that the goons wanted me dead.

My car was parked in the driveway along with Eleanor's Caddy. They knew I was home. They must have been watching me! Were they still doing so? I thought it best to wait until the fire department arrived to get up, just to be safe. I trembled, but I knew this was the best place to be as the thick smoke drifted toward where I lay on the ground. If the fire department failed to get here soon, I feared as much for my life as the house.

I felt something rub against my arm and jumped, but it was just Duchess. She trembled, apparently as freaked out as I remained. Everything I had worked for, for the last twenty years was evaporating before my eyes.

I lay my head down and cried, for how long I don't know, but long enough for the thick cloud of smoke to shift toward me even more. I lifted my head. Tears clung to my lashes as I watched the flames lick upward.

If the fire department didn't get here soon, more than just my house would be lost. I had no way to call 911. Helpless, I watched and waited, but the smoke was making it hard to breathe.

I had to move.

I had no choice.

I heard a soft sound at first, growing louder. Could it be? Yes, sirens, and now I could see the flashing lights as help arrived.

I stood and rose out of the blackest of smoke and moved toward the sound. From the way they looked at me, I must have looked a fright. Looking down, I saw squashed tomatoes smeared on my clothing, but all I could think about was how damn lucky I was.

I coughed and stumbled out of the way, and a fireman helped me to sit. Well out of range of the blaze now, the fireman applied an oxygen mask over my nostrils and mouth. The fireman asked, "Is anyone in the house?"

I shook my head.

Firefighters assembled the hoses that snaked across the ground.

Six of them sprayed along the ground and toward the tops of the trees surrounding my house. They knew, as did I, my house couldn't be saved. It would be a greater loss if a fire spread into the woods. At least I had insurance, not that it would make up for losing everything I owned.

More fire trucks blazed up my drive from six neighboring communities, followed by an ambulance, the sheriff, and two state cruisers.

The sheriff made his way toward me. "We need to get you to the hospital," he said. I didn't glance toward him. My eyes were glued to my house, or what was left of it. "Agnes, you need medical attention." Peterson's voice sounded sympathetic to my plight.

I nodded. "But what about my cat, Duchess? She's out here somewhere. I can't just leave her here."

Trooper Sales walked forward, holding Duchess. For once, she had allowed a stranger to hold her. "You go to the hospital, and I'll look after the cat."

"Are you sure?" I cried. "She can be so fussy sometimes."

"I promise."

My chest felt tight, and I tried to choke out another word but couldn't. I was loaded into the ambulance, but I had more problems catching my breath, even with the oxygen applied.

I felt the burning sting of an IV needle enter my arm and saw the IV bag dangling above my head.

I glanced down and saw the soot covering my clothing and skin. Rubbing my hand across my face, I saw it was equally dirty.

"Calm down, ma'am," a paramedic said. Her young face looked blurry. "It's going to be okay. Remain calm, and all's going to be just fine."

Being strapped to a gurney reminded me of my last ride in an ambulance. This wasn't my first trip to the hospital, nor would it be the last.

Andrew was in my thoughts. What if I hadn't thrown a fit and told him to leave? What if I hadn't gone outside to water my plants?

What if Duchess hadn't followed me outside? The strange part was my insane worry over whether the mice had gotten out, too. Sure, I wanted them out of the house, but I didn't want them barbecued.

The sheriff's concern seemed genuine. Maybe I had been focusing on him a bit too much. I also know it was perfectly normal not to mesh well with everyone.

I was always a firm believer that not everyone has compatible personalities. Mine could be a bit harsh for people, and my know-it-all attitude could be a bit annoying. I knew that I was more like that than I'd ever admit. In times like this, I saw all my faults more clearly, and I admitted to myself that I had plenty.

I wondered if these were the kind of thoughts a dying person has, forgiving everyone who wronged you while facing your own vulnerability.

Andrew remained one of the most caring men I had ever known, and all I had accomplished in regard to him was to push him away. Maybe it would be best if everyone thought me dead. Tears came to my eyes, and I felt like going to my knees, and I would have if not hooked up to an IV.

I yawned and hoped I wouldn't fall asleep. I had to let Eleanor know that I was alive. I hated the thought of her going over the deep end. Who knew what the poor dear would do?

I tightly closed my eyes. I felt so tired that I couldn't fight it anymore.

* * *

I woke up to the smell of coffee. There's not another reason for me to open my eyes.

I looked straight into Andrew's eyes. He smiled wide, but it was more of an are-you-okay smile, not his usual warm smile.

"You okay?" I asked him.

He shrugged. "If you call waiting at your bedside for two days for you to awaken then I'm—"

"Okay?"

"Worried. You gave me quite a scare, and I still can't get the sight of your house in flames out of my mind."

"Me, either. Did the police call you?"

"You left your purse in my Lexus. I returned to bring it back to you, but I saw your house burning, and I thought..."

"That I was dead?"

He nodded, and I saw a flicker of emotion, but he held it in check. "Yes, Trooper Sales stopped me from running inside the blaze. He told me you had just left in an ambulance."

"Someone threw a firebomb inside while I was outside watering my plants."

"That's what the police think, too. I wouldn't worry about your plants this year, though."

I sat upright. "Why?"

"I hate to tell you this, but they were trampled by the firefighters and police. Did you know you had marijuana plants growing on the edge of the woods?"

I rolled my eyes. "No! Peterson will have me in jail for that for sure!"

"The police confiscated the plants."

I sighed. "Good thing for me that I have other connections." I winked. "You look awful."

"Thanks, Agnes. I sent Eleanor home yesterday. She needed to be medicated."

"She must be out of her mind with worry."

"I think it was time for her medication, and I'm sure she was out of her mind. She babbled some nonsense about hunting the goons down herself."

I sat up, pulled my legs off the bed, and stood. "What are you waiting for, Andrew? We have to go find her before she gets into trouble."

"You'll need some clothes, unless you want to sport your bare butt all the way to the door."

"Where are my clothes?"

"They cut them off. As far as I know, that's standard procedure."

I looked down at my hospital bracelets and gasped. "Why am I wearing a do not resuscitate bracelet?" I squeezed the purple bracelet over my hand.

"Oh, that; Eleanor carried on about how you always said if your heart stopped, you didn't want to be worked on. Claimed it was against your religion."

Oh what a liar, I thought. I felt steam rise, and I stomped my way to the nurses' station and waited until a nurse looked up. Her eyes grew round as saucers. Obviously, I'd interrupted her from lunch, as the aroma of Chinese food filled the air, and stains covered her light blue scrubs that identified her as an RN.

She stammered, "Wh-What are you doing out of bed?"

I scanned her nametag. "Cindy, I would like to sign myself out of the hospital."

"But I don't think..."

"You just call the doctor ASAP and get the paperwork started. Don't give me any excuses or backtalk, either. I'm a patient and have rights. I insist, no, I demand that you release me now."

I knew I was being unreasonable, but I needed to get out of here to check on Eleanor.

Cindy ran to the phone, made a call, and a security guard approached a few minutes later. "Ma'am, I think it would be best if you go back to your room now. There are patients trying to sleep."

The young man talked in a soothing tone of voice, but he had no idea who he was dealing with.

"Back the hell off. I have important business to attend to. A friend of mine needs my help."

His eyes widened. "Calm down. I don't think your friend would like it if you stopped by at two in the morning." He was trying hard to reason with me.

I jacked my head to one side. "It's two?" I glanced at Andrew. "Why in the hell didn't you tell me it was two in the morning?"

"You were so gung-ho on leaving, I didn't have a chance to say anything."

"Did you want to watch the man over here slap me into restraints first?"

Andrew laughed. "I'd love to see you slapped in leathers."

He may have thought himself just being funny, but I wasn't amused in the least. I narrowed my eyes and walked with my head held high back to my room. I didn't bother trying to cover my ass either.

Cindy snickered behind the counter.

Once in my room, I climbed into bed and pretended to go back to sleep.

"What's the plan?" Andrew asked.

"Wait thirty minutes and go downstairs. I'll meet you in the car. You're going to pull up to the front door."

"They'll be watching you."

"No, they won't."

Just then, a large woman strolled into my room and sat down. "Hi, I'm Connie. I'll be sitting in your room until morning."

"Why?"

"I have no idea. I was just told to come here."

I looked at her pudgy cheeks and saw her Cheetos-stained lips. She pulled out a book with a garish cover by Robert W. Walker and began to read, but her eyes looked heavy to me.

Andrew smiled. "Okay, Agnes, I'll see you tomorrow." He rushed out of the room.

I flipped my eyes toward Connie and feigned sleep until her head began to rock forward, and she began to snore over Walker's crime novel. Some sitter.

I rolled out of bed and peered down the hall. I ran down the hallway, hit the stairwell, and I next descended the stairs in record time. When I made it to the ground floor, I saw Andrew waiting outside with his Lexus running. I walked calmly out the front door, jumped inside the LX, and ducked down.

"What took you so long?" he asked.

"I didn't think the sitter would ever go to sleep." I grinned.

"She fell asleep?"

"Yup, and I hope she comes up with a convincing story about how I slipped out. I'd hate for anyone to lose a job."

"If you truly felt that way, dear, you'd have stayed 'til morning."

"Drive to Eleanor's before they call in the SWAT team."

"No offense, dear, but I hardly think you're SWAT material."

I gasped. "You don't think I'm dangerous."

"Oh, you're dangerous all right, but only in the naked kind of way. I have to admit, you have quite the appetite for a woman your age."

"Just drive."

Andrew drove toward Eleanor's house, passing a deputy's car. "I told you so."

"You are a hardened criminal. I heard walking around half-ass naked is a crime at your age." He added. "Stealing a hospital gown may be a capital offense."

"Remind me again why you came to the hospital? What? There's nobody to harass at the manor?"

Chapter Thirty-Three

Andrew turned sharply into Eleanor's drive, and I tried to exit the Lexus without flashing anything too important. He'd seen it all before, but the hospital gown made me feel a great deal less than sexy. I pulled the thin gown around me, making my way toward the door, but a breeze blew the gown up just as Eleanor swung the door open.

"Now, that's what I call a hello," Eleanor said.

I yanked the hospital gown down, trying to regain my composure. I felt so glad to see her here at her doorstep and not trying to scamper after a goon in some sort of Clint Eastwood vengeance-is-mine endeavor.

Eleanor shot me a look. "Where're your clothes?"

I shrugged. "Hospital waste bin, I imagine. They love cutting your clothing off there."

"You make it sound like a place I'd like to go." She giggled, making snorting noises.

I rolled my eyes. "You wouldn't say that if you were held prisoner there! Not allowed to leave."

"I'd pop one of 'em in the mouth."

Visions of Eleanor in shackles made me smile. "They sent up a security guard and a sitter."

"Sitter? Like babysitter?"

"You know, one of those people who come into your room to watch you ... make sure you stay put."

"A guard's more like it," commented Andrew, who'd come in behind me and had parked himself in an easy chair.

Eleanor leaned forward, her eyes dancing. "Oh, my. So what did you do?"

"She just loves a good story, doesn't she?" I asked Andrew, and turned back to Eleanor. "I waited until my sitter fell asleep. That's how boring I can be. Bored her right to sleep."

"Oh, my, that won't bode well for her job." She snickered. "So you flew the coop, then?"

"Yes." I groaned, my gaze scanning the kitchen, falling on an apple pie.

"This is great. Now you're a fugitive." El clapped her hands. "Do you think they'll send the cops to look for you?"

"I hope not."

I yanked open a cupboard, pulled a plate out, and scooped up a generous slice of apple pie. Shoving it into my mouth like I hadn't eaten in a week, I parked myself at the dining room table.

"You better slow down. If you get sick, I'll have to take you back to the hospital in time for your guard to wake up to redeem her job with dignity." Andrew winked, and I threw him a challenging glance.

"Excuse me, but I have been through a horrible ordeal. Someone tossed a firebomb through my window and set my house on fire! All I could do was lie there in my garden and watch everything I own go up in flames. Things I can't replace ... like-like my wedding pictures and pictures of my children throughout the years, before they decided to stay long gone."

"I'm sorry about your memorable items, but at least you weren't in the house," Eleanor consoled with her words and hands on my shoulders. "You're the only friend I have. Don't worry so about your children, they'll return someday. I'm sure of it."

I didn't want to focus on how I almost died, and still no sign of my Martha and Stuart. I had told Eleanor in no uncertain terms to not ever try to contact them, so why should I expect my children to suddenly appear? I had tried to contact Martha after Sophia's disappearance, but came up empty. It felt like I had lost my entire family since my Sophia was gone. Instead of focusing on my sad thoughts, I suggested, "You could make more friends, Eleanor."

"Not at my age. Besides, folks don't much like me." She came around to face me, sitting close. I could sense that she remained shaken at my new set of harrowing circumstances.

"You shoot your mouth off too much," I finally suggested with a smile.

"I say it like it is."

"Sometimes people can't handle the truth!" Andrew added from his perch on the chair in the other room.

"That man has the best pair of ears," I whispered.

"I heard that!" Andrew shouted.

Meanwhile, Eleanor had ducked her head down, and I felt bad for being so hard on her. "I'm sorry."

"That's okay, you're right." She sniffled. "Where do you plan to stay now?"

I hadn't thought about it. Where would I stay? "I'm not sure yet. I do have a camper in storage." I shrugged. "Could get the ol' Winnebego plugged into what's left of the plumbing and electrical."

"Are you flippin' kidding?" El burst out. "You're planning to sleep in a camper?"

"Like hell you are!" shouted Andrew, who'd shot to the dining room on hearing this. "There is no way you're sleeping in any camper until we find out who's responsible for firebombing your house."

"Is he kidding?" I asked El before I turned on Andrew. "Did you just try to tell me what to do? I'll do just as I please, Mr. Hotshot Lawyer, and you can't stop me."

"They have crime scene tape across your drive, and you won't be allowed anywhere near until the investigation is done."

I slumped my shoulders. I hated that he had completely sucked the wind out of my sails with his lawyerly pragmatic stance, which was so damnably reasonable. "I have to get Duchess."

Andrew and Eleanor laughed at this.

"What?" I asked.

"You're going to have to extricate her from the trooper's house," she replied.

"Trooper Sales has birds, and the last I heard, Duchess was having the time of her life," Andrew added.

"He won't feel that way when she eats one of them."

"She better have improved her skills from the last time I saw her trying to have a go at it."

"She can't even catch a mouse," Eleanor added.

"Yes, she can." I defended poor Duchess. "She just doesn't choose to kill them."

The apple pie having disappeared, I walked out to the deck and watched the sunrise. It looked to be a beautiful day brewing, but maybe not for me, because I didn't have any clothes to wear. Eleanor didn't have anything my size either.

I sat back on a lawn chair and closed my eyes. Sometime later, I felt a blanket cover me. I breathed deep of Andrew's scent and hoped I hadn't made a mistake by pushing him away. It would be a mistake I'd live to regret, if I made it through the week.

Chapter Thirty-Four

I woke up and noticed a neatly folded pile of clothing lying on the table next to me. I struggled to stand, like I always did in the mornings, and felt stiff and sore in more places than usual. It'd teach me to fall asleep on a lawn chair.

I slid into the house and jerked on the clothing, a blue matching capri set with tiny flowers embroidered near the hemline. It felt nice to have a bra and underwear on, and everything fit. I wondered how Andrew knew my size, then figured maybe he had an eye for things of that nature. I wandered into the kitchen and made coffee that smelled of cinnamon. I wondered if he had gone or stayed?

As I made my way to the front door, I spied Andrew standing just outside, animatedly talking to Dr. Thomas.

Oh, shit, I'm busted.

I opened the door and let Dr. Thomas inside, followed by Andrew. Dr. Thomas's hands shook, and for once, I saw him in a different light.

"Agnes, the next time you are in the hospital, wait until I release you before you leave. You really caused quite an uproar this morning."

I bit my lower lip. "I'm sorry about all that, but I did ask them to call you."

He dropped a bag onto the table. "I think these are all the medications you lost in the fire." He grinned. "Rosa Lee Hill is doing a fundraiser to help out."

I could well imagine what kind of fundraiser she'd have.

"Thanks, and it won't happen again, I promise."

"Not only do I not want to see you in the hospital again, I don't think they do, either," he said with a chuckle.

He left. I should feel bad about the ruckus, but I snickered.

"The fundraiser is today," Andrew said. "We are so going."

I gazed at him with the best scowl I could muster. "Fine talk from a former lawyer."

He handed me a brand new pink revolver, which I pocketed. "Thanks, Andrew. I lost mine in the fire."

"I thought as much. I can't have my girl investigating crimes without having the proper fire power," he said with a wink.

"Is it loaded?"

"Yup. Try not to shoot you foot off with that thing, or more importantly, me."

We waited for Eleanor to dress for the fundraiser. How could I not attend? It was for me. All I had to do was slide into brown sandals, which miraculously fit. Andrew really was a rare man, as he understood the feminine needs in great detail.

Eleanor managed a feat of amazement by squeezing into purple leggings and a white shirt with a sparkling array of sequins in the shape of a butterfly. I insisted she wear a hat to keep the sun off her fair skin. As it so happened, she had one handy, and it just so happened to be purple.

I whispered to her, "Purple People Eater," which she responded to with a rolling giggle that made her belly come alive like some kind of alien was trapped inside.

We walked to the Lexus, and I noticed a huge scratch over the hood. "Is that new?" I asked.

He nodded. "It happened at Walmart today, but it beats the windshield being blown out any day."

"I'm hoping for calmer days," I said. "I'm beginning to wonder if I'll ever find Jennifer."

"Don't be discouraged. Look at all the enemies you're collecting."

Usually, I would care less what people thought of me, but since the firebomb, things had taken on a sinister tone. It just wasn't safe for me to be anywhere, and I was beginning to think ... for anyone to be near me. If I stayed with Eleanor much longer, her life might be in jeopardy, too, and I couldn't have that.

We climbed into the Lexus, and Andrew roared up the road. He pulled into Rosa Lee's driveway, which appeared to be filled with an odd display of flashing bubble lights, which came from five state police cruisers. From the looks of it, the whole damn town had turned out.

Andrew hit the gas and planted his Lexus atop Rosa Lee's rose bushes. I was unsure how she'd feel about that, but if someone did that at my house, I'd be burning mad. Considering the events that led up to this fundraiser, I decided burning might be the wrong word to use.

I made my way into the backyard in time to see Jack Winston slammed to the ground. Two troopers struggled to keep him on the ground, while another slapped the cuffs on him.

"You goddamn pigs better get the hell off!" Jack shouted.

"If you don't stop fighting us, you'll leave me no choice but to call your son, Jack! Do you want me to call Frank?"

Jack's glazed-over eyes looked as if he were giving this some thought. "Frank?"

He went limp, with what some might misconstrue as defeat. "You call my son, you son of a bitch, and I'll be calling your momma, boy."

"You don't know my mother," the young trooper said.

Jack's eyes danced about. "She sucked my winkie just last week."

The trooper picked him up and pushed Jack toward the car. "Shut your yap and keep walking," he ordered.

Eleanor gasped. "Is this an episode of *Cops*?"

It did look like an episode of *Cops,* too; a senior redneck version. Two old men were engaged in a battle with a trooper, one swinging a cane and the other a walker.

"Please stop. I don't want to hurt an old man," one trooper said just before he ducked.

"You're the one who's going to be in pain!" Mr. Wilson yelled.

How had I not recognized him before?

I envisioned someone having a heart attack, or at least a trooper getting a contusion. This madness had to stop.

"Pop off a shot into the air. It might calm them down," I shouted at Trooper Sales, who had just cleared the woods carrying a large garbage bag.

Sales pulled his gun out and fired into the air. The explosion rattled my ears, and I watched everyone hit the deck, except for Frank Alton, who fumbled with his hearing aid.

"What did I miss?" Frank asked.

"Oh, Frank!" Dorothy Alton exclaimed. "You were almost shot to pieces."

It might not have been the smartest of ideas. I knew most of the seniors here were veterans.

Rosa Lee sat where she always did, in her lawn chair, but this time handcuffed.

She smiled and shrugged. "They do this at least once a year."

I popped a look at Trooper Sales. "Is this necessary? This was a fundraiser for me."

He scratched his head. "Looks like a pot party to me."

I sniffed the air. "Smells like a pig roast. Why don't you just take the weed and leave it at that."

"I can't do that," he said.

"Rosa Lee, aren't you registered to grow marijuana for medicinal purposes?"

"Sure am."

"It's still breaking federal law."

My hands moved to my hips, "Are you an FBI agent, Sales?"

He drew his lips together and gazed around at the foray.

"Think about how much it'll cost the county. Most of these folks will drain the budget in medical costs alone," I insisted.

As if listening, Sales replied, "Keep talking."

"Take the weed and come back and enjoy the barbecue. Except for Jack. I'm afraid he assaulted an officer."

"Nothing new." He smirked.

Trooper Sales gathered the troopers in a circle as if negotiating. When they separated, they rounded up more bags and filled them with weed, enough to keep the entire state high for a month, from the looks of it.

When Rosa Lee was free of her cuffs, she gave me a quick hug, the most expression of emotion I would likely ever get from her.

"Sorry about your plants, Rosa Lee."

"Oh, don't worry about that."

She didn't elaborate, but I knew she had more, much more. I was glad she didn't elaborate because I didn't want to know.

The crowd of seniors returned and started eating chips.

"Looks like the munchies have kicked in," Andrew said. "I wish we had gotten here earlier."

I noticed Roy had arrived with a man I didn't recognize. He looked dark-skinned like the other goons, with his black hair slicked back, and dressed mighty fine for a barbeque, wearing a black suit. Could he be one of the goons? I had only taken a brief glance at the goons at Roy's Bait & Tackle, but if this fellow was one of the them, why would Roy be anywhere near him?

Roy's cheeks were red and became even more so when he laughed. I watched him and his friend with interest. I felt something odd was unfolding before my eyes. Damn, Roy was up to no good again. I could feel it.

"What's the matter?" Andrew asked.

"I wonder who that stranger is with Roy."

"Oh, no, stranger danger." He rolled his eyes. "I swear small towns are all the same."

I let Andrew's voice trail away. I was too busy concentrating. Offhandedly, I said to Andrew, "Why not ask Rosa Lee if she has a hidden stash?"

He raised an eyebrow. "With the cops here?"

I motioned him off. "She's got ways."

I watched Andrew trail after a laughing Rosa Lee. I searched for

Eleanor and spotted her giggling like a schoolgirl as she spoke with a group of troopers. She was in her glory, and when I spotted Mr. Wilson, I saw why. He was talking to a rather young woman with enormous breasts that resembled water balloons. It made no sense to me why the young folks these days do that to themselves. She should get a job as a lifeguard, I nastily told myself. Her boobs would make good floatation devices.

I walked over to Roy, and he smiled. "Hello, Agnes. If you get tired of your lawyer man and want to rock on the Roy boat, just call me."

I frowned and shook my head. Roy did look like a boat, though, and not one I'd want to be rocking on. "Who's your friend?"

Roy turned to his companion. "Agnes here is what we call the town snoop. I wouldn't get too close to her, Anthony."

"Why's that?" asked Anthony, a permanent grimace on his face.

"Why, Mr. Cicero? 'Cause trouble seems to find her everywhere she goes."

"You mean like a firebomb being tossed into my house?"

"She must have made many enemies," Anthony said. "My name is—"

"I heard as much."

"It is a pleasure to meet such an experienced investigator such as yourself."

I stared at him. I wondered if I knew him. "Do I know you?"

"You should, but I doubt you'd recall ruining my marriage ten years ago."

I tried to remember, but couldn't. Being seventy-two, jeez, what did he expect?

"I think you must be mistaken. The only people I have ever investigated were scumbags. Are you a scumbag?"

Anthony seemed less than amused. I was sure this man had something to hide. The two of them were up to something, but what?

Obviously, Anthony had heard enough and walked toward the bimbo Mr. Wilson was trying hard to rub against. "Time to go,

Glenda!" Anthony shouted. He again proved himself to be a pig; not that it was a surprise because most men fell into that category. Except Andrew, of course.

"You would do well to stop sticking your nose into things that aren't your business," Roy said.

"How long have you been living in Tadium?" Not waiting for an answer, I continued. "I know you were living here when the Robinson murders occurred."

His eyes bulged slightly at the questioning. "That would describe half the town."

I knew the Tadium area was more of a retirement destination. "No, not half at all. The list is smaller than you'd think."

"I thought you were searching for that missing rich girl?" he sneered.

"I am, but I now know there is a connection between the Robinson murders and the missing girl, Jennifer." I curled my lip. "Roy, what do you know about Jennifer Martin's disappearance?"

He shifted his eyes nervously, indications of a lie about to come out of his mouth. He rubbed his bald head to dot away the sweat that beaded up. "I had hoped we could be friends, but you are making that impossible," he whispered to me. "I'm sorry, but I'm afraid you'll never see your granddaughter again."

He walked away, while fireworks lit up inside my head. He knew where my granddaughter Sophia was.

I whirled around toward the bimbo, Glenda. She was gone, along with the mystery man, Anthony, and when I turned my head back toward Roy, I didn't see him either. He had disappeared in the crowd! It then occurred to me that everything was related.

I ran to Rosa Lee, who had just returned, followed by a stumbling Andrew.

"Does Roy have a boat?" I searched her face frantically for her response. Something about the whole boat reference struck home to me.

"Sure does. He used to run charter trips. I did always wonder why he quit." She stretched her arms.

Wheels, although a bit rusty, turned inside my head and everything came full circle and collided together. Sophia! Oh, God, poor Sophia!

Chapter Thirty-Five

I didn't waste another moment, and without another word to either Rosa Lee or Andrew, I raced across the lawn and entered the woods. As voices drifted toward me, I was convinced it was Roy and his accomplices. I gave no thought to going for help, even though I knew Andrew and the troopers were close by. If I went for help, I might lose the trio, and what then? I was more than convinced if I followed them, they'd lead me straight to both Jennifer and Sophia. I just hoped I'd catch up to them without being discovered by the miscreants.

I ducked behind a pine tree as I heard voices directly ahead.

"She's harmless," one voice said.

"You wouldn't say that if she had destroyed your life. You have no idea how much I lost in that damn divorce. My wife took me for everything that wasn't nailed down."

I heard giggles next.

It had to be Roy and the mystery couple, Anthony and Glenda.

"There is no point in worrying now. It's too damn late for that. If we don't move soon, the buyers will withdraw their offer."

"Why in the hell would they do that?"

"There's only one night they can make it ashore without being seen."

"The authorities monitor the boats coming from Canada these days."

"Yes, but they can't keep track of all of them, not on the Fourth of July."

I shook inside. Why was a boat coming ashore? And what, if

anything, did it have to do with Jennifer or my granddaughter? I stepped back. I had to tell Trooper Sales what I'd heard.

I stepped on a branch.

Snap!

I stood there, shaking. I felt frozen, and it occurred to me that I should duck back behind the tree again and conceal myself, but in a panic, I knelt. I knew it was too late!

"There she is!" Anthony Cicero shouted.

I jumped up fast, jarring my hip. The pain shot up my spine, and I gasped at the intensity. I hobbled toward the line of trees ahead of me. I focused on the smell of cooking pork, and in my delusional state, I hadn't noticed the stranger who had jumped ahead of me and now blocked my way.

He grabbed my arm and gave it a vicious twist that brought me to my knees. Then, even my knees buckled beneath me, and I fell to the ground. I lay on the ground, helpless, my face pressed against fallen pine needles and dirt. I tried to catch my breath and inhaled sharply, but all I could smell was earth.

Pain shot into my head when the stranger grabbed me by the hair and yanked my head backward. I fell forward when my thin hair gave way.

He kicked at me, rolling me to my back. I struggled to open my eyes, and when I did, I was facing the barrel of a gun.

"Get up!" Anthony ordered.

Roy came forward and helped me to my feet. I saw the regret reflected in his eyes. "Get up, Agnes."

I rose to my feet, and I was pushed forward, moving deeper into the woods. Where were they taking me? I feared they planned to kill me somewhere out in the forest.

"I'd much rather we shoot her right here," Anthony said.

"No, we're not doing that. Someone would hear," Roy insisted.

"We'll pose her body like the other two."

Roy threw his arms up. "We need to move before someone comes looking for her."

"That bunch of stoned old folks won't miss her until tomorrow."

"I'm taking her to the cabin." Roy firmly gripped my arm and led me down a trail I had never seen before. All the twists and turns made me feel dizzy, and I felt the need to sit down.

Tall pine trees loomed overhead, blocking out the sun. We neared what looked, based on the fact that discarded tin cans littered the ground, to be a deserted cabin. I followed Roy inside the cabin. What else could I do?

Inside stood a table centered in the room. He pushed it aside and lifted a trap door, revealing a set of steps going downward. I saw death below if I made one false step, something that would be easy to do at my age. My head hurt, my hip hurt, and I felt dizzy. Roy, who'd guided me inside, stood staring into my eyes as if he knew what I was thinking.

"Take your time, Agnes. I can't have you falling," Roy said.

Not sure why Roy showed a sudden concern for my welfare, I gulped and felt nauseous at the stench of mold and unwashed bodies that filled the tiny space as I descended. I thought it was Roy, until I made it to the bottom of the steps.

Once at the bottom, I stood in an open room, surrounded by six barred doors. It appeared to be a jail of some sort. The dirt floor felt hard, as if it had been packed by hundreds of feet walking over it.

I moved toward the barred doors and saw ten women looking up at me with tear-streaked faces. They wore what appeared to be rags, but upon closer inspection, I saw they were simply dirty and unwashed, their filthy hair covering most of their faces. Glazed-over eyes stared through the bars, but they didn't register or respond to me or anyone else in the room. It was as if they were numb inside, like empty shotgun shells.

Whatever was happening here, it wasn't good. I searched the faces for Jennifer and Sophia, but I didn't see them. These women had been herded here like animals for some purpose, but what?

I looked ahead to a solid door as it opened. Once it opened, I could see Jennifer and Sophia, each wrapped in a towel. Their white-knuckled fingers were gripping the towels like a lifeline.

Following them out was a woman dressed in green camouflage. Her gray hair was pulled back tightly. She looked like a drill sergeant, and about my age.

"Who's next to look pretty for the buyers?" the woman asked. She yanked open a barred door and pulled out two women. One clung to the bar, but the woman struck her full across the face. I was torn. I felt the urge to protect Jennifer and Sophia, yet compelled to help the poor girl being abused at the same time.

"Stop hitting her, Marge," Roy shouted. "They won't want her if she's damaged!"

Marge turned and sneered. "They're all damaged goods, if you ask me. Isn't that right, girls?"

The women trembled, and pure terror shone from their eyes.

Anthony tossed clothing at Jennifer and Sophia, and they turned their backs and quickly donned them. I stood in front of them, determined to keep the men's hungry gazes away.

I saw the bimbo, Glenda, shake with the realization of why she was here. "What, what's going on?" she asked, her voice quivering.

Anthony led Glenda to a cell and threw her inside. "I should have done it this way all along. You were so eager to get your claws into a rich man. I could have led a hundred of you stupid bitches here to sell." He glared at Roy. "Kidnapping rich girls with families who give a damn about them just isn't a good idea."

Roy's eyes flicked back and forth from Anthony to me. "You shouldn't have kidnapped Sophia. She doesn't deserve to be here."

Anthony pointed at me. "I did that to get back at this old crone. Sophia's medical knowledge has worked well for us, anyway. It's the only thing that kept the Martin girl alive."

"Roy, I take it Stella isn't your daughter," I said. "I found out she was adopted, and there was no way you could have known she was your daughter."

Roy hung his head. "I always liked Stella, and I tried to help her, but—"

"You needed the money more," Anthony spat. "If not for your connections, Roy, I'd have no use for you."

"I'm just as invested in this as you, and once Agnes is out of the picture, it will be smooth sailing. Nobody suspects me."

I hugged Sophia and Jennifer close as we were shoved into a cell. Roy slammed the door shut and whispered in my ear, "Sorry it has to be this way."

This seemed so wrong. Why would Roy do this? I couldn't wrap my mind around the fact that someone I knew so well would be involved in human trafficking.

I gazed at him with imploring eyes.

I sat down, watching as the women were shuffled into the shower room by twos. I huddled the girls together.

Tears poured from my eyes as I looked into Sophia's startled face. She touched my face in wonder, and I hugged her so tightly that she gasped slightly. I released her when I realized I had about squeezed the life out of her. I was just so glad to see her again. I had all but given up hope of ever seeing her alive, but here she was ... right in front of me, not a corpse like I figured. I was overcome with emotion and lost for words, for a moment.

"Grams, how ever did you find me?"

"It was an accident, really." I wiped the tears back. "I never gave up on you, though, sweet Sophia." I hugged her again. "Not for a single moment."

I pulled away and inspected her rosy cheeks for any marks or signs of abuse. These people would rue the day they took my Sophia from me.

She was wearing a white dress that clung to her curves. She looked so thin that it brought more tears to my eyes, and her wet brown hair felt cool to my skin.

My heart swelled with love as I gazed at her. She was so beautiful, even in her fragile state. I had to figure out a way to get us out of here, somehow. It would be so unfair to find her only to lose her again.

I heard the door open, and Marge returned with the next two young women. As they dressed, I felt a surge of anger pulse through my veins.

"What is the meaning of this?" I asked Marge, who seemed to be in charge, the boss of the outfit.

She turned and gritted her teeth, displaying them. "Whose idea do you think this operation was? My stupid son, Anthony? He's too busy screwing every stupid bitch he can, just like his father." Brushing her nails across her shirt, she shook her head to indicate how sad it all made her feel. "They call my husband The Hammer, and I'm not just talking about his bedroom skills."

"Sounds like a real character," I said, hoping to keep her talking. The more I learn, I figured, the better to fry these bastards with if and when we got free.

Muscle-woman continued as if starved for conversation. "My husband and I came here in 1968 for a vacation. One night, when he returned to our cabin, he was covered in blood."

"In '68? Oh, my ... covered in blood?" I immediately thought of the Robinson family murders.

"Bruno told me there was a woman in town whom he fancied, and when he couldn't get into her pants, he followed her home. He then raped her. He told me how she begged him to leave afterward. She promised not to tell. She tried to protect her family, you see, but what she didn't know was that The Hammer always does what he does best, and that is to kill without mercy."

I shuddered involuntarily. "Let me guess, the goons in town are your sons, too."

Marge nodded. "You killed two of my boys, and I had hoped my other boys had killed you, but I see they botched the job. You'll be seeing my son, Timothy, soon. I may give him and Anthony a round or two with your granddaughter."

I felt my revolver in my pocket. I may not be able to shoot our way out of here, but if those goons come anywhere near my Sophia ... they'd be the first to die. It had been a miracle it hadn't fallen out of my pocket during my fall in the woods.

I had five bullets and needed to use them wisely.

"Why were they in town searching for Stella?"

"I was afraid that Stella might go to the police when her daughter went missing. She knew what my family was capable of."

"She did?"

"Bruno raped Stella years ago and threatened to kill her family, but when she disappeared, it became pointless."

"How did she know your sons had kidnapped Jennifer?"

"Roy let it slip, and she went into hiding," she said with a snarl. "She had to be killed before she told someone."

"Why kill the handyman, then?"

"Billy Chambers stumbled upon Anthony in the woods, and he recognized his face. He does look so like his father. Anthony thought it conceivable that the handyman would kill Stella, and then himself."

"How could he hang himself from a clothesline when he was confined to a wheelchair?" I shifted to my good hip. "If he saw your husband kill the Robinson family, why didn't he tell the police?"

"He may have, but my husband wasn't known to the area. They believed it was the handyman all along, and they probably thought that he was making up another suspect. Police make mistakes all the time."

I was almost afraid to ask my next question. "What happened to your husband?"

"You'll be meeting him soon enough."

Marge strolled away, lit a cigarette, and took a puff while keeping an eye on me.

When I turned to Jennifer, I saw her huddle toward Sophia. Her face was white as a ghost. She was sick. She needed medical attention, and soon, or she might well die.

I asked Jennifer, "Have they given you any medication?"

She shook her head no.

"Your father, William, is here searching for you."

Her expression became animated. "Really? He's really here?"

"Of course, and he has been ever since you went missing."

She began to cry. "I can't believe it."

William was obviously more concerned with business than his

family under normal circumstances, but it was plain to see he had put that all aside to search for Jennifer. He was a good man, and I felt more determined than ever to bring the two of them together again—even if I had to die trying.

Chapter Twenty-Six

I was jarred awake as I was pulled to my feet. Why? I had no idea. I had drifted off to sleep, and I had no clue whether it was day or night. I shivered involuntarily, not only from the dampness of the cellar, but also from full-blown terror, more for Sophia and Jennifer than for myself. Lord knows, I'd had my time to live. Although, I hadn't ever imagined I would meet my end by the hand of goons led by a thug momma and family in the business of pure evil, seemingly genetically predisposed to it, thanks to a serial rapist and killer for a father, and a mother without moral compunction.

I followed the other women as they climbed the steps, but I panicked when I lost sight of Sophia and Jennifer. I would have scaled the steps at a much faster pace, but it wasn't like any of the women ahead of me were in any hurry to meet an uncertain fate.

When I reached the top, I saw Sophia held fast by a goon. He was touching her ... stroking her cheek. My steady hand reached into my pocket, but as I brought the gun nearly out, Marge cuffed the man on the back of the head.

"No touching, Timothy." Her eyes met mine as she added, "Not yet."

She smiled a suggestive, leering smile that I felt compelled to rip from her lips. "We need to get moving before the Fourth of July fireworks start," Marge added.

Relax, Aggie, all in good time.

I pushed the gun back into my pocket, thankful nobody had noticed it.

We made our way through the woods, only flashlights lighting our way, and when we emerged from the trees, we stood across from Roy's bait shop. The sight of the place turned my stomach as I thought, *Isn't this where I started my search?* It made me feel both foolish and as if I'd gotten nowhere, just spinning wheels and getting no traction. I reviewed every step of my investigation in my head.

The wheels inside my head kept spinning, too, and as if reading my mind, Roy popped a glance my way. I couldn't read his facial expression because it was dark.

I wondered how long I had been asleep as Anthony pushed and prodded us across the road. I hoped someone, anyone, would drive by, but no such luck. When the bait shop door closed behind all of us, I felt my heart leap into my throat.

Standing before me was a dark man, probably Italian, with a neck as thick as a tree trunk. His gray hair shining in the darkness, I knew it must be Marge's sick-o husband, Bruno The Hammer—the one they all worked for and feared.

He flipped on the lights and pointed at me. "You!"

Oh, my God. I trembled and stammered. "I-I think you-you must have me confused with some-someone else."

"You are like a cat with nine lives." His eyes shot to his sons' faces. "You stupid fools! Can't you do anything right?"

"Her car was in the driveway," exclaimed Anthony. "Father, sir, I thought she was home."

"Nothing I hate worse than a snoopy bitch."

I spat at his shoes. Sophia pulled me back, but I felt the blow strike my forehead.

I dropped to my knees as stars danced before my eyes.

"Who do we have here?" Bruno asked, leering at Sophia.

"I d-d-don't know what you mean, sir," Sophia replied.

Bruno yanked Sophia forward, and I watched him rip Sophia's dress through blurred vision.

"Bruno The Hammer has something for you." He viciously pinched Sophia, and she cried out. He threw her on the counter and lowered his pants, but Sophia kneed him in the groin. He slapped her face and held her down with one hand, and raised his erection toward her innermost parts.

Bam!

The Pink Lady .38 to the rescue.

I shot him right in the crotch. He howled in pain but lunged toward me. His eyes were huge and protruding. As he wrapped his hands about my throat, I unloaded my revolver into him.

He shuddered once, and a surprised look came across his face. Roy pulled him off me, and I jumped up, grabbed Sophia and Jennifer by their hands, and pushed them toward the back room known so well to me.

I opened the door, and when I saw the glowing red eyes of the little beastie staring back, I yelled. "Jump!"

Jennifer, Sophia, and I made it over the rabid-looking raccoon with its equally vicious-looking babies. We jumped atop a counter, metal pans tumbling noisily to the floor, while Anthony chased after us. It was then that momma raccoon attacked.

She bit Anthony on the leg, and he screamed in pain. In an effort to escape, he tripped on pots and pans, fell like a brick onto his back, moaning in pain, and the raccoons went for his face. The way the babies attacked Anthony's flesh suggested that they hadn't been fed in a while.

I dropped to the floor, trying to shoulder the back door open. Sophia and Jennifer helped, and the door came off its hinges. We rushed out into the still darkness and toward the lake.

"Don't quit running!" I shouted.

We ran, and I could hear a wail coming from the bait shop as bullets whizzed over our heads. We continued up the beach in the darkness. It was too dark to see much, but then came the Fourth of July fireworks blasting into the night sky, lighting our way.

I heard the rumble of a motorboat close by. I glanced fearfully over my shoulder and tried to run faster, but Jennifer collapsed ahead of me.

"Jennifer?" a voice echoed, from the direction of the lake.

It was William Martin! A spotlight hit us, and I saw another boat making its way toward shore, but it circled around and went back where it came from. I ran toward the edge of the beach.

I cupped my hands around my mouth and yelled to him, pointing toward the boat. "Get on the phone and tell the coast guard to follow that boat!" I saw more spotlights appear as the coast guard, obviously on hand to help William in his search, raced after the fleeing boat.

William dove from the boat and swam to shore. He ran to Jennifer and dropped down on one knee, scooping her into his arms.

"Daddy," Jennifer cried. "I-I'm s-so h-happy t-to—"

"Save your energy, honey," William responded.

"The people that kidnapped her are in the bait shop, and they're armed," I said.

William pulled a cellphone from his pocket and dialed 911. Sophia held her ripped clothing against her as best she could, trying to cover herself.

Andrew, who'd been on the boat with William, had secured it to an overhanging tree, and now he appeared out of the darkness, took his sports coat off, and held it out to Sophia. She donned it quickly, and we made our way up the beach and squeezed between two cabins.

When we made it back onto US 23, we saw lights flashing everywhere. I let out a sigh of relief.

Trooper Sales ran toward us, shouting, "An ambulance is en route."

I quickly summarized for Sales and the others what I'd discovered of Roy, that his bait shop was a front for human trafficking, and how the ringleader was responsible for the Robinson family's murders. Almost out of breath, I added, "There are still ten young girls at the bait shop held against their will, but there is also a wounded asshole who calls himself The Hammer and his hag of a wife, Marge, both of whom are running the show, and the goons—all of them were their sons!"

My eyes were glued on Sales for his reaction.

"So that's what this is all about?"

I nodded. "I shot a man calling himself The Hammer; the one who actually murdered the Robinsons. I suspect he's bled to death by now. Slowly and agonizingly, I hope."

"Grandma Aggie shot him in the crotch," Sophia added with pride. "He was trying to rape me at the time."

"Self-defense, sort of," I put in. "Bastard dared try to rape my granddaughter." I began to cry as much from nerves and disbelief it was finally over as from fear of how it might have gone.

Trooper Sales' eyes roamed Sophia's face, observing her disheveled appearance.

Within minutes, the ambulance arrived, and the paramedics rushed forward. They took Jennifer from William and gently placed her on the gurney while William detailed her heart condition. One paramedic lowered his head, doing the look, listen, and feel, and checked for a pulse. He shook his head toward his partner.

Her chest wasn't moving!

Sophia stumbled forward. "Is she...?"

Tears gathered in all of our eyes as we watched the paramedics begin CPR, counting aloud.

I couldn't move or breathe.

None of us could.

Until we saw Jennifer take a deep breath in, and her chest rose and fell.

She was alive.

I nearly swooned in relief.

An oxygen mask was placed over Jennifer's nose and mouth, and an IV started as the EMS workers rushed her into the ambulance, and they roared away.

I suddenly heard Godzilla-like footsteps to the left of me. "You killed my husband, you bitch!"

I turned and saw The Hammer's wife, Marge, her gun pointed at me. I squeezed my eyes shut as Andrew leapt in front of me.

When I reopened my eyes, I saw, as if in slow motion, Trooper Sales draw his gun. Shots rang out in the night air, but Eleanor, who'd come tearing onto the scene in her Caddy, was now the fastest draw, the one to shoot first. El's bullet tore through Marge's head. The evil bitch took three more shots from Trooper Sales. Her bullet-riddled body did a really awful, zombie-like dance before falling to the ground.

Eleanor walked forward and shook the trooper's hand. "That's how you do it."

El then puffed out her chest and ran toward me. I met her halfway and gave her the biggest hug ever. It kind of reminded me of some damn sappy Lifetime movie ending, but this was for real.

"Where did you learn to shoot like that?" I asked, giddy, smiling.

"Agnes, you know you taught me everything there is to know about handguns."

Andrew joined us for a hug, but my eyes shot to Sophia as she was being led to another ambulance, and I watched as they closed the door behind her. "I can't let her go alone. I will see you at the hospital. I'm riding in the ambulance."

"You know that's against their rules, Aggie." Andrew stopped me. "Ride with us."

"Rules? Since when do I listen to rules?"

It took some persuading, and Eleanor beside me with her gun, to get the emergency response workers to agree that it was a good thing a grandma wanted to ride with her granddaughter to the hospital, but it got done.

Epilogue

One month later.

I arrived at Hidden Cove and was directed toward the deck outside with a view of Lake Huron. It was a clear day, and I could see a number of sailboats looming in the distance.

I adjusted my pearl earrings and searched Sophia's face. "Are you sure you're up to this?" I asked as we joined the throng of people awaiting our arrival.

Sophia smiled and smoothed her white shirt tucked into her khaki shorts. Her white sandals left her ankles exposed, which would likely be permanently marked by rope burn scars. I hoped they would fade in time.

Barbecued chicken was cooking on the grill, and glasses were being clinked together. The celebration had already started.

I led Sophia to a table, where Eleanor, Andrew, and Trooper Sales sat. Sales still insisted I call him Bill when he was not in uniform. I saw a sad-looking Sheriff Peterson leaning against the railing, gazing out across the lake as if gathering his thoughts.

Eleanor leapt up and gave Sophia and me a hug. Andrew's eyes met mine with an expressionless look. He had distanced himself from me since the ordeal, and I was thankful for the space. I was getting to know my granddaughter again.

Sophia made her way to a chair near the railing, where she sat and pulled her legs up, hugging them.

I broke my gaze and sat on the chair held out by Trooper Sales, or Bill, as I now call him if not in uniform.

"I know you have been waiting for an update, Agnes," Bill said.

"Roy and the remaining goon were arrested, and with the death of The Hammer, his wife Marge, and Anthony, the others sang easy enough."

I had mixed feelings about Roy. "I'm a bit shocked Roy had anything to do with this. I know he's a bit out there, but a plot of this sort is too much, even for him."

"He ran into financial difficulties, the best I can tell, and he was so terrified by Bruno and Marge that he was led like a puppy to the slaughter," Sales concluded.

"Yes, but that's no excuse for kidnapping Jennifer, and he planned to sell my granddaughter. I just can't forgive him for that."

"Who knew? Human trafficking in a small town such as this," Eleanor said. "Did the sheriff and the Coast Guard catch up with the traffickers on the boat?"

He shook his head. "They made it to Canada and were placed into custody there. We're letting Canada deal with them. They're all facing murder charges there, or so the FBI informed us."

"Doesn't that let Roy and the goon off the hook, though?" I asked.

"Hardly. Roy has been charged with kidnapping, false imprisonment, and conspiracy to commit human trafficking, as well as murder—and attempted murder conspiracy against you, Aggie."

"And the goon?"

"The so-called goon, Timothy Cicero, faces the same charges. Roy also faces charges for tossing a pipe bomb into your house, and attempted murder."

"State charges?"

Bill picked up a beer and took a swig. "Nope, federal charges, but no need to worry. None of them will see the light of day again."

I folded my hands in my lap. "How did you know where to find us that night at Roy's along the lake?"

"When you disappeared, Rosa Lee told me you had asked about Roy having a boat," Andrew answered. "So the state police staked out the bait shop and the nearby stretch of Lake Huron. Even Sheriff Peterson helped out with the use of his department's marine patrol boats."

I sighed, relieved it was all over; or was it?

I glanced toward Sophia, and when she turned, her face lit up. I followed her gaze and saw Jennifer headed across the room. I smiled as I watched Sophia stand up and squeeze her tight. They had formed a bond, something that might surely help them both to fully recover.

Jennifer's boyfriend, Kevin, followed her, with William Martin close by. Kevin looked at William, an uncomfortable glance. I had heard William had a change of heart and had hunted Kevin down. He brought him to Taduim to be with Jennifer while she recovered. When Jennifer and Kevin's eyes met, the love between them was clear for us all to see, and she wore the engagement ring I had found in her backpack. I had returned the ring to Jennifer after our ordeal, and she admitted when asked that she had never had an abortion at all. The supposed pregnancy had simply been a ploy for her to get her father to believe Kevin was the right man for her.

William smiled and joined our table. He slid an envelope toward me. "I can't thank you enough for finding my daughter." He took a beer a waitress handed to him and popped the top, tipping it back. Not quite something you'd expect from a man of his wealth.

I took the envelope. "I'd rather not take the money. I had an interest of my own."

"I know, but you earned it. You had quite an ordeal of your own. A lesser person would have run off and said forget it."

Andrew laughed. "You don't know my Aggie. She doesn't run from danger. On the contrary, she runs toward it."

I rolled my eyes. "I'll take that as a compliment, and I'll use this money to set up my detective agency."

"*Our* agency, you mean," Eleanor interrupted.

"Yes, I couldn't do it without you."

"Have you thought of a name for the agency yet?" William asked.

"Yup, sure have. I'm thinking, 'Pink Ladies.'"

Everyone laughed.

"What? The Pink Lady saved my ass. You have no idea how hard it was to keep that gun concealed until it became absolutely necessary. When you only have five bullets, you need to use them wisely."

"I'd say you did a fine job," Sales said. "I'd also say you made the right choices, but how do you feel about it?" he asked, his eyes searching my face.

"How do I feel about killing someone who tried to harm my granddaughter to get back at me? Great, that's how I feel." I coughed. "How are the other kidnap victims faring?"

"Physically, I hear they are fine, but mentally, it may take a while."

I nodded and glanced at my granddaughter. "I know what you mean. Sophia has yet to tell me what happened after she was kidnapped, and to tell you the truth, I'm not sure if I want to know."

"Is she having nightmares?"

With tears in my eyes, I nodded. "It's hard to see someone you love in such pain. I'm glad Jennifer and Sophia are close, and that gives me comfort."

Sheriff Peterson approached the table. He looked down like he wanted to say something to me, but was hesitant. "Agnes—"

"I know, Sheriff. I want to say thanks, too." I smiled. "If it's worth anything, I'm sorry about accusing you the way I did."

"And I'm sorry for having you arrested … almost." He snickered as he strolled away.

It was brought to my attention that the sheriff had been trying to cover for his father. It's hard to believe that, for so many years, he had thought his own father guilty of being involved in the Robinson murders, and I wondered who had planted that seed in his head. Gossip mills have never been known to be just or correct, at least not all the time.

I said to the others at the table, while nodding at the retreating sheriff, "I heard he took his father out for a fishing trip last week. I wonder where the old man peed."

Everyone laughed, but I just watched the sheriff stride off, a proud man. I knew we would never be friends or see eye-to-eye about anything. He knew how I felt, and I knew how he felt. And that was enough for me.

I sipped the wine brought to me earlier by a waitress who had said it was on the house. Over my glass, my eyes met Andrew's. I rose from the table, and he followed me to the handrail.

He grabbed my arms and turned me, lowering his head, and when his lips met mine, I melted.

I pulled away. "I hear you're leaving town soon."

His eyes briefly trailed away, and when they met mine again, he smiled. "I have some business to attend to, but I'll be back soon. Don't think for a moment that you can get rid of me so easily."

I kissed him and felt myself taken to a place where guns and goons didn't belong.

About the Author

When Madison Johns began writing at the age of forty-four, she never imagined she'd make it onto the *USA Today* best-selling books list with her first cozy mystery, *Armed and Outrageous*, as an independent author. Sure, this book is an Amazon bestseller, but *USA Today*?

Although sleep-deprived from working third shift, she knew if she used what she had learned while caring for senior citizens to good use, it would result in something quite unique. The Agnes Barton Senior Sleuths mystery series has forever changed Madison's life, with each of the books making it onto the Amazon bestseller's list for cozy mystery and humor.

Madison is a member of Sisters In Crime. Madison is now able to do what she loves best and work from home as a full-time writer. She has two children, a black lab, and a hilarious Jackson Chameleon to keep her company while she churns out more Agnes Barton stories, with a few others brewing in the pot.

Agnes Barton Senior Sleuths Mystery series, in order:

Armed and Outrageous
Grannies, Guns and Ghosts
Senior Snoops
Trouble in Tawas
Treasure in Tawas
Sign up for my newsletter.
https://www.facebook.com/MadisonJohnsAuthor/
app_100265896690345

Made in the USA
Lexington, KY
06 April 2014